THE ACCIDENTAL COUNTESS

"The references to Oscar Wilde's play are more of a tribute than a straight retelling, which keeps this hilarious and lively story from becoming too predictable. Bowman is one to watch." —*Kirkus Reviews* (starred review)

"Readers will take the well-drawn, likable characters into their hearts, enjoying every moment of their charming love story as it unfolds in unexpected ways. Simply enjoy the humor and tenderness."
—*RT Book Reviews* (4½ stars)

"Merry, intelligent, and wholly satisfying. The plot is elaborate, and Bowman handles it with grace to spare."
—*USA Today*

"A fun, sexy read that will have you laughing and crying. Valerie Bowman has outdone herself with this one . . . a true gem." —*Single Titles*

THE UNEXPECTED DUCHESS

"Smart, witty, sassy, and utterly delightful!"
—*RT Book Reviews* (4½ stars, Top Pick!)

"Engaging characters, snappy banter, and judicious infusion of smoldering sensuality will have readers clamoring for the next installment in this smart and sexy series."
—*Booklist* (starred review)

"A fun, smart comedy of errors and a sexy, satisfying romance." —*Kirkus Reviews* (starred review)

ALSO BY VALERIE BOWMAN

THE PLAYFUL BRIDES
The Untamed Earl
The Irresistible Rogue
The Unlikely Lady
The Accidental Countess
The Unexpected Duchess

THE SECRET BRIDES
Secrets of a Scandalous Marriage
Secrets of a Runaway Bride
Secrets of a Wedding Night

E-NOVELLAS
The Unforgettable Hero
A Secret Affair
A Secret Proposal
It Happened Under the Mistletoe
(Also featured in the anthology *Christmas Brides*)

The Legendary Lord

VALERIE BOWMAN

St. Martin's Paperbacks

This is a work of fiction. All of the characters, organizations, and events portrayed in this novel are either products of the author's imagination or are used fictitiously.

THE LEGENDARY LORD

Copyright © 2016 by June Third Enterprises, LLC.

All rights reserved.

For information address St. Martin's Press, 175 Fifth Avenue, New York, NY 10010.

ISBN: 978-1-250-07259-7

Our books may be purchased in bulk for promotional, educational, or business use. Please contact your local bookseller or the Macmillan Corporate and Premium Sales Department at 1-800-221-7945, ext. 5442, or by e-mail at MacmillanSpecialMarkets@macmillan.com.

Printed in the United States of America

St. Martin's Paperbacks edition / November 2016

St. Martin's Paperbacks are published by St. Martin's Press, 175 Fifth Avenue, New York, NY 10010.

10 9 8 7 6 5 4 3 2 1

For my sister, Sarah Bowman-Steffes,
for showing me where Mrs. Goatsocks lived
and being a fabulous Veronica Darling.

CHAPTER ONE
Scotland, November 1816

Someone was inside his house. Christian Forester, Viscount Berkeley, stood outside the small hunting lodge and watched as a plume of smoke from the chimney billowed into the darkening sky. He made his way slowly toward the front door, pushed it open with his boot, and tightened his fist around the pistol he kept inside his coat pocket whenever he traveled. He'd spent the last sennight on the road. He was tired. He was dirty. He hadn't shaved. And he was in as foul a mood as he ever got. It was bitter cold. The wind was picking up. And from the looks of things, the sky was about to open up and dump an unholy amount of snow on this place. All Christian wanted was a warm fire and some food. Instead, it looked as though he would first be forced to dispatch a thief. He took a deep, calming breath and slowly pulled the pistol from his inside coat pocket.

He pushed farther with his boot and the front door creaked open, revealing the great room. The *empty* great room. Christian glanced around the space. There was a fire in the grate, a pleasant woven rug he didn't recognize set in front of the door on the wooden planks, and a boiling pot of what smelled suspiciously like stew bubbling over a fire in the kitchen. Christian stepped inside. Yes. It was obvious. *Someone* was here. Someone *other* than Mr. Fergus, the caretaker, and his little black Scottish dog with pointy ears who also happened to be named Fergus. The odd man once explained to Christian that if men could name their sons after themselves, then by God, he could do the same with his dog. Christian had always thought that sounded about right. But no, Fergus I and II (human and canine) weren't here now. In addition to the stew, the room smelled vaguely of flowers. Lilies, to be precise. There were no flowers in the Scottish Highlands at this time of year. He'd made it up here just ahead of the looming storm that was already blowing freezing gusts up the mountaintop behind him. The smell of lilies meant one thing: perfume. A woman was here. An uninvited, unknown, unwanted woman. And he'd left London to get away from women.

He shut the door behind him, stomped his boots on the rug, and cleared his throat. Perhaps she would show herself, introduce herself. Oh, and explain what the bloody hell she was doing here.

There was no movement. No sound. Nothing. He swung his heavy wool overcoat from his shoulders and placed it on the rough wooden coatrack he'd made himself out of a felled oak tree one summer here. He might be Viscount Berkeley in both London and Northumbria, but here in Scotland he was just Christian. Or Master Christian, according to Mr. Fergus. There was no pomp and circumstance at the hunting lodge, which was why Christian liked it so much. One of many reasons.

A small opening in the bottom of the door at the back of the house flapped to and fro for a moment and Fergus II, the canine variety, came rushing into the room like a black dart. He had the manners to stop and shake the snow from his back and paws as Fergus I had taught him when he'd created the little door for him. Fergus II came rushing up to Christian, wagging his tiny tail furiously and hopping about on all four paws. Christian put his hands on his hips and stared down at the handsome little pup. What in the—? Christian nearly rubbed his eyes. Was it his imagination or was Fergus II wearing a small red woolen coat?

"Well, what are you doing?" Was Christian mistaken? Was his caretaker here after all? Had Fergus I begun to do things like cook stew, place homey rugs near the door, and wear perfume? Or had he taken to entertaining a companion? A female companion? Perhaps she had made the stew. Yes, that surely made more sense than Fergus I wandering around smelling like lilies and dressing his dog in sweaters. But knowing the irascible man, Christian decided that scenario was equally implausible. No. More likely a vagrant had happened by the dwelling and, finding no one home, had decided to take up residence. It wasn't uncommon in these parts. But Christian wanted to get to the business of dispatching the drifter (male or female) posthaste.

After sliding his pistol back into his pocket, he leaned down and scooped up the little pooch. Fergus II licked him squarely upon the nose. "Thank you," Christian said, wiping off the slobber with the back of his gloved hand. "I don't suppose you'd be so kind as to tell me who's here?"

The dog blinked at him and cocked his stout head to the side.

"No?" Christian rubbed the back of his neck. "Very well, then. I'll follow you. Lead on."

He set the short, solid dog back down and motioned for him to precede him down the corridor. The entire lodge consisted of a great room with the kitchen instruments in one corner and a sofa and two aged leather chairs near the fireplace in the other corner. A plump cushion for Fergus II sat near the sofa. There was a wooden table and four matching chairs (also made by Christian one long-ago summer) near the kitchen area. A corridor led to two small bedchambers, each populated with a feather bed, a chair, some books, and a rug. If Mr. Fergus was here, he was either outside in the snowy forest or in one of the bedchambers. The man usually slept in the small room at the back of the barn, but Christian had just come from there after seeing to his horse. That room had been empty and Fergus's mount was gone.

"Go on, mate, show me," Christian said. He followed the dog's determined little trot down the corridor to Christian's own bedchamber door. Mr. Fergus wouldn't have any business in that room. Christian frowned. The dog placed his paw on the door and whined.

"Go on, then," Christian prodded, his chin in his hand. Fergus II glanced back at him as if confirming his permission, then he pushed open the door slightly with his paw and trotted inside the dark room. A few moments of near silence passed. The only sound was the dog's toenails clicking against the wooden floor. A moment later, a distinctly female voice floated out into the corridor. "Why, there you are. Are you here to wake me from my nap?"

Christian's eyes widened and his hand fell away from his chin. By God, there was a woman in his bed!

CHAPTER TWO

Someone was in the house with her. Sarah Highgate's pale hand froze on the dog's slightly rough fur. There was no mistaking it. She'd just heard a man clear his throat. At least she thought she'd heard it. The long shadow moving outside the bedchamber door confirmed it. Someone was there. And the odds of it being the dog's owner were low. Mr. Fergus would have called out, asked her how she was, given her news of Mrs. Goatsocks. No, it was certainly *not* Mr. Fergus.

Fear clutched at Sarah's heart. It was true that she was in a stranger's house. Well, not *entirely* a stranger. His name was Master Christian, and Mr. Fergus had assured her that she had nothing to fear from him. He was a gentleman. But the fact was that she didn't know it for certain and Mr. Fergus wasn't here now and neither was Mrs. Goatsocks—and, worse, the shadowy man outside the door could be a stranger, a Scottish ne'er-do-well, a killer. No. No. There went her imagination again. She mustn't overreact. She must keep calm and be reasonable. Perhaps the shadow simply belonged to someone who'd wandered off the beaten path and ended up in the wrong place . . . just as she had. Fergus the dog wagged his tail. She envied his calmness. She was anything but calm. What exactly should a lone female with an overly friendly dog do in such circumstances? She could call out and ask the man if he was Master Christian. She quickly discarded that thought. "Of course I am" would no doubt be his answer, and fool that she was, she might just believe him, given that she'd never actually *seen* Master Christian. She'd already been idiot enough coming here. She needed to gather her wits about her to survive this misadventure and make it back home. Giving a potential murderer the name of someone he should pretend to be was the opposite of wise.

Her heart hammering in her chest, Sarah contemplated the rest of her options. She could call out and ask him to name himself. But if he was a murderer, she would be identifying herself as a female and letting him know she was there, ready to be murdered or raped, perhaps both. Though now that she thought on it, no doubt he'd already heard her speak to the dog. *Bother. Bother. Bother.*

She held her breath and pressed her shaking hand against her middle. *Be calm. Be calm. Be calm.* There was only one sane course of action. She must find a weapon. He, whoever he was, would make the first move, and she would not be cowering meekly on the bed when he did.

Resolved, she slid off the feather mattress as quietly as possible in search of a weapon. She tiptoed across the wooden planks, wincing whenever one of them creaked. She glanced around wildly. What looked like a medieval sword was propped against the far wall of the small room. She'd already decided that Master Christian must be an eccentric old man. The sword confirmed it.

Whoever was in the corridor, however, might be a young man. Young and spry and dangerous. Regardless, she would at least attempt to defend herself. For the thousandth time, she cursed her own stupidity over the circumstances that had brought her so far from her home and placed her in so much potential danger. Putting her finger to her lips to shush the dog (as if he knew what that meant), she finished her slow journey to the sword, grabbed it with both trembling hands, and took a deep breath. If only London Society could see her now. Lady Sarah Highgate, eighteen-year-old so-called belle of the Season, wearing maid's clothing, huddled in a Scottish hunting lodge, and arming herself with a broadsword. She blew out her breath from trembling lips. Life could be downright odd sometimes.

Sarah braced her feet apart, adjusted her grip on the sword's handle, and heaved upward just as the door to the bedchamber flew open.

In his thirty years of life, Christian had never seen a sight quite like the one that greeted him when he kicked open the bedchamber door. A beautiful woman stood there brandishing a sword at him. Well, *brandishing* might be a bit of an overstatement. She could barely lift it an inch from the floor, but she was obviously *attempting* to brandish it.

Normally, Christian was at a loss in front of a beautiful woman. Well, other than his friends, of course. And this woman was *extremely* beautiful. She had lush black silky hair that fell in fat curls past her shoulders. She'd obviously unpinned it for her nap. She had pale skin, red lips, an adorable upturned nose, and eyes of palest green, almost crystalline. They were tilted, like a cat's, and framed by long, sooty lashes. She was dressed as a servant. Had she run away from some estate? Only there wasn't an estate near here. She must have come far. Regardless, whoever she was, she was an incomparable beauty. And a stranger.

"Get out of here right now, or I'll cut you in half." The sword quavered in the woman's grip, but her eyes narrowed to slits. "I mean it. Leave now. You won't want to see me angry. I promise you. I'm quite good with a sword." Again, the sword quivered up another inch.

In other circumstances, Christian would have stuttered in the face of such beauty, wouldn't have known what to say, would have made an ass of himself. God knew such lack of debonair sophistication was a large part of the reason he'd failed to find a wife in London after all these years. But the audacity of this particular woman—or, more correctly, his anger at her audacity—mixed with his exhaustion, made his encounter with *this* beautiful woman quite different from all the others.

"What if I told you I have a pistol?" he asked dryly, studying her face to gauge her reaction.

She tossed her curls and lifted her chin higher, but her eyes flashed with a hint of fear. "I have a sword," she announced, her voice quavering slightly.

"I see that. But I'd like to think we would both agree that a pistol would trump a sword were this little confrontation to turn into actual combat." He stepped toward her, all the while assessing how carefully and quickly he might disarm her.

Her eyes flashed again. She took a step back. "I . . . I don't believe you have a pistol. You'd have shown it by now. And I will slice you in half if you take another step closer."

He pressed his lips together to keep from smiling. "Well, you see," he said, squinting, "I don't usually point pistols at ladies. But I'm quickly beginning to consider making an exception in your case. Especially if you continue to threaten me and refuse to put down that sword."

She did exactly the opposite. She lifted the sword even

higher, but the muscles in her upper arms quivered. It had to be a chore for her to keep the thing aloft.

"If you have a pistol, show it. I dare you to," she said, her jaw clenched.

"Oh, my dear Miss House Thief, don't tempt me. Now, I'm going to ask you one more time to put down that sword before I *force* you to put it down. It's entirely your decision."

"You'll have to kill me first. And I'm no house thief." Her quaking arms lifted the sword even higher, and she had the audacity to jab it toward him slightly.

That was it. Christian was through with this farce. He had to disarm her before she hurt herself or him or, God forbid, the dog, who'd sat in between them watching this peculiar exchange, his ears switching from side to side, no doubt in an effort to hear each of them more clearly.

Christian reached her in two long strides, wrenched the sword out of her hand, twisted her arm behind her back, and pulled her sharply against his chest. "You say you're not a house thief, but let me see if I have the right of it. You've broken into *my* home and you're trying to kill me? With my own sword?"

The woman struggled to pull her arm free, but Christian held her fast, her backside squirming against him. He wasn't about to allow her to scramble away from him. God only knew what she'd scoop up to fight him with next. The dog, perhaps?

"*Your* home? How do I know this is *your* home?" she asked in a tone that was both demanding yet edged with fear. And in an accent that was obviously not that of a maid, but of a lady. Unexpected.

Her breath came in panting gasps, and her breasts—which Christian had quite a good view of, actually, given that he was close to a foot taller than her—were heaving.

She was frightened. Good. Thieves shouldn't get too comfortable.

"I damn well know it's not yours, Miss Thief."

"I told you. I am *not* a thief. Let go of me." She struggled harder to break free of his grasp.

He tightened his hold on her arm. "Is anyone else with you?"

"No."

"How long have you been here?"

"This is my third night."

"You have been in my home three nights?" Outraged, he glanced around the room, searching. "What have you taken?"

"Nothing. How many times do I have to say it? I'm no thief." She attempted to elbow him in the ribs. He stepped back just in time, mentally thanking his fencing days at Eton for his quick reflexes.

He secured her elbow so she couldn't do it again. "I don't want to hurt you," he said calmly, "but unless you can tell me in the next five seconds who you are and why the hell you're in my house, I'll be happy to toss you out in the snow, thief or not."

She stopped struggling and made a small gasping noise. That was more like it.

"*You're* Master Christian?" Her head snapped to the side, and he saw the outline of her patrician profile, though she still had her back to him.

Christian tightened his grip on her warm wrist. "I'm the one asking questions here, not you," he growled near her ear. The lily scent was definitely coming from her. Her ebony hair was giving off the essence. It smelled . . . good.

"I'm trying to prove that I'm not a thief," she insisted. She'd stopped struggling for the moment. "How else would I know your name?"

"I'm certain it's written on some paperwork in here somewhere, and it appears you've made yourself at home. But you'll have to do better than toss about a name to convince me you haven't broken into my house."

She took a deep breath. "Mr. Fergus knows I'm here. He said I might stay." She tossed her head after that pronouncement, obviously proud of herself for getting another name right.

Christian considered this a moment. It seemed unlikely that such a slip of a woman had done something violent to Mr. Fergus, but she *had* drawn a sword on him and his man wasn't here at the moment. For all Christian knew, Miss Thief's husband was hiding outside somewhere having disposed of Fergus's body, waiting to spring a trap.

"What is the dog's name?" Christian asked slowly. He nodded toward the animal.

Miss Thief's chest rose and fell, her breathing shallow. Christian tried to ignore the enticing view of her décolletage.

"Fergus also." The note of triumph in her voice was unmistakable.

But Christian wasn't through. "Where is *Mr.* Fergus?"

Her gaze quickly dipped to the floor. "He took Mrs. Goatsocks to town. She was in need of a doctor."

He hitched up her arm again and she yelped. More out of surprise than pain, he suspected.

"I don't know anyone named Mrs. Goatsocks," he ground out.

"Of course you don't. She's my chaperone."

That did it. Christian spun the woman away. She whirled to face him, her bright crystal-green eyes flashing. He eyed her up and down. She was actually more beautiful than he'd first thought. Stunning, if truth be told. High cheekbones, a delicate jaw, and the body of a goddess. But that didn't make up for the trespassing. And he'd *seen* many beautiful women before. Perhaps he had trouble speaking to them, but he'd seen them. This one needed to explain herself. *Immediately.*

He crossed his arms over his chest and eyed her down the length of his nose. "So thieves have chaperones, do they?"

She rubbed her wrist and gave him a condemning glare. The dog sat in between them and glanced back and forth, as if he were watching a fascinating game of battledore and shuttlecock.

"I told you, I'm *not* a thief, and Mr. Fergus led me to believe that you are a *gentleman*." She sneered the last word.

"Mr. Fergus takes care of this house and the accompanying property. I don't pay him to make assessments of my character. Now finish telling me who you are, and don't lie to me. Because if I don't believe you, I may still throw you outside."

Her eyes widened. "According to Mr. Fergus, there could be *wolves* out there." She sounded more affronted than frightened.

"He's right about that," Christian replied. "I suggest you make your story extremely convincing."

Two black brows snapped together over eyes filled with anger. She glanced about as if looking for another potential weapon. Christian crossed his feet at the ankles and leaned back against the doorjamb. "There's a longbow on the wall in the other bedchamber." He didn't uncross his arms. "But you'll have to get by me to get it. And we're staying right here until I'm satisfied." He gave her a challenging glare.

She gasped and put her hand to her throat. Then she rushed back over to the bed and pulled the patchwork quilt off of it. She wrapped it around her back and shoulders, covering herself completely. She sucked in air through her nostrils, and Christian could tell she struggled with her next words.

Her voice quavered slightly. "Sir, I must inform you that I am the daughter of the Earl of Highfield, and if you intend to dishonor me—"

Christian's laughter stopped her. She snapped her mouth shut and glared at him. "What is funny about *that*?"

He gave her a tight smile. "I have no intention of dishonoring you, Miss Thief. But I don't care if your uncle is the pope, which I doubt, by the by, given the manner in which you're dressed. If you don't explain your presence in my house *right now,* your father will have to come fetch you from a pile of snow in Scotland, and something tells me he's not nearby at present."

After delivering that little speech, Christian braced both elbows against the door and eyed her carefully. "Give me one good reason to allow you to stay."

CHAPTER THREE

Sarah glared at the man resting casually against the bed-chamber door, blocking her only chance at escape. Though where she'd escape to, she had no idea. The thought of the snowy, dark, wolf-filled Scottish woods held little appeal. She considered attempting to overpower him but quickly discarded that notion. She'd wrestled with her brother upon occasion when they were younger, and Hart had always won. This man was at least Hart's size, if not bigger. She had no chance of beating him at hand-to-hand combat. Especially now that she'd been divested of her sword.

Very well. She had no choice but to stay here and reason with him. She eyed him up and down. He had the voice of a gentleman, indeed. Though she was somewhat surprised to hear that it was the voice of an *English* gentleman. Mr. Fergus was Scottish, and she'd simply assumed his master was as well.

Yes. This man was clearly English, and his accent indicated he had *some* breeding, but he was clearly not of the Quality. The man himself was wearing coarse wool trousers, a rough linen shirt with a rumpled white cravat, and a simple black overcoat. His boots looked expensively made, but they were the only things he wore that appeared to be of any value. Still, she suspected they were not from the fashionable Hoby's in St. James's.

It was true that she herself was dressed as a maid, but that was for a very good (or very bad, depending upon how one interpreted the matter) reason. This man, whoever he was, had threatened to toss her out in the snow. Twice. He couldn't possibly be a gentleman. A *gentleman* would have instantly recognized her father's name. A *gentleman* would have immediately inquired after her health and safety. A *gentleman* wouldn't have threatened to feed her to wolves.

She eyed him up and down again. What did she expect from a man like this? A man who lived in a tiny house in Scotland and had one servant to his name? Despite Mr. Fergus's assurance, clearly Master Christian here— if indeed that was with whom she was dealing—was a barbarian. Not only was he sporting several days' growth of beard, he looked grimy and smelled as if he'd been sleeping in a barn.

No. He was no gentleman. He was a ruffian. Albeit a somewhat handsome ruffian. His nose was straight. His jaw was square. His shoulders were broad. *Was* he Master Christian? If so, she'd been mistaken about his age. But she was quickly beginning to suspect that the tall, arrogant blond man with the crystal-blue eyes was probably the son or some poor relation of Master Christian. There was no help for it, however. She would have to tell him her name. She cleared her throat. "I'm Lady Sarah Highgate, daughter of the Earl of Highfield."

The man glanced at the dog as if *he* might be able to verify her identity.

"And what are you doing in my house, Lady Sarah Highgate, daughter of the Earl of Highfield?"

Nervousness made her voice far harsher than she intended it to be. "In London people take such titles quite seriously," she informed him, clutching the quilt tightly around her shoulders.

"I'm certain they do. Too bad for you that we're in Scotland."

Her mouth nearly dropped open. "But I'm Lady Sarah . . ."

"You might try explaining that to the wolves. I'm certain they will be impressed."

Sarah's face heated. He was right. She hated the pomposity with which she'd spoken. She never used her title for any special favors in London. But here, here she was frightened and uncertain of herself, uncertain of this man. She needed to use whatever means she had at her disposal to convince him not to toss her out on her ear, and she was quickly coming to realize that the things that mattered most in her world apparently made little difference in the Scottish Highlands. She decided to try a different tactic. "Have you never been to London?"

"Not when I can help it," he replied vaguely, "and you still haven't answered my question."

Her virtue being somewhat assured, Sarah allowed the quilt to drop from her shoulders. She heaped it back onto the bed sheepishly. She hadn't answered him because she hadn't yet decided how to answer him. The truth was ridiculous, but a lie might be exceedingly more so. In the end, she decided to tell the truth. Her former governess, Miss Hawthorne, would demand it. Besides, she'd already told Mr. Fergus the truth. Mr. Fergus had been far more sympathetic and far easier to trust, of course. But when he returned, he'd repeat it and contradict any lies she might dream up now. Finally, she decided to tell the truth because of her own innate sense of fairness. She was clearly in the wrong here. She *had* broken into his home, even if Mr. Fergus had eventually invited her to stay. And she *had* subsequently attempted to attack this man with his own sword. She felt an adequate sense of chagrin. She was not chagrin-less.

She straightened her shoulders and cleared her throat, but she did not meet his eyes. She would answer his questions truthfully, but there was no need to blurt out the *entire* story.

"My father owns a hunting lodge nearby," she said evenly.

"But why are *you* here?"

All right. She had to bend the truth *a bit*. "On . . . holiday?" Bother. She hadn't meant it to sound like a question. She was obviously rubbish at lying.

"On holiday, dressed like a maid?" Skepticism positively dripped from his deep voice.

Double bother. That was a difficult question to answer without revealing more details.

She smoothed her hands over the white apron she hadn't remembered to remove when she'd lain down for her nap. "I didn't wish anyone to know I left London."

"You left London?"

"Yes."

"Secretly?"

"Yes."

"And you came to Scotland?"

"Yes."

"Why?"

She tugged at the wide white collar of her plain gray gown. "Be . . . cause." Her face heated again. "Because I *had* to get away, only . . ."

He waited, watching her for a few moments of silence before prompting, "Only?"

She pressed a clammy hand to her forehead. "Only I've

never been here before and the direction I was given wasn't entirely accurate and I picked the wrong house."

A few moments ticked by before she could tell he was struggling not to laugh. The corners of his mouth turned up and his firmly molded lips shook suspiciously.

"You mistook my house for your father's?" he asked.

"Yes." Her cheeks were flaming now. She pushed at the rug with the tip of her stockinged toe.

"I take it your father was not the one who gave you the direction?"

"No, I . . . er . . . that is . . . my maid bribed my father's valet for the information, and—"

"Bribed?" His blond eyebrows snapped together. "Am I to understand your father didn't allow you to come here?"

She bit her lip but forced herself to meet his eyes. *Bother. Bother. Bother.* She'd have to come out with it. "That's correct. The truth is I ran away."

CHAPTER FOUR

Christian eyed the young woman carefully. With her upper-crust English accent and haughty airs, there was little chance she was truly a servant, despite her clothing. She was telling the truth. At least part of it. The Earl of Highfield *did* have a hunting lodge near here. The two men had hunted together on more than one occasion through the years. And Highfield had a family he'd never brought with him to Scotland. Christian seemed to recall him mentioning a daughter who would be about this woman's age. He couldn't recall if her name was Sarah, but he'd met the countess in London a time or two, and while she was nowhere near as gorgeous as her daughter, there was certainly a resemblance. Yes, Christian had no doubt that Highfield's daughter was standing in front of him right now. She was telling the truth about that. But he wasn't through questioning her yet.

He narrowed his eyes on her. "Why didn't you leave my house when you discovered your mistake?"

"We did," she replied. "But we got lost in the forest and it was getting dark, so we came back to spend just one night. We met Mr. Fergus and he kindly offered to show us the way the next morning."

"But?"

Color continued to ride high in her cheeks. "But on the way back into the house, Mrs. Goatsocks tripped over a branch hidden in the snow and twisted her ankle and—"

"Fergus took her to town while you remained here?" Christian finished for her.

She nodded. "He said the only doctor nearby was the one in town. I'm sorry for the trouble, Mr. . . . What is your surname?"

"Forester. Christian Forester at your service." He bowed at the waist to her. He never went by his title in Scotland, and he'd already decided he wasn't going to inform this chit that he was a viscount. She'd made it clear how impressed she was by such things, going on as she had about her own title. He didn't want to impress her.

"Mr. Fergus wasn't entirely certain when you'd be arriving," she continued.

"You weren't expecting me?" he drawled.

"No." She shook her head this time. "I'm sorry about the sword." She looked so contrite and innocent that Christian chuckled.

He didn't, however, know what sort of trouble she was in, and given that she was a young lady who'd obviously recently made her debut, he could only guess that the trouble involved a man. Lady Sarah here just might be carrying some London blue blood's by-blow. He eyed her up and down again. He certainly couldn't fault the chap for not wanting to wait till the wedding night. The woman would tempt a saint, and Christian should know. He was practically a saint given the state of his own years-long self-induced celibacy. But there would be time to talk about her circumstances later. She was obviously frightened, and given her confession, she might well be in the family way. He felt a bit sorry for her, really. He might be tired and hungry and put out, but he hadn't been raised to be churlish or unkind.

He took a deep breath. "What say we start again? Good evening, I'm Christian Forester. Welcome to my home." He pushed himself off the door and bowed.

When she smiled, relief made her crystalline eyes sparkle. "Thank you, Mr. Forester. I'm Lady Sarah Highgate." She lifted her drab skirts and executed a perfect courtroom curtsy.

"I take it you are responsible for the stew pot on the stove?" he asked.

She nodded hesitantly. "Yes."

He quirked his lips again at that. "Does it taste any good? I am famished."

"I don't know," she admitted with a grin that Christian could only categorize as sheepish.

"Do you care to find out?" he asked. "At the moment I'd be willing to eat my own glove if it were properly seasoned."

"I'm game if you are." She smiled at him sweetly.

"Good." He stepped forward and offered her his arm. She threaded her arm through his and they turned and made their way into the corridor.

Christian kept his eyes trained ahead, but if she'd bothered to glance up, she would have seen the half smile still planted firmly on his lips. "While we eat, Lady Sarah, you can tell me all about why you ran away."

CHAPTER FIVE

Once they made it to the kitchen, Sarah hurried over to the cabinets and pulled out two bowls and two spoons. Christian raised his brows at the speed with which she went about busily preparing the meal. She'd obviously made herself right at home. She seemed to know where everything was, including the peppercorn, which she shook from a small glass bottle that she produced from the back of a cabinet.

"I didn't even realize I *owned* peppercorn," he announced with a friendly smile.

"Apparently you do. Peppercorn and salt and sage, too. Mrs. Goatsocks refused to leave with Mr. Fergus until she'd inspected the cupboards and ensured I wouldn't starve while she was gone."

"And how does the daughter of an earl know how to cook?"

"Oh, uh, er, Mrs. Goatsocks . . . left me instructions."

He eyed her carefully, wondering at her hesitation. "Well, if the smell is anything to go by, her instructions must have been perfect and your execution flawless."

"Wait until you try it," she said. "But I must make the biscuits before we eat."

There was indeed a roll of dough lying on the counter. Christian hadn't noticed it when he'd first walked in.

Lady Sarah knew how to make biscuits, too? How interesting.

"I left them to rise while I was napping," Sarah admitted with another sheepish smile. She went about flipping the dough in the flour and slapping it on the countertop before using a round cup to produce biscuit-sized amounts of the stuff. Christian watched her in fascination. Surprising that a London blue blood would know how to cook and appear so natural doing it. It seemed strangely homey to him. His chest felt tight. All he'd ever wanted was a wife, a home, a simple life. He'd spent the last several Seasons in London looking for a wife. With no success. Seeing a woman in the kitchen of his lodge, making biscuits, suddenly felt very intimate.

"You do that as if you've done it before," he murmured, crossing his arms over his chest.

"The truth is I have." Her cheeks reddened. "I used to sneak down to the kitchens at our country house and watch the cook. She let me help her after I begged. I know how to cook lots of things, actually."

"You *wanted* to help cook? Why?" Christian couldn't keep the incredulity from his voice.

Sarah gingerly placed the biscuits in a pan that she was preparing for the hearth. "It always seemed like a more useful thing to do than sit around in pretty gowns and not get mussed all day."

Christian shook his head. His arms dropped to his side. An earl's daughter dressed like a maid and preferring kneading dough to buying fripperies? What a singularly odd combination. But then again, he reminded himself, she wasn't the typical earl's daughter or she wouldn't have taken off to Scotland dressed as a maid, would she have?

Christian filled Fergus's water bowl from a pitcher sitting on the table. "I'll be back in a few minutes," he announced.

"Take your time," Sarah replied in a singsong voice.

Shaking his head, Christian strode back to the guest bedchamber. He changed into a clean shirt and washed up as best he could using the bowl and basin on a wooden stand in the corner of the room. The water was nearly freezing. In London, his valet would have had a fresh set of clothing waiting and a hot bath. But Scotland was a different matter altogether, and his valet was at his country estate in Northumbria. Before he left the room, Christian glanced at his reflection in the looking glass above the washbowl. He hadn't shaved in many days. He looked a fright. It was a wonder Lady Sarah hadn't shrieked at the sight of him. He wouldn't have blamed the poor girl.

When he returned to the great room, Lady Sarah had ladled out a large bowl of stew for him and another for herself. She'd poured two glasses of red wine from one of the bottles that he'd had stored in the pantry. The biscuits were hot and fresh from the pan on the hearth, and Sarah had placed two on a small plate near his bowl of stew on the table.

Sarah sat at the small wooden table, quietly waiting for him. From his place a few paces away, Fergus II sat up straight and licked his chops, staring at them both expectantly. Sarah tossed the dog a bit of crust from one of her biscuits.

"Shall we try it?" Her voice seemed oddly high. Was she nervous?

"By all means." Christian grabbed his spoon, dunked it into the thick stew, and scooped up a large mouthful. He allowed it to cool for a moment before taking a bite.

Sarah bit her lip, watching him with the obvious apprehension of an anxious cook.

"It's delicious!" he declared, and it was true. Rich, flavorful, thick, and hearty. By God, this little pampered daughter of an earl had managed to create a fine pot of stew. The girl was obviously talented.

A look of relief washed over her face and she took her own first tentative bite. She blinked. She blinked again. "It is good!" she agreed, incredulity dripping from her voice. "It's quite good."

"You're surprised?" He took another healthy bite.

"Yes, I'm exceedingly surprised, actually."

Christian pulled off a piece of one biscuit, dunked it into the stew, and ate it. Sarah watched him carefully, a slight frown marring her brow as if she'd never seen anyone eat in that manner before. But soon she, too, pulled off a piece of one of her biscuits, dunked it into her bowl, and ate it. A giant smile spread across her face after she swallowed, as if she'd just discovered the most delicious thing in the world.

"Why are you surprised it's good?" Christian asked after swallowing his bite.

"Because I haven't cooked in an age. I've been . . . well, I made my debut this past Season and Mother insisted that I spend my time doing . . . other things."

Christian dunked another bit of biscuit in his bowl and arched a brow at her. "Other things?"

"Yes."

"Such as?"

She took another bite. "Such as . . . find a husband."

"And?" Christian countered. "Any luck?"

Lady Sarah began coughing uncontrollably. She beat her chest and her eyes watered. Then, just as Christian was contemplating circling around the table to slap her on the back, her breathing returned to normal. "My," she said. "It must have slipped down my windpipe."

He quickly handed her her wineglass. "Are you all right?"

"I think so, now."

"Well, the stew is delicious. Thank you for making it for me. You're obviously an accomplished cook," Christian said.

"Mother always says I'm capable," she replied, the smile not quite reaching her eyes.

Christian grimaced. Lady Sarah might just need to be capable indeed if she'd run off to give birth to a bastard. They ate in awkward silence for a few moments. The only sound was the clicking of the spoons on the bowls and the wine being sipped.

Finally, Sarah cleared her throat. "Don't worry, Mr. Forester. As soon as Mr. Fergus returns, he shall escort us to Father's lodge and we'll no longer be a burden to you."

Christian sipped his wine and stared out the window, where the snow was falling swiftly, piling up in big, fluffy flakes. He shook his head slowly. "On the contrary, given the severity of the storm, I doubt Fergus will be returning."

Sarah blinked. She lowered her spoon back into her bowl as if in a trance. "Ever?"

Christian dunked another piece of biscuit into his stew. "No time soon, I'm afraid."

"But that's impossible. That means . . . Why, that means . . ."

He popped the biscuit into his mouth, chewed, and swallowed. "That you're stranded here with me. Alone."

Sarah gulped, braced an elbow on the table, and let her forehead fall onto her palm. "What am I to do?"

Christian took a sip of wine. Then he lifted the glass and stared into its dark depths. He'd forgotten he had this wine. Madeira. He'd collected some damn fine Portuguese wine during the wars. "Why don't you tell me the reason you're here? Perhaps I can help you."

"I doubt it," she groaned.

"Tell me," he prompted. "I've helped many a fair maiden out of trouble. My friends, mostly. I've a great deal of experience."

Sarah lifted her head and studied him for a moment, as if trying to decide whether she believed such a claim. Finally, she sighed and rested her chin on her palm, her elbow still braced on the table. "The truth is I've made a series of very poor decisions in a very short amount of time, and the more I consider them in hindsight, the more I am convinced I have ruined my entire life. Mother always says I'm too impetuous. Apparently, she is right."

"Capable but impetuous?" Christian said.

"Seems so," Sarah replied, her face still scrunched in a grimace.

Christian set his wineglass next to his bowl. "I hate to be indelicate . . . but are you . . . do you happen to be . . ." He cleared his throat. *"Enceinte?"*

It took a moment for the word to register, and when it did, he could tell by the look of horror on her face that he'd been wrong. An unexpected wave of relief washed through him.

"Pregnant? No! Absolutely not!" she gasped.

He lifted his spoon to take another bite of stew. "Forgive me. But the usual course of action for a young lady who is in that sort of trouble would be to run to Scotland at the first opportunity, though admittedly she usually drags a potential bridegroom along with her."

Sarah groaned. "It's the exact opposite in my case, actually."

That was intriguing, to be sure. "What do you mean?"

She raised her glass in a silent salute. "You're looking at London's most sought-after young lady of last Season."

He arched his brows. "Am I?"

"Yes, I wouldn't call *myself* that, of course. I think it's horrid. But the papers, the scandal sheets, they all seem to agree—Lady Sarah Highgate, the belle of the Season."

He narrowed his eyes on her. "And you find that horrid?"

"Entirely."

His eyes narrowed further. "May I ask why? Seeing as how I've managed to be the exact *opposite* of the bachelor of the Season for several Seasons past, I can't imagine why anyone wouldn't relish popularity."

"What do you mean, you've been the exact opposite of the bachelor of the Season?"

"I've been searching for a wife for years now with absolutely no luck whatsoever. Ladies barely seem to know I'm alive. The ones who do, quickly become my friends, with nary a word about marriage."

"Oh, that doesn't sound pleasant. Not in the least." She shook her head and gave him a sympathetic look.

Christian tapped his fingertips along the tabletop. "So, you'll understand why I'm curious to know the reason you believe being the belle of the Season is horrid."

She waved a hand in the air. "Oh, it's quite simple, really. It's because being the belle of the Season drew the attention of the most eligible *bachelor* of the Season."

"Who is?" Christian took another bite of stew.

"Lord Alistair Branford."

Christian set down his spoon and scratched his chin. Damn beard was itchy. "Branford? I admit, the man can be a bore, but he's good *ton*. What do you find so objectionable about him?"

"You know good *ton*?" She looked entirely skeptical. "Forgive me," she rushed to say. "That was rude. I just . . . it's just that you . . ."

"You're wondering how a man dressed like me and living in the Scottish Highlands knows anything about the ways of the Quality in London?" he asked.

She nodded slowly, a guilty look etched on her fine features.

"You might say I'm loosely connected to the Quality. I've been to many a ball in London. Even made an appearance at Almack's a time or two."

"You have my sympathy," Sarah said, making Christian realize that in addition to being able to cook, the young woman had a dry sense of humor. Another surprise from Lady Sarah Highgate.

"Are you of the gentry?" she asked.

"Something like that." Christian grabbed his spoon again. "But you never said, what is the matter with Branford?"

Sarah uttered a labored sigh. "You've clearly never been a young lady suffering his attentions."

"True." Christian grinned at her.

"The man is a complete bore. No. He's *more* than a complete bore. He's constantly talking about himself. It's his favorite subject: his looks, his clothing, his money, his estates. There's nothing about himself that he doesn't find endlessly fascinating."

Christian took another bite of stew and swallowed. "I take it you don't share his fascination."

Sarah folded her hands in front of her on the tabletop. "I do not."

"So you were forced to suffer the attentions of the Marquess of Branford and that made you run away?" Christian asked.

Sarah's eyes widened and a look of disgust mixed with a bit of hopelessness crossed her face. "No. I ran away after my father informed me that I was betrothed to the awful man."

CHAPTER SIX

Christian contemplated the young lady sitting across from him. He'd never considered such aspects of an arranged marriage before. Most of the ladies he knew, like his friends the Duchess of Claringdon, the Countess of Swifdon, and Mrs. Upton, had all chosen their husbands, fallen in love with them, actually. It had to be difficult to be a female forced to marry in accordance with her family's wishes. It was done all the time, of course. This wasn't an extraordinary circumstance, but Lady Sarah obviously had chosen to flee rather than obey. At great potential risk to her reputation. He could well imagine how her imperious father would react. The Earl of Highfield was a good man but could be pompous when the occasion arose.

"The worst part is," she continued, "that everyone keeps informing me how fortunate I am. How lucky to have drawn the eye of the marquess, what a boon it is, et cetera."

"You don't feel fortunate?" Christian took another bite of stew.

"I've *tried* to feel fortunate. I have. I truly have. There must be something awfully wrong with me to *not* feel fortunate. But then, one night, I got a funny feeling in my chest. I can't explain it other than to say that I couldn't breathe. The room seemed to be closing about me. I felt frightened. I only knew I had to leave."

"Leave?" Christian narrowed his eyes on her.

"Flee. Get out. Be anywhere but there."

He watched her carefully. "And you decided to come here?"

"It was the only place I could think of."

"Did you leave just before the wedding, then?"

"No." She groaned again. "That's what is even more mad. The wedding isn't to be until spring. But I just had to go. Oh, I know I sound positively insane. It's quite difficult to explain." She shook her head sadly and pushed her stew around in her bowl with her spoon.

Christian had never heard of a lady who had the same sort of reaction to worry that he had. Tight chest? Fear? Walls closing in? He'd experienced the same sensations himself on more than one occasion. It was some sort of attack of the nerves that he dreaded. It didn't sound positively mad to him in the least. "You plan to remain here till spring?"

Sarah's hand paused on the spoon. "No. Of course not. I've never done anything like this before. I've always done everything I've been told. Never broken one rule. I cannot imagine Mother's shock. I feel absolutely awful. I don't know what I was thinking."

Christian rubbed his chin. "What did you think would happen if you ran away?"

She sighed. "I'm not a complete fool. I did have a plan. I took clothes and all the pin money I'd been saving for years. I decided to dress as a maid so I wouldn't need help with my clothing."

"Very astute of you." He inclined his head. "But you brought a chaperone with you?"

"I never intended for Mrs. Goatsocks to come."

Christian let that part go for the moment. "Why did you save your pin money?"

"No particular reason. I simply abhor shopping. The only things I ever bought were gifts for Mother and Father and Hart and Mrs. Goatsocks and my maid."

"Hart?"

"My elder brother."

"Ah, yes, Highfield's heir. What was your plan once you got to your father's hunting lodge?"

She took such a long draught of wine that she drained the glass. She stood to retrieve the bottle from the table near the hearth. "I hoped to create a scandal. Hopefully one that would be bad enough that Lord Branford would ask Father to destroy the marriage contract."

Christian's lips twitched with humor. "And if that didn't work?"

"That was my entire plan. How could it not work? Who would want a wife who'd been missing and unchaperoned?"

Christian eyed her up and down. Clearly the young woman had little idea how appealing she was. He doubted Branford would let some idle gossip stop the wedding.

"And now I feel like an idiot," Sarah continued, "and dear Mrs. Goatsocks has been injured and poor Mr. Fergus had to go out in the snow just before a storm and it's all my fault."

His bowl clean, Christian leaned back in his chair and folded his hands over his middle. "Well, the stew you cooked is a sight better than anything Fergus has ever made, so I'm glad you're here for the moment, at least."

She tried to return his smile but couldn't. "I'm sorry if I can't quite see the humor in it. I've ruined my life."

"You must have felt quite strongly to have taken such a risk."

"I did. But now, now I feel as if I'll never be able to fix it. Oh, why? Why did I run away so hastily?"

Christian rested his forearm atop his head. "It sounded to me as if you didn't have a choice."

"Father will never forgive me."

"Do you forgive him? For betrothing you to Lord Branford?"

She blinked at Christian quizzically, as if she didn't understand the question. "I've been expected to make a desirable match since I was young. If you've been to balls in London, you must know how these things go. And to marry a marquess? Well, it's Father's dream for me. "

Christian nodded. "I do know how these things go, but I also know that it isn't unheard of for parents to take their children's feelings into consideration when making such decisions."

The look of confusion on her face deepened. "I never told them I didn't want to marry Lord Branford."

Christian's arm fell away from his head and he sat up straight. "My dear girl, why ever not?"

"I was trying to be brave. Do the right thing. You know? Keep a stiff upper lip and all that."

"And if you go back, will you tell them then?"

"It doesn't matter now." She grabbed the wine bottle and returned to her seat. She tipped the bottle into her glass, refilling it. "I've been awful and selfish, I know. It's all I can think about. I must return home to face the scandal and the censure. Perhaps someday I will find a man willing to look past my tainted reputation."

Christian settled back against his chair again and righted his shoulders. "What if Branford still wants you?"

Her eyes widened with surprise. "Why would he want a wife steeped in scandal?"

Because you're exceedingly beautiful. "Trust me, it's more than possible."

She sighed, holding her glass just beneath her red lips. "I hadn't even considered that. I've been such a fool. I regret it. I do. I regret it horribly. I've been a hideously disobedient daughter."

Christian narrowed his eyes on her. "You truly believe that?"

"Yes. I feel absolutely sick. Now that I've had a chance to calm down and think about everything, I'm certain. I'd do anything to get back to London with no one being any the wiser, but the longer I stay here, the less chance I have of that happening. I fear it's too late for my reputation. And now I'm stuck here with . . ."

Christian plucked up his own wineglass and grinned at her again. "Me."

She nodded miserably.

He lifted the glass and eyed her through the dark liquid. "Well, Lady Sarah Highgate, what if I told you that I can help?"

CHAPTER SEVEN

Sarah watched him carefully. Why had she never noticed this man before? If he had been to London, surely she'd have met him among the scores of men she'd encountered during her come-out. It would be rude to ask him if they'd met. She couldn't bring herself to do it.

He was quite handsome. True, his face bore the ill-kempt shadowing of many days' growth of beard, his hair was a bit too long, and his clothes were a bit too coarse. But his smile was charming, and he was kind and witty. And he smelled a bit better ever since he'd gone to apparently wash up. Soap had definitely been involved. He was tall and lean, and those blue eyes were positively mesmerizing. The man had potential. That was certain. And now he was offering to help her.

"Whatever do you mean?" she asked. "How could you help me?"

Mr. Forester stood and stretched his long, lean frame. "I've found over the years that all hope is not lost until all hope is lost."

Sarah tilted her head to the side. "What does that mean?"

"Precisely what I said," Mr. Forester replied. He paced to the fireplace, where he tossed two more small logs onto the pile. "Let's begin with the facts. I presume you left a note for your parents."

Sarah nodded. "Yes, for my mother."

"What did the note say?" He grabbed a poker and jabbed at the logs.

"It simply said I was sorry but I *had* to leave."

Mr. Forester turned to her. His white teeth flashed in a wide grin. "Is that all?"

"Yes."

"You're quite certain? No more details?" he asked.

"That's correct. Mother must know Mrs. Goatsocks is gone, too, of course, but that's only because I tried to tell her good-bye and she insisted upon coming with me."

"A fine chaperone," Mr. Forester said. "And she just might well have saved your reputation."

Sarah's forehead burrowed into a frown. "How?"

"You've been quite properly in the company of a chaperone this entire time, so all hope is not lost."

"The entire time until *now*," Sarah pointed out.

"Yes, but the only people who know that are you, and me, and Mr. Fergus, and Mrs. Goatsocks herself." He nodded toward Fergus II. "And this dog here, of course, but something tells me if you give him a biscuit, he'll agree to keep your secret."

Sarah grinned and tossed the dog another crust. "It's true," she said. "I didn't leave any details in the note I wrote Mother. She has no idea where I've gone or why I left."

"Excellent," Christian replied. "When Mrs. Goatsocks returns, the two of you can go back to London and tell everyone you were merely visiting friends to the north."

A kernel of hope slowly unfurled in Sarah's chest. She

sat up straight and leaned toward him over the table. "Do you truly think that would work?"

Mr. Forester propped the poker next to the fireplace. "I think there's no reason whatsoever not to try. Your mother certainly wouldn't want to contradict you, would she?"

"Absolutely not. Scandal is the last thing my parents would court. Why, they're more concerned with their reputations than with the air they breathe."

"Perfect," Mr. Forester said. "I suggest you do just that. Much more outlandish things have been known to be believed by the good people of the *ton*. Fergus and I will never tell what we know. You may depend upon it."

An enormous smile began to form on Sarah's face. It started as a small quirking of the lips and soon spread into a wide grin that reached nearly from ear to ear. "Oh, Mr. Forester. Thank you for your hospitality. I'm certain I shall never be able to properly repay you for your kindness."

He crossed back over to the table, braced his hands against the back of the chair he'd been sitting in, and met her gaze. "I'm not entirely certain about that."

Christian watched as the smile slowly faded from Lady Sarah's face, to be replaced with a look of confusion. Her brows were drawn together and her smile had turned into a frown.

"How could I ever be able to help *you*?" she asked.

Christian scooped up his wineglass from the table and made his way back over to the counter where Sarah stood with the wine bottle. He refilled his glass, emptying the bottle. "I find myself with the opposite problem from yours."

"The opposite?" Her hands braced against the counter, she eyed him warily.

"Yes," Christian replied, taking another long sip from his glass. "As I said, I am whatever the opposite of the most eligible bachelor of the Season is."

"Why exactly is that?" she asked, still blinking innocently at him.

"Would you believe me if I told you that I normally have an unfortunate habit of stuttering whenever I am in the company of a beautiful female?"

"I haven't heard you stutter once. Oh . . ." She trailed off, obviously wondering if he found *her* beautiful enough to stutter in front of.

"Present company withstanding," he hurried to reply. "I daresay you shocked me by breaking into my house. It may come as a surprise to you, but I've never had a beautiful woman do that to me before."

She laughed and clapped a hand over her mouth. Then she asked hesitantly, "I don't scare you?"

He shrugged. "I suppose not."

He smiled at her. She smiled back.

"You seem perfectly nice to me so far," she replied. "Well, aside from that bit when you threatened to toss me into the snow for wolves to eat. But I suppose that was understandable given the circumstances."

"I'm glad you think so," he replied, fighting another chuckle. "But my problem isn't not being nice. My problem perhaps is being *too* nice."

The look on her face told him she was certain he was half-mad. "Too nice? How could that possibly be a problem?"

"I told you I've rescued my fair share of damsels in distress."

"Yes."

He sighed. "I have the unfortunate problem of turning into the *friend* of all the young ladies I meet. Don't misunderstand me. I value my friendships, but I would like to find a wife, sire an heir. Locate a female who is interested in being more than my *friend*."

She blushed and after setting down her glass, she turned to walk over to the fireplace. "I'm not certain I follow, Mr. Forester. How do you think I might help you with that?" She swung around to face him again.

He met her gaze, a challenging glint in his eyes. "I want you to advise me. Help me become eligible. Teach me what a young lady such as yourself is looking for in a mate. I promise not to be a bore and talk about myself overly much."

"Oh, but I—"

"Don't play coy and be polite," Christian demanded. "I know there is something wrong or I'd have been married long before now. I want you to tell me what it is. I want you to be honest with me, Lady Sarah. You're the belle of the Season. You must know a great deal."

"Well . . ." He could tell the moment she took his proposal seriously. The proper polite tone had left her voice and an interested sparkle lit her eyes. She stood and walked around him, taking in his face, his clothing, his stance. "Your clothes are a bit out of fashion," she admitted. "I could tell you which tailor to go to."

He looked down at his clothing. "These aren't what I'd normally—"

She'd obviously warmed to her subject, for she interrupted him with nary a breath. "Your hair is a bit long, and that beard must go. Close-cropped hair on a gentleman is all the rage in London these days."

He stroked his chin. "I've been traveling and—"

"I could tell you what to say, how to behave, and which venues to frequent to make you irresistible to women. To begin with, Almack's is out of the question."

This time he grinned. "That is precisely what I'm looking for. I've spent many a boring evening sipping tepid lemonade at Almack's."

"A pity," she said, just before rubbing her hands together with obvious glee, the sparkle still firmly alive in her eyes. "It would be a challenge for me. The very thing at which I excel." She paced back and forth in front of the fireplace and tapped her cheek with a finger. "Can I do it? Can I turn a young gentleman from the Scottish Highlands into the most eligible bachelor of the Season?" She turned in a sudden swirl to face him, a catlike grin on her face.

He eyed her over the rim of his wineglass. "I don't know, Lady Sarah, *can* you?"

"Is that a challenge?" she asked.

"Indeed it is, my lady." His gaze met hers in an obvious dare.

"Mother always says I cannot resist a challenge." She lifted her skirts and curtsied to him. "Very well, Mr. Forester. I accept. I'm going to turn you into a legend."

CHAPTER EIGHT

"So tell me, what have your efforts been to date?" Sarah asked. She stood, gathered up the plates and wineglasses, and located the wash bucket under the counter. She filled the bucket with water from another pitcher, pushed up the sleeves of her gray gown, and began scrubbing the dishes as if she'd been born to the role of scullery maid.

Christian watched her for a few moments in awe. If everything else she'd told him didn't seem plausible, he'd wonder if she was indeed the daughter of an earl. For some reason, despite her cooking skills, he'd expected the belle of the London Season to perch on the sofa while he catered to her. But she did nothing of the sort.

He shook his head and refocused his attention on the question she'd just asked. "My efforts?"

"At courting young ladies."

"Ah, that." He pushed up his sleeves and grabbed a dish. Their fingers touched in the wash bucket and Christian swallowed. Sarah froze.

Sarah took a step away from him to the side.

Christian shook his head again. *Focus. Focus.* "My

efforts have been positively abysmal. If I'm not stuttering, I'm saying something entirely wrong. However, it is how I made some of my closest friends. I cannot say it's been entirely bad."

Her head snapped up to face him. "Friends?"

"Yes. Some of my closest friends are ladies who weren't a bit interested in me." He chuckled.

"And you were interested in them?" she ventured.

He shrugged. "Not all of them."

"Who?"

He picked up a bit of linen to wipe the plate he'd just finished washing. "Let's see. One is my friend Lucy." He wasn't about to admit that she was also known as the Duchess of Claringdon.

"Who else?"

"Cassandra and Jane."

Sarah frowned, perhaps wondering why he was referring to his lady friends by their Christian names. But Cass was a countess and Jane a future countess. Sarah would wonder why he was acquainted with such highborn ladies. "Anyone else?" she asked.

"Most recently, I did a good turn for my friend Alexandra. Though I cannot say we were ever enamored of each other."

Sarah scrubbed a bowl. "And these ladies live in . . . London?"

"Yes."

"I cannot believe you and I didn't meet in London." She winced. "Did we?"

"No." He chuckled. "I'm certain I would have remembered you."

She expelled her breath. "I'm so relieved."

"Difficult to keep track of everyone, eh?"

She nodded.

"And you don't attend Almack's?" he asked.

"I did. Once. It was hideous. As you said, tepid lemonade and even more tepid conversation."

"Can't that be said about most of the *ton* events?" he drawled.

"Not if you know whom to speak to and whom to avoid."

Christian cracked a smile. "I see. Something tells me I've chosen exactly the right person to assist me in becoming fashionable."

Sarah returned his smile. "Indeed you have. I have little to recommend me, Mr. Forester. I'm not particularly well learned. I was rubbish at maths. I'm not a fine horsewoman and am abysmal at the pianoforte. But if you're in need of someone who knows the way of the *ton* and its young ladies, you've found the right person, I can assure you."

They finished washing the dishes, studiously avoiding each other's eyes.

"I must see to Oberon," Christian announced.

"Oberon?" Sarah blinked.

"Yes. My horse."

The hint of a smile touched Sarah's lips.

"What is it?" he asked. "Are you not an admirer of Shakespeare?"

"On the contrary. *A Midsummer Night's Dream* is my favorite of his works."

"Is it?" Christian arched a brow. "Mine too. And you just finished telling me you're not particularly well learned. Tsk, tsk, tsk."

"Well, *reading* is different."

"Tell me. Why were you smiling?"

She bit her bottom lip. "I was smiling because my horse is also named Oberon."

Christian's eyebrows shot up. Contemplating that interesting bit of information, he pulled on his boots and overcoat and braced the freezing wind and snow to go to the barn to see to the horse. When he returned, he found Lady Sarah in the yard next to the front door, wrapped in a wool coat, ushering little Fergus II to a spot she'd obviously cleared in the snow so the dog might relieve himself. Apparently, she wasn't even above seeing to the unmentionable needs of an animal. Full of surprises was this Lady Sarah Highgate.

"Did you make Fergus Two that coat?" he asked, pausing next to her.

"Yes," Sarah replied.

"Why?"

"Because I thought he might be cold, of course," she said, giving Christian a look that told him she thought the question a bit daft. She sauntered ahead of him back into the house, and Christian tried to ignore the swing of her hips.

When they got inside, Christian closed the door behind them. They stamped the snow from their feet, hung up their cloaks, and removed their boots. Fergus II wiped his paws on the rug accordingly and trotted over to his little bed near the fire. He paced around in a circle a few times before curling up into a tight ball.

"Care for another drink?" Christian asked Sarah, moving back into the kitchen.

"What are you having?"

"Only tea. I've had enough wine for one evening."

"As have I. Tea sounds lovely."

Christian strode over to one of the cabinets, where he found two teacups. He pulled a bag of leaves out of the cupboard and put the kettle on to boil. Once the water had heated, he poured two cups over the leaves and left them to steep for a bit. Finally, he brought the mugs to where Sarah sat on the sofa in the great room. She'd discarded her slippers and her feet were curled under her.

"No cream or sugar?" she asked with a bit of a pout to her lips.

"My apologies." Ah, here was the moment when she would no doubt indulge in daughter-of-earl-like histrionics.

"I'll make do," she said gamely.

Blinking back his surprise, Christian handed her one of the cups. "Are you certain?"

"What choice do I have?"

"What choice indeed." He set his own cup on the side table and made his way toward the fireplace, where he added more logs to the crackling fire while Fergus II's little snores filled the room.

After stoking the fire, Christian moved back toward the sofa and took a seat across from Sarah on one of the large leather chairs that rested near the fireplace. He picked up his cup again and took a sip.

"So, tell me, what do I need to know? To finally attract a wife?"

"First, I am curious . . . If you're such good friends with Lucy, Cassandra, and Jane, why haven't they helped you find a suitable wife already?"

Christian couldn't help laughing. "Lucy? Are you serious?"

"Yes. Doesn't she have the right connections?"

He nearly choked. "Oh, er, ah, she has the right . . . connections, but . . ."

"But what?"

"My friend Lucy has many talents, but choosing a wife for me hasn't been one of them. She's tried countless times to matchmake for me, to absolutely no avail. Every single one of the ladies she's attempted to introduce me to is either already madly in love with some other chap or firmly disinterested in me altogether. Why, Lucy didn't even realize her own match was directly under her nose for the better part of two months."

Lady Sarah smiled at that. "She's too close to you to know what's good for you, is that it?"

"Partially," Christian replied. "And it's also that she doesn't understand why anyone wouldn't *enjoy* parties and balls and meeting strangers. She has no earthly idea why meeting some ladies makes me stutter, why dancing isn't my forte, and why anyone on earth would want to retreat to Scotland for peace and quiet."

Lady Sarah glanced at him from behind her cup. "I have a confession to make," she said. "I also quite enjoy parties and balls and meeting strangers. And dancing. But I understand why you don't like it. My brother, Hart, doesn't like any of it either. Neither does Meg. Hart calls it all nonsense. But he must find a wife because he's an heir and a future earl and . . . well, just be glad you don't have any of that title nonsense to deal with."

Christian tugged at his collar and didn't meet her eyes. "Who is Meg?"

A bright smile lit Lady Sarah's face. "Oh, Meg is my dearest friend."

"Another belle?"

"No . . ." Lady Sarah sighed. "Unfortunately not. Meg is the opposite of the belle of the Season, I'm afraid. She's more the wallflower of the Season."

"Why is that?"

Lady Sarah shook her head sadly. "Her father is a terrible gambler. He's reduced their family to poverty, and Meg's dowry is gone. Her gowns are hideously out of fashion and she's attracted nary a suitor. It's quite sad, really. I've tried to give her some of my gowns. I have far too many. But she's proud. She refuses any charity. She's gossiped about horribly by some of the other ladies, though not within my earshot. I would not stand for it. Meg is perfectly pretty and sweet and funny. I adore her."

Christian pushed back in his chair and crossed his legs at

the ankles. He took another sip of tea. "Meg sounds lovely. Is she still in the market for a husband? Say, someone tall and blond who lives in Scotland?" He cracked a grin.

Another smile crossed Sarah's lip and she took a sip of tea. "I'm afraid not."

Christian did a double take. "She's looking for someone titled?"

"No. It's just that Meg, much like the ladies Lucy has introduced you to, is already helplessly, hopelessly, in love with another man."

"Ah." Christian shook his head sadly. "A story I've heard all too often. Who is the lucky man?"

"*That* is a story for another time," Lady Sarah replied. "For now, let's get back to your predicament." She took another tentative sip, the grimace on her face less noticeable this time at the lack of cream and sugar.

"By all means," Christian replied, raising his cup in the air in salute.

Sarah smoothed her skirts with her free hand. "Let's begin with the obvious. Pardon my forwardness, but I assume you are eligible?"

"Eligible?" Christian nearly choked on his tea. He drew his brows together.

"Yes. You know. Not already married? Have a steady income? That sort of thing."

He laughed and settled back into his chair again. "No. I'm not already married."

"No heavy debts?" Lady Sarah drew an elegant finger around the rim of her teacup.

"None."

"And your income?" she prodded.

"Steady enough." Why was the smell of lilies slowly driving him mad? The woman was helping him find a wife, for Hades's sake. He shouldn't be fantasizing about kissing her rose-red lips.

"No madness in the family?" she ventured.

Christian scratched the back of his ear. "None of which I am aware."

"No scandal that's marred your reputation?"

"Ironic, *you* asking *me* that."

She pushed her nose in the air, but she smiled. "We're talking about you now, not me."

"Fine, no scandals," Christian said. He still couldn't shake the image of what it would be like to kiss her.

"No former wives dead under unusual circumstances?" she asked.

This time his head snapped up to face her. "Good God, no."

She laughed. "I didn't think so, but I felt it necessary to ask. Anything else to declare that might make a lady in any way reticent to accept your suit?"

Christian quirked a brow. "Other than the stutter and the fact that my home is far from London?"

She contemplated that for a moment. "Scotland isn't so bad."

Christian didn't correct her. She obviously believed this was his only home. He didn't know why he hadn't told her the truth yet. "Some young ladies don't like the idea of being so far from the amusements of London, and . . ."

"And?"

"I'm not overly fond of town, so my lady might well find herself living in the north for a good part of the year."

"I don't see why that would be so bad. London can be tedious after a bit."

"You may not see why, but I assure you, some do. Lavinia Hobbs said I was the least eligible man in London because of it." She'd actually said he was the least eligible *lord* in London, but that was neither here nor there at the moment.

Sarah wrinkled up her nose. "Lavinia Hobbs is a shrew. How she has such a dear of a sister, I'll never know."

Christian took another sip of tea. "You know Lady Alexandra?"

"Yes. She would be a good catch for you, though I hear her parents are set on Lavinia marrying first. And of course, without a title, you'd be hard-pressed to gain the favor of her father, the duke."

Christian grinned. "No matter. I have it on good authority that Lady Alexandra already has her sights set on Lord Owen Monroe."

One of Sarah's fine eyebrows arched. "Lord Owen? *Really?* That is an unlikely pair, but I suppose he's somewhat eligible."

Christian grinned again. "More eligible than I am?"

"Well, he's set to inherit an earldom one day. However, given his scandalous reputation, I daresay you'd still be a fine catch compared to him, even without a title."

"Ah, yes. A title is important, isn't it?"

"Quite. But don't worry. You said you're gentry, correct? We'll find someone perfect for you."

He hid his smile. "There's a viscount in my lineage."

"A viscount? Why didn't you tell me? What was he? An uncle? Twice removed?"

"Something like that." Christian lifted his cup as if to dismiss the question.

"What's the title?"

"Berkeley." He studied her face for any sign of recognition. There was none. "Have you heard it before?"

"No." She bit her lip. "I haven't."

"Not at all?"

"I'm certain I read the name at school when I studied *Debrett's*. Unfortunately, my memory for such things is rubbish."

"That's my entire problem. It seems no young ladies remember me. Obviously, aside from my stutter, I have left absolutely no impression at all. I am the man to whom all the ladies lament about the men they *do* remember."

A touch of a smile graced Sarah's lips. "It can't be all that bad. As I said, I've yet to hear you stutter even once."

"I assure you it's quite real and it's quite humiliating, but that's precisely why I need you. I need you to tell me what I must do to become memorable. I'm not greedy. I don't require a flock of ladies vying for my attention. I am only in need of one. One kind, thoughtful, happy one who won't mind spending quiet days and nights in the country. One who is in want of a faithful, healthy, equally kind husband."

Sarah leaned back and rested her head against the sofa. "It sounds quite lovely," she said wistfully. "So much more lovely than anything Lord Branford has ever said."

"Branford that awful, eh?"

"Yes." She sighed. "The sacrifices one must make for family and lineage and all of that. As I said, you're fortunate to not have to deal with such nonsense."

He glanced at her, his throat tight. "Yes, of course. You and I, *we* could not possibly be—"

"No. No! I mean . . . that is to say . . . my father would never consider a man without a title. Without an estate. A healthy income. All utter nonsense, I assure you."

"Ah, yes. A pity." He took another sip of tea. *That's* why he hadn't told her he was a viscount. And his income was quite healthy. It didn't matter. She could give him all sorts of advice and the belle of the Season still wouldn't be interested in him. No. This wasn't about Sarah. It was about his future wife.

"Don't worry," she hastened to add. "By the time I'm through with you, you *will* have a flock of ladies vying for your attention."

Christian rubbed his beard. "It's better than the alternative, I suppose. So, tell me, what do you think it will take to make me memorable?"

"Well, it's certainly not a problem with your looks," she blurted out, then blushed and pressed her lips together tightly. "I mean, you seem quite easy to look at."

"I'm pleased to hear that, at least," he replied with a chuckle.

"And your physique is also pleasing."

Yours is, too.

He opened his mouth wide, spreading his lips back, and turned his head from side to side. "Care to examine my teeth?"

She snorted but proceeded to lean forward to examine them. "Your teeth are bright, white, and perfectly aligned. Quite a fit set, actually. I see no problem."

He tried not to look at the décolletage she displayed when leaning forward. He cleared his throat and glanced toward the front door. "I have no limps or injuries. And the only scar I've managed to earn is one from putting out a fire that was consuming my cousin Harriet's dollhouse when I was ten years old."

"Oh, dear. However did your cousin's dollhouse manage to catch fire?"

"She tried to light the tiny fireplace with a candle. It was a near ruin. I spent most of my summer holiday rebuilding it for her."

Sarah glanced down into her teacup. "That was kind of you."

Leaning forward, he showed her the small scar that spanned between his thumb and forefinger. She touched it and immediately pulled her hand away. "I'm sorry, Mr. Forester. We might be quite alone together in this hunting lodge, but that doesn't give me leave to behave like a hoyden."

"You're far from a hoyden, Lady Sarah." The scent of lilies filled his senses.

"You don't think people will speak ill of me? If they don't believe my story, I mean." Her frightened eyes searched his face. "You don't think Lord Branford will cry off?"

Christian leaned forward and touched her shoulder. "I wouldn't think ill of you even if I knew the truth. And if you were my betrothed, I would *never* cry off."

She gave him a tentative smile. But there was something in her eyes he couldn't read. "You do know the truth," she murmured.

"Precisely." He moved away from her and settled back into his seat. "You care far too much what others think of you."

She eyed him over the rim of her cup. "Perhaps you haven't cared enough, Mr. Forester."

He inclined his head toward her. The lady was astute. He'd give her that.

She glanced away, shook her head, and cleared her throat. "My apologies for changing the subject. Tell me, what, in your expert opinion, is the reason you've been relegated to a friend of every young lady you've fancied?"

His grin was unrepentant. "Why, my lady, that's what I was hoping you could tell me. For I cannot for the life of me discern the reason myself."

"You're handsome, eligible, connected to the Quality, have a steady income, seem nice enough, and have good teeth. There is no reason I can think of why you haven't made a good match yet."

"Precisely what my cousin tells me." He rested his wrist atop his head.

Sarah was busily tapping her cheek in thought. "Perhaps it's the ladies you're choosing to court. It sounds as if they all had other gentlemen in mind before they met you. That's interesting, isn't it?"

Christian narrowed his eyes. "It's true. I suppose I never thought of that."

Sarah took another small sip of tea. "Is there anyone else? Anyone you fancy?"

He swallowed and looked away into the fireplace. He slowly shook his head.

"That may also be part of the problem," Sarah said. "Ladies like to feel special, singled out, as if the man who is courting them is interested in absolutely no one else."

Christian set aside his cup. He stood and picked up the poker and nudged the burning logs in the fireplace again. "Ah, I see. Does Lord Branford show interest in anyone else?"

"Indeed." Sarah laughed. "Himself, and I'm afraid there's no competing with the strength of that particular affection."

Again, Christian admired her sense of humor.

A singularly loud snore from Fergus II tore through the room. Sarah glanced over at the little dog. "I suppose it's past time to retire. I'll take Fergus to bed with me if it's all right with you. I've got quite used to sleeping with him since I came here."

Christian jabbed at one of the logs. *The bloody dog's making more headway with a woman than I ever have.* "Perfectly all right with me."

She nodded toward the bedchambers. "The room I'm in . . . it's all right for me to remain?"

"Yes. You're perfectly welcome to stay there. I'll be in the other bedchamber." He wasn't about to tell her she'd been sleeping in his bed. "With the door firmly shut and perhaps locked so that I won't have to defend myself against a sword-wielding woman in the middle of the night."

She crossed her arms over her chest and eyed him up and down. "You shouldn't have a thing to worry about as long as you don't do anything that would make me grab my sword."

She was playful, this Lady Sarah. She made him feel younger, lighter. He'd smiled and laughed more tonight than he could remember having done in the last six months.

She stood, stretched, and moved over to the kitchen, where she set her teacup on the countertop. "Tomorrow we'll begin by examining your clothing."

"My clothing?" Christian glanced down at his attire. Not particularly his finest hour, he acknowledged.

"Let's go, Fergus." Lady Sarah clapped her hands and the little dog's brown eyes popped open. He scrambled up from his spot and hurried over to her.

Christian watched as an English earl's daughter went to bed with a Scottish dog wearing a red coat in his hunting lodge. A piece of wood snapped and crackled in the fireplace. Christian rubbed the back of his neck and cursed silently to himself. It was the first time in his life he was jealous of a dog.

CHAPTER NINE

The next morning, Sarah woke to the smell of bacon. Bacon and . . . coffee? Yes, coffee. Mrs. Goatsocks must have returned! Sarah pushed herself out from under the pile of quilts, pulled on a dressing gown, and hurried toward the kitchen. Fergus II scampered at her heels. Awaiting her in the kitchen was a delightful sight: a platter of crackling bacon, a pot each of coffee and tea, and a plate of golden-brown biscuits, with syrup and honey set out beside them. But where was Mrs. Goatsocks? And Mr. Fergus? Sarah turned in a circle. She was quite alone. Who had made this? Surely not . . .

"Good morning," Mr. Forester said in a cheerful voice as he came through the door with a pile of wood braced against his shoulder. Fergus II took the opportunity to trot through the open door to see to his morning needs.

Sarah gasped, from both the rush of cold air that found her bare skin and the fact that a man was seeing her in her dressing gown. She pulled the gown tighter around her neck and held it together with one hand. What in heaven's name was Mr. Forester about? First of all, the man looked far too good for this hour of the morning. He'd clearly cleaned himself up a bit, and even though his hair was still longish and his beard hadn't been shaved, he looked even better in daylight. His broad shoulders were outlined in a rough plaid shirt and the coarse linen breeches he wore outlined his backside in a way that made Sarah swallow unintentionally. He'd surprised her in another way as well. A gentleman, even one of the gentry, wasn't normally up at this hour. Why, her father and brother slept till well past noon. And cooking breakfast? She couldn't imagine her father preparing any sort of meal. Perhaps the gentry were more different than she realized.

"Would you like some tea? You don't strike me as the coffee-drinking sort." He dropped the stack of wood into a pile near the fireplace and brushed the dust from his shirt, his hands moving against his flat abdomen. Forcing her eyes away from the sight, Sarah struggled to breathe evenly.

"Don't you have any servants?" The words left her mouth before she had a chance to examine them. "Oh dear. Forgive me. That was terribly rude."

He laughed. "I'm sorry, my lady. I'm certain it's more rustic here than you are used to, but Mr. Fergus is the only one in my employ up here, and as you've informed me, he is unavailable at the moment."

"I've just never known anyone like, er, you to cook and—" She couldn't bring herself to admit that she'd just assumed a maid or someone else would arrive in the morning to see to such things.

"You cooked last night, didn't you?" he asked. "Besides, I've not only been cooking. I've seen to Oberon and cut this wood for the fireplace." He gestured toward the stack near his feet. "If I don't miss my guess, this storm is only going to worsen. We'll be quite snowed in before nightfall."

"Snowed in!" She froze. Her hand tightened at her throat till it ached.

"Yes. Don't look so alarmed. We've plenty of food and wood for the fire. I always ensure the lodge is well stocked before coming for the winter."

Sarah's heart raced. "It's not that. It's . . ."

"Don't much like the idea of being snowed in with me?"

"It's not proper—" Her voice cracked.

"Perhaps you should have thought of that before you took off into the Highlands alone."

She gave him an unamused look. "I had Mrs. Goatsocks."

"By accident." He pushed the curtain aside and looked out the window at the rapidly falling snow. "At any rate, by the looks of things, Mrs. Goatsocks won't be journeying back here today or anytime soon. You'll just have to make do with me."

Sarah bit her lip. "Yes, yes, of course. I don't mean to sound ungrateful and I'm . . ." She glanced down at her dressing gown. "I'm sorry for my . . . my . . . lack of proper attire."

"I won't tell anyone if you won't."

She couldn't squelch her smile.

He winked at her. "And Fergus Two only speaks Gaelic."

"Is that right?" Releasing the garment at her throat, she put her hands on her hips and stared through the snowy window at the little dog outside. "No wonder he hasn't listened to a word I've said."

"Would you care for some breakfast?" Mr. Forester asked.

Sarah's stomach growled fiercely and she gave him a sheepish grin. Seemed sheepish grins were quickly becoming her specialty around this man. "Yes, please." She frowned. "But I should dress first."

"There is no one here to report it if you don't." He crouched down and added two more small logs to the fire. Yes, his backside was definitely noteworthy. "And I certainly won't tell." He stood again and dusted off his hands. Sarah shook her head and willed herself to stop thinking about his backside.

She gave him a half grin. Eating breakfast with a bachelor in her dressing gown? This was positively scandalous, but it was so tempting to just sit at the table and gobble down bacon in her dressing gown the same way she would at home if she were served a tray in bed.

"Very well," she said, warming to the idea.

Fergus II came back in the front door and Mr. Forester shut it behind him. Then he walked over to the kitchen and served them each a plate of biscuits and bacon.

The snow fell steadily outside the window, and the wind whipped along the eaves. The sky turned progressively more gray, and soon wind and snow were battering the small house—so much snow that they could see only pure white out the windows.

"What did you say you were going to teach me today?" Mr. Forester asked with a wide grin when Sarah finished clearing away the breakfast dishes.

"I want to take a look at your clothing," she announced.

"Ah, that's right. But I'm hardly dressed for a London ball while rusticating in Scotland. What would be the point?"

"I understand completely, but as you know, in London, clothing is quite important. All the best-outfitted gentlemen buy their hats at Yardley's, their coats at Weston's, their shirts at Martin's, and their boots at Hoby's. And yes, I do see the irony in the fact that I'm lecturing you about clothing while I myself am in my dressing gown."

He returned her smile. "By all means, lecture away. I'm quite fond of you in your dressing gown already."

Sarah's face heated while Mr. Forester took another drink of his coffee, obviously unrepentant over his remark.

"As for Yardley's and Weston's," he continued, "I believe I've heard Owen Monroe mention those places a time or two."

"You're acquainted with Lord Owen?"

Mr. Forester nodded.

"Well, Lord Owen would certainly know. The man rivals Brummel himself for well dressed."

"You remember Monroe?"

"Yes, of course, he . . ." She trailed off, realizing how rude it sounded that she remembered the earl's son and not Mr. Forester himself. "The point is that Lord Owen knows how to dress."

"I've always thought the simpler the better," Mr. Forester said.

"Simple, yes. But quality counts, and there is nothing more attractive than a man outfitted well in fine black evening attire and a perfectly tied white cravat."

"And here I thought ladies liked wit and charm."

"We like those things, too." She grinned at him.

"Very well. I'll go fetch my clothing. What little there is of it. And you may examine it at your leisure."

He was back in the span of a few minutes, his arms loaded with garments. He dumped the pile on the sofa and turned back to Sarah, gesturing toward the mound of clothes. "I await your advice, my lady." He bowed to her.

Sarah stood and dusted her hands on her dressing gown. She was entirely improper at the moment. Not only was she indecently dressed, she was about to go pawing through a man's clothing. Positively unthinkable in London. Scotland was an odd place. It was as if none of the rules and strictures of Society mattered up here. It was a bit freeing, actually. She felt positively wicked.

She folded her arms across her chest, walked over to the pile of clothing, and stared down at it. It all seemed perfectly clean, if rumpled. Her father's valet would faint if he saw such poor treatment of clothing. She picked up a dark blue woolen coat and shook it out. "This is . . . adequate."

"Adequate?" Mr. Forester frowned.

"Yes, I mean, the cut seems fine, but—"

"What about this?" He pulled a shirt from the pile and held it in front of her in his fist.

"I'd have to see it on before I could properly judge."

Before she had a chance to protest, Mr. Forester ripped off his flannel shirt and proceeded to put on the other. Sarah gasped. She was studying his chest in the firelight. Her throat worked as she swallowed. She quickly spun on her heel, facing the opposite direction.

"I beg your pardon," Mr. Forester said. "I didn't think—"

"It's quite all right," she called over her shoulder. "Just let me know when you're decently . . . I mean properly . . . I mean—"

"I have a shirt on," he announced, putting Sarah out of her misery.

Despite his assurance of being properly dressed, she decided to count to ten first, to be safe. The entire time she was counting, she remembered the look of his skin in the firelight. His flat abdomen. His rippled muscles. Her mouth went dry. The man obviously did something for sport.

When she finally did turn around, his shirt was on as promised and he had an untied cravat hanging over his neck. She examined the shirt. "It's a bit wrinkled, but it's a fine cut. Where do you have your shirts made?"

"Not at Martin's," he admitted with a guilty grin.

She nodded toward the cravat. "What is your favorite knot?"

"I'm supposed to have a favorite knot?"

She shook her head and tried to squelch her smile. "Show me how you tie it, then."

He tied it quickly in a modest, imperfect knot.

"This is how you wear it, to a ball, in London?" she asked, her hands on her hips.

"Yes, is there something wrong?"

"Well, it's a bit . . . simple, isn't it?"

"I like simple."

"May I?" She nodded toward the cravat again.

"By all means," he replied.

She moved closer to him. He smelled like freshly cut wood. When she reached his chest, she looked up into his blue eyes. They were twinkling with mirth. "Do you find this amusing?" she asked.

"A little. I've never worried much about my clothing before."

"I'm trying to help you, as you requested." She'd never noticed before how very good freshly cut wood smelled. It was positively distracting. She swallowed hard.

"Yes." He nodded, pressing his lips together to keep from smiling. "Of course. I'm willing to do whatever you recommend."

She arched a brow at him and reached up to untie the knot he'd created. Why were her hands trembling ever so slightly? "I'll show you one of my favorite knots."

"You are an expert at tying cravats?" he asked.

"I've helped Hart more times than I can count."

"Instead of his valet?"

This time she steadfastly tried to ignore Mr. Forester's

scent. She was certain she would never be able to smell freshly cut wood again without remembering him. Without remembering him shirtless, that is. Another swallow. She also tried to ignore the fact that her hand had brushed against his short beard, sending a trail of shock down her arm. She concentrated on keeping her fingers steady. "Hart's valet drinks." She shook her head. "Half the time the poor man is passed out in the silver closet."

"What? Why doesn't your brother sack the man?"

"Hart's too kindhearted. Father threatens to sack him on nearly a daily basis, but Hart won't hear of it. He's extremely loyal, my brother. Perhaps to a fault at times."

"Funny," Mr. Forester said, his eyes fixed above her head. "My father used to say the same thing about me."

"It's not a bad trait." She kept her eyes trained on the cravat she was tying.

"Try telling that to my father. Which is an impossible task for more than one reason," Mr. Forester said. "Given that he's dead."

"Oh, I'm terribly sorry."

"I'm not. He never approved of a thing I said or did my entire life."

"I know exactly how you feel." Sarah sighed. "It's the same with me and my mother."

"But the difference is you seem to put a great deal of stock into what your mother says about you," Mr. Forester added. "You've mentioned her more than once."

"Did I?" Did she? "I can well imagine what she's saying about me now."

"If she had any heart, she would be wondering why her beloved child has fled and is worried sick that you're missing."

"I can assure you, neither of those things is likely."

"Why not?"

" 'Do as you're told, Sarah,' " she mimicked in a stern,

matronly voice. "That is my mother's very favorite thing to say to me. I was supposed to be at half a dozen parties since I've been gone. No doubt Mother is lamenting the fact that I've been unavailable to Lord Branford and am ruining my reputation and putting my highly sought-after engagement at risk."

He glanced down at Sarah briefly. "That's why you feel guilty for running away? Because for the first time in your life, you didn't do as you were told?"

She nodded. "I don't know what came over me."

"You said your parents don't know that you don't love Branford?"

She snorted at that. Her hands nearly fell from the cravat. "Of course they know. I think they'd be surprised if I did."

Mr. Forester's eyes narrowed. "What do you mean?"

She concentrated on the knot, weaving the stiff fabric through itself and pulling tight. "My parents have raised me like a prize heifer since the day I was born. Status, power, position at court, reputation. Those are the things that matter to them most."

"And not their daughter's happiness?"

She tugged a bit too hard on the cravat. "It's not—it's more complicated than that."

"Is it? You're not a piece of chattel to me and I've only known you two days."

She tugged hard again, trying to ignore those words. "I've always known what was expected of me. It's my duty to make a good match."

"But can't you make a good match and one you actually might enjoy at the same time?"

"There is no better match than Lord Branford."

"That's your parents' opinion, not yours."

" 'Do as you're told, Sarah,' " she whispered. She gave him a smile that didn't reach her eyes, then tugged the cravat one last time. Mr. Forester was pulled off balance. He grabbed her shoulders to steady himself. His large hands cupped her shoulders and Sarah closed her eyes.

He righted himself and pulled his hands away.

"I obviously don't know my own strength." She laughed and reached up again to pat the cravat. "There, a mathematical knot."

Mr. Forester's jaw was rock hard and he was staring above her head. "I heard those are quite fashionable."

"You heard right."

She moved away from him and walked over to stoke the fire with the poker. She tried to banish the memory of his bare chest from her mind, the smell of him, like soap and firewood, and the look in his eye when he'd told her she wasn't a piece of chattel to him. Then the feeling of his hands on her shoulders . . . Dear God. For the first time in her life, she'd wanted a man to kiss her.

She quickly shook her head, clearing it of such unhelpful thoughts. " 'Do as you're told, Sarah,' " she murmured. She wrapped her arms around her middle. She was engaged to another man, for heaven's sake. "I hope the weather turns soon. I must leave as soon as possible. I need to get home."

CHAPTER TEN

The wind had howled throughout the night and the endless snow piled up high around the little lodge. It was snuggled up to the windowsills, peeping inside. Poor Fergus II had a difficult time finding any space to go outside. Christian had gone out to see to the horse and pushed aside a mound of snow for the little dog. The storm worsened by the minute, but Christian managed to carve a path to the barn.

When he returned to the house, he stamped the snow from his boots and rubbed his freezing hands together. He surveyed the room. Sarah, in her maid's dress, was running around the table chasing Fergus II, who had a small cloth toy in his mouth.

Christian pulled off his wool cap and nodded toward the toy. "Where did he get that?"

"I sewed it this morning out of a bit of cloth left over from the wool Mr. Fergus said I might use for his coat." Sarah continued her standoff with Fergus II. When she darted to the right, the dog took off around the table legs to the left. "I made it for him," she said breathlessly, looking at Christian over her shoulder. Her cheeks were rosy and her smile was enchanting. One dark curl had fallen against her cheek. She looked positively breathtaking, and Christian had to remind himself for the dozenth time that not only was she engaged to another man, but she wouldn't look twice at *him* even if she weren't. He concentrated on his reply to her admission about having made the dog's toy.

"You surprise me again," he said, pulling off his overcoat near the front door.

Sarah stopped for a moment. The dog stopped, too. "Surprise you? How do you mean?"

Christian hung his coat on the rack. "When you told me you were the belle of the London Season, I assumed you were . . . that you were . . ."

"Vain? Full of conceit?" She darted toward the dog again. He eluded her.

"I wasn't going to say that." Christian turned back from the coatrack.

"But you were going to say something like that, weren't you?" This time she darted in the opposite direction. So did the dog.

"Aloof, perhaps?" Christian offered.

She turned to face him. "Which is a prettier word for being full of conceit."

"I'm merely surprised that you cook and clean, seem perfectly happy wearing a maid's gown, and are willing to spend your time making coats and toys for a dog."

Fergus II took the toy into the corner and busily chewed on it with the side of his mouth.

Sarah smoothed her skirts and exhaled. "First of all, I've precious little else to do here than make a coat and a toy for a dog. But secondly, I've never seen the need to be high-handed because of my position in life. It's not my fault that I was born the daughter of an earl any more than it's Fergus's fault that he was born a dog."

Christian bowed to her. "A progressive stance, my lady."

"You don't agree?"

"On the contrary, I agree completely. I'm just a bit surprised that *you* feel that way. Though I admit, it's my own prejudice. The belles of the Season haven't been particularly kind to me in the past."

"You seem to have preconceived notions about the peerage. Your friend Lucy wasn't a belle?"

Christian snorted. "Never think it. Lucy was known for her barbs and sharp tongue. She frightened off more suitors than she attracted, I assure you."

Sarah folded her arms across her chest. She watched him carefully. "What would you say if I told you that you surprise me, too?"

Christian had made his way across the room and was busy warming his hands in front of the fireplace. "I do? How?"

"To be blunt, I've never known a handsome man to be so ready to admit his faults."

Christian threw back his head and laughed at that. "You've been associating with the wrong sorts, then. All of my friends and I *live* to point out each other's faults. And more than one of them is good-looking."

"I simply mean that most of the young, handsome gentlemen I've known are more concerned about their reputation. I can't think of one who would be so honest about the trouble he is having finding a wife."

Christian shook his head, still laughing slightly. "Oh, I've had plenty of trouble. And I'm not above admitting it. How else would I plan to remedy the situation? You can't fix what you won't admit to."

She curtsied to him. "A progressive stance, sir."

"I'm glad you agree." He moved over to the table and held out a chair for her. "Now, speaking of my trouble. What else can you teach me?"

Sarah made her way toward him and took a seat. She folded her hands in front of her on the table. "Let's see . . . We've discussed your clothing. Let's talk about your speech."

"My speech?" Christian moved around the table and sat across from her.

"Yes, what you say to a woman is as important as your eligibility and your aspect, I'm certain you're aware."

He cracked a grin. "You mean what I say to her when I'm *not* stuttering?"

She waved a hand at him. "I'm beginning to doubt you've stuttered a day in your life."

"I assure you, I have." He glanced away.

Unconsciously, she reached across the table and touched the top of his hand with hers. "Tell me . . . why?"

Christian drew a deep breath. He didn't pull his hand away. It felt comforting, her sitting there, touching him. When was the last time a woman other than his friends had touched him? And she seemed to genuinely care.

It's not that he didn't know why he stuttered. He remembered the day it had started. Would never be able to forget. But telling someone else? A woman? A beautiful woman? That was a different matter altogether. But even as he had the thought, he knew he was going to tell her. Because somehow here with Sarah at his hunting lodge, he wasn't the shy stutterer whom the ladies in London knew. He was . . . comfortable.

"Please tell me," she repeated, still touching his hand, her eyes meeting his.

"I was always a shy boy. Didn't like to speak to strangers. Hid behind my mother's skirts." He chuckled.

Sarah smiled encouragingly. "It sounds adorable to me."

"It drove my father mad, I assure you. He used to grab me and pull me out from behind Mother, insisting that I talk to whoever was visiting."

Sarah nodded. "That must have been awful for you."

"Excruciating. He'd yell at me also, right there in front of whomever he wanted me to speak to. 'Say something, lad, don't just stand there like a deaf-mute!'"

Sarah winced. "How positively horrid of him."

"One day, he was meeting with potential governesses for me. I must have been no more than four years old. My current governess planned to marry and they needed to replace her. He called me down to his study, and when I poked my head in the door, the most beautiful woman I'd ever seen before was sitting there, across from my father. Mind you, at the ripe old age of four, I hadn't seen many women, but she looked like a goddess as far as I was concerned." The ghost of a smile touched his lips.

"Don't tell me. Your father yelled at you to speak." Sarah shook her head sympathetically.

"I was frozen halfway in and halfway out of the door. I couldn't move. I couldn't say anything.

"'There he is,' my father said. 'The little half-wit. You'll have your hands full getting that one to speak.'"

"No!" Sarah's hand squeezed around two of Christian's fingers.

"Yes," Christian replied. "And of course that made it all the more awful. 'Come in now, Christian!' he demanded. And when I didn't move, he stood, stalked over to me, and pulled me by the ear inside the room to stand in front of the beautiful governess."

Sarah gasped. "Why, I'd like to slap him. How could he be so unkind to a child?"

"It's funny you should say that, because that's exactly what he did. Slap me."

"No!" Sarah's hands flew to her cheeks and her eyes filled with tears.

"Yes. And he continued to slap me over and over again until I said something."

"Oh, Christian, no." Tears dripped from her eyes.

"Yes." His jaw was tight. It was a memory he didn't often allow himself to dwell on. It was one that made him feel as if the walls were closing in on him. But somehow, here, telling it to Sarah, he felt safe.

"I finally spoke," he said. "But whatever I said—and I swear, to this day, I have no idea what it was—came out with a horrible stutter. A stutter my father promptly mocked."

"I hate to say it, but I'm beginning to be glad your father is dead, too. I can't imagine meeting such an awful man."

"And that's it," Christian said, pushing back on the legs of his chair. "I've stuttered ever since. At least in the presence of beautiful ladies. Sometimes in front of men, too. Especially powerful ones. As I said before, your arrival was quite different. Something about a sword being drawn on me must have knocked me out of my habit."

She wiped the tears from her cheeks. "Well, your father was an idiot. And I'm glad I pulled a sword on you if it kept you from being uncomfortable around me. I'm also sorry to have been improper and used your given name."

Christian grinned at her. He desperately wanted to revive the lightheartedness they'd had earlier. "Don't worry about that. I've seen you eat bacon in your dressing gown, and now you know a very humiliating secret about my past. I'm certain we can survive calling each other by our given names."

She pressed her handkerchief to her nose and laughed.

"I believe you're right. You may call me Sarah. When we're alone, of course."

"Of course." He winked at her. "Very well, my lady. Before I shared that less-than-entertaining tale, you were telling me that we must examine my speech. Tell me, what is the matter with my speech?"

"Oh, no. I didn't mean your speech. That is to say, the *way* you speak. I meant the content of what you say."

"Ah, I see."

"There may, of course, be nothing the matter with it. But I'll have to examine it."

"How, precisely, do you propose we do that?"

"Well." She cleared her throat. "Let us pretend that you are at a ball and you are asking me to dance. We've met, but only once."

She stood and made her way to the corner, where she began to have an earnest conversation with absolutely no one.

Christian watched her and scratched his head. "What are you doing?"

She glanced back at him. "I'm pretending to be speaking with my friends. Come over and interrupt us."

Christian exhaled his breath. He'd already learned that Lady Sarah was a bit unusual, but if the woman could help him attract a proper wife, he'd try anything. He stood, grabbed a coat from the pile on the sofa, put it on, pulled on the lapels, and strode over. "Good evening, Lady Sarah. May I have this dance?"

She glanced at him over her shoulder and batted her eyelashes at him. "Good evening, Mr. Forester. Have you met my friends, Lady Kate and Lady Mary?" She gestured to her imaginary friends.

"I have not, but I am here to ask *you* to dance," he continued.

Sarah stopped, turned, and put her hands on her hips. "See, right there. That was shortsighted of you."

Christian frowned. "You said a lady likes to be singled out."

"Yes, but her closest friends are the ones to whom she will speak about you after your dance. If you aren't solicitous of them, they will not like you and will not say particularly kind things."

His frown deepened. "Should I ask them to dance, too?"

"Certainly not. Then the lady you are attempting to court will not know whom you are interested in."

Christian shifted his weight to his right foot and stuck out his left one. "Does this honestly make sense to all of you?"

Sarah blinked at him innocently. "Of course it does. And it would make sense to you, too, if you would pay attention."

"I don't see how it can possibly—"

"Try again," she interrupted.

Christian gave her a thunderous expression but walked away, turned, grabbed his lapels again, cleared his throat, and walked back. "Good evening, Lady Sarah, Lady Kate, Lady Mary. A pleasure to see you all this evening."

"Good evening, Mr. Forester," Lady Sarah replied, batting her eyelashes again.

"Don't do that."

"Do what?"

"Bat your eyelashes at me. It's distracting."

"The lady you're courting may well be distracting to you. In fact, she'd better be distracting or you probably ought not to court her." Sarah's tinkling laughter followed. That was distracting, too.

Christian tried to ignore her laughter and her lily scent and concentrate on his lesson. "I hope your lovely friends here won't mind if you take a turn dancing with me. Can you spare her, ladies?" He bowed to her imaginary friends.

"Yes, thank you. I would love to dance," Sarah said prettily.

He offered his arm and she placed her hand on his.

"We've no music," he pointed out when they walked over to stand in the open space between the table and the sofa.

"Use your imagination. Pretend a waltz is playing." She held out her hands as if they were about to begin a waltz.

Christian took a deep breath and pulled her into his arms. He spun her around in time to music that was only in his head. Sarah apparently knew the song because she began to hum the exact one he'd been thinking of.

"How did you—?"

"I told you, I've done this quite a lot. I've been learning to dance since I was barely out of leading strings."

They danced for a bit and Christian tried to ignore the lily scent of her hair and the soft feel of her in his arms. He reminded himself that he must concentrate on his witty repartee. That was what they were about, wasn't it?

"Lady Kate isn't as pretty as you are," he whispered, leaning down so she could hear.

Sarah slapped at his arm with an imaginary fan. "That's horrid."

"Lady Mary isn't either," he said with a wicked grin.

"You are insulting my friends, sir." She raised her nose in the air.

Christian stopped for a moment. "You don't truly have friends named Kate and Mary, do you?"

"No," Sarah said with a wink. "I invented them entirely."

"Good." Christian exhaled. "I'd hate to be insulting real people. Insulting imaginary ones is amusing, though."

"How are you enjoying your evening, Mr. Forester?" Sarah asked, obviously intent upon resuming their lesson.

"It's better now that I'm in *your* company, my lady."

"You do know how to flatter a girl," Sarah said, with more eyelash batting.

"It's impossible not to flatter one as lovely as you," he replied smoothly.

"Hmm." Sarah stopped dancing. Christian stopped, too.

"You're doing a fine job," she said.

"Dancing?"

"Yes, but I was referring to your speech. You obviously have no problems being charming."

He snorted. "I'm glad to hear you think so. Was my repartee witty enough?"

"I think so."

"Was my speech enticing enough?"

"Quite."

"It's because we're just here, you and I, in my home in Scotland. There's nothing intimidating about it. No reason to be shy or uncomfortable. When I'm in London, however, things will be different."

"The answer to that particular dilemma is simple."

"It is? How?"

"When you are in a London ballroom speaking to a beautiful lady, you must pretend that you are here in Scotland, dancing and speaking only to me."

Christian lifted his chin and glanced away. Why did he have the feeling that when the time came, that was precisely what he would wish he were doing?

CHAPTER ELEVEN

By the evening the snow seemed to have stopped, but it was already halfway up the windows and the wind continued to blow mercilessly, howling between the trees in the nearby forest. Fergus II returned from his business outdoors with a fine layer of ice resting atop his coat. Sarah removed the little garment to dry it by the fire and rubbed the dog vigorously with a blanket to warm him. He yipped and stuck out his tongue, clearly happy for the attention.

When Christian came in from doing his chores, he smiled at her. "My apologies for myself and this dog being your only company, my lady."

"Nonsense. You are both excellent company. In fact, I was just thinking of how peaceful and lovely it is to be able to sit and enjoy myself in a room with another person even though no words are shared between us. You're obviously comfortable with silence."

"Perhaps too much so," Christian replied.

"It's so different here from my life at home," Sarah said. "Father and Mother and Hart are always talking.

There's a constant bustle in our houses either in London or in the country. But here, with you, I can just be quiet and relax without feeling . . . alone."

"I understand," Christian said quietly.

"I've never felt that way before. I don't think I've ever met anyone else comfortable with sharing silence."

"Nor have I," Christian murmured.

"What was that?" Sarah asked.

"Nothing. What say we have dinner? I'm famished."

They had cured meat and cheese and wine for dinner. Afterward, Christian brought out the wood pieces he'd been working on and set them on the table along with his knives and small chisel.

"What is that?" Sarah exclaimed. She was wiping her hands on her apron, having just finished cleaning the dishes from the meal.

"A chessboard."

"I can see that," she said, rolling her eyes but smiling. "What are you doing with it?"

"I've been slowly carving it over time. I was planning to work on it more this evening."

She came over and stared down at the board. "You *made* this?"

"Yes."

"The entire thing? The pieces, too?" She picked up one of the rooks and turned it over in her hand, examining it carefully.

"That's right," he said. "I've always enjoyed fashioning things out of wood. I made this table. And the coat-rack too."

"What is it made from?" Sarah asked, setting the rook back down and running her fingers over the checkered board.

"The dark pieces are made from cherry and the light, hawthorn."

"It's so well done." There was an unmistakable note of admiration in her voice.

"Thank you."

"You're just going to let this sit up here? With no one to see it?"

"I don't get many visitors here," he replied. "Which is how I like it. Present company notwithstanding, of course."

She twisted a dark curl over her finger. "I love to play chess," she said, a twinkle in her eyes.

"Do you?" Another surprise. "How did you learn?"

She pulled out a chair and settled in. "Father was forever trying to teach Hart how to play. Hart hated it. So one day I asked Father if he'd teach me. He laughed at first, but when he stopped laughing and realized I was serious, he decided it would be a lark. Hart never did learn how to play properly, poor man." She grinned. "I, however, never lose."

"Never?" Christian whistled. "That's a strong word."

"Yes. And a true one."

"Careful. I might just begin to think you're full of conceit after all."

She lifted one shoulder. "It's not conceit if it's true."

He gestured to the board. "By all means, then, my lady. Show me your skill."

"With pleasure." She rubbed her hands together.

Halfway through the game, Christian realized he was going to be beaten soundly. He and Sarah had spent the better part of the last hour teasing each other over the game. He decided to change the subject. Perhaps he might distract her.

"What's next?" he asked. "In your lesson plan for me?"

"Trying to divert my attention, Mr. Forester?" Her alert eyes didn't leave the board.

"Absolutely," he replied with a grin.

She paused, stretched her arms high above her head,

and continued to study the board. "I believe that would be reputation."

"Reputation?" He crossed his arms over his chest. "What exactly do you mean by that?"

"You know, reputation? A sort of popularity. What the gossips say about you. That sort of thing."

"I can tell you exactly what the gossips say about me. Absolutely nothing."

"Precisely, and that's a problem. I always tell Meg, better to be gossiped about than to be ignored."

He snorted. "Does that comfort Meg?"

"Of course not, but I have to say something uplifting. She's my dearest friend."

He smiled at her and shook his head. "So I'm to make the gossips' tongues wag?"

"It's all about making them wag in the right direction. I could give you the best clothing, teach you the best manners, and provide you with the most witty repartee, and none of it matters a pin without word spreading that you're sought after."

Christian groaned. "Marvelous. How on earth am I to manage that?"

Sarah's eyes remained pinned to the board. "All you need is a young, popular, *unmarried* lady to tell her young, popular, *unmarried* lady friends that *you* are the catch of the Season. She must be unmarried. Hearing such gossip from the matrons is sure to send the unmarried ladies running in the opposite direction. It's like hearing it from our mothers, I'm afraid."

"Which is another reason why my friends Lucy, Cassandra, and Jane can't help me," Christian replied.

"Precisely."

"You truly believe that will work? Spreading a bit of gossip among the unmarried ladies?"

"Of course." Sarah shrugged. "How do you think the catch of the Season becomes the catch of the Season?"

The side of Christian's mouth quirked up in a grin. "A coveted title, a huge estate, and lots of money, of course."

She finally met his gaze. "No. It's never that. Last Season the marquess was a catch because of his title, of course, but the Season before last it was Baron Bolt. And he was neither particularly rich nor particularly well titled."

Christian rubbed his chin. He still hadn't shaved. No valet. No proper shaving utensils. He'd long since decided that Lady Sarah was just going to have to forgive him for his beard. That's what she got for arriving unexpected at his hunting lodge.

He considered her words. She was right. Baron Bolt had been the catch of the Season two Seasons ago. The man had half the female members of the *ton* chasing after him. "I always assumed it was because Baron Bolt was particularly handsome, or so the ladies seemed to think."

"No more handsome than you," Lady Sarah said just before making her next move on the chessboard.

"I'd thank you for the compliment if you hadn't just captured my bishop."

"You're welcome," she replied with a grin, clutching the vanquished bishop in her fist.

Christian studied the board, plotting his next move. "So you're saying it isn't about one's clothing, money, or title?"

Sarah propped her elbow on the table and rested her chin in her hand. "It is about those things if they're missing or inadequate, but if they're there, it's merely a matter of generating the right sort of word of mouth."

Christian continued to study the board. "That sounds preposterous, you know."

Sarah laughed. "You're the one who suggested I waltz

back home pretending I've been visiting. You understand how it works."

Christian rubbed his beard again. "God help me, I believe you're right. But who would be willing to spread such gossip? I'm not exactly rich in unmarried, young, popular lady acquaintances. I might add that if I were, I might not have this problem to begin with."

"Why, you ask one of them for a favor, of course. Haven't you ever asked for a favor?"

Christian stared blankly at the chessboard.

"You haven't, have you?" Sarah's voice was incredulous.

"Haven't what?"

"Ever asked for a favor."

"What does this have to do with chess?" Christian made an idiotic move that put one of his knights at risk. He cursed under his breath.

Sarah stopped studying the board to look at him. "It's all right, you know."

"What is?"

"To ask for a favor. People do it all the time. You've granted me a favor by allowing me to remain here."

"What if it doesn't work?" he asked softly.

"What if what doesn't work?"

"The rumors? The reputation?"

"That's simple," she said, returning her attention to the board and easily capturing his knight. "If the rumors don't work, set your sights on the most sought-after lady in the crowd. If she notices you, all the others will, too."

Christian shook his head, marveling at her words. "You ladies are devious."

"No, we're practical."

"Practically evil."

"Not at all."

"Very well. Any suggestions of whom I might ask for such a favor?"

She crossed her arms over her chest and gazed at him skeptically. "Really?"

"Really what?"

"You cannot be that dense. You happen to have a young, unmarried, popular female sitting directly across from you and, by the by, she owes you a favor."

CHAPTER TWELVE

"You're going to help me?" Christian asked, blinking at her incredulously.

"Why wouldn't I? As soon as Mrs. Goatsocks and I return to London and say we've been visiting friends to the north, hopefully the gossip will die down soon enough. If you return to London just as the next Season begins, I'm certain I can help you before I become an old married lady myself." She grinned at him and rubbed her hands together as she studied the chessboard.

Christian sighed and contemplated his defeat. "Go ahead. There's my queen. Finish me off."

Sarah did so in two easy moves.

"You're quite good at chess," he admitted.

"And you are quite good at carving." She examined the queen closely. "It's absolutely amazing how detailed the pieces are."

"It's just something I do to pass the time."

"If this is something you do to pass the time, I'd like to see what you're *truly* skilled at."

That statement hung in the air for a bit, making Sarah

blush until Christian chuckled and said, "Obviously not at attracting ladies." He gathered the pieces together to put them back in the wooden box he'd carved for their storage. "Anything else to teach me? About the fairer sex, I mean."

"Oh, yes. I nearly forgot. When you pay the lady of your choosing a call, don't bring roses. Anything but roses."

"Why not roses?" He set the pieces gingerly inside the velvet-lined box.

Sarah rolled her eyes. "Everyone brings roses. It shows absolutely no imagination whatsoever."

He cracked a smile. "Shouldn't you merely be glad to have received flowers?"

"Well, of course, but if you want to stand out in a crowd of suitors, you'll have to do better than roses."

"Fine. No roses. Duly noted. Anything else?"

"Yes. Tell her that her hair looks pretty."

"What if it doesn't?"

Another eye roll. "Tell her regardless. We spend a great deal of time on our hair and we're excessively fond of it."

Sarah made her way across the room and curled up on the sofa, her feet under her, a quilt surrounding her. Soon, Fergus II was similarly curled up on the rug beneath her. Sarah reached for the knitting needles that sat on the side table next to the sofa and resumed knitting a second coat for the dog. If this snow didn't let up, the pup would have a large wardrobe.

She glanced over at Christian, wondering for the dozenth time what he looked like without his beard. She'd drifted off to sleep last night wondering about it, actually.

"Did you bring those knitting needles with you from London?" he asked, jolting her from her thoughts.

She dragged her eyes away from the stitch she was

making. "No. I found them in a drawer in the bedroom. Don't worry, I have no intention of stealing them. I'm merely borrowing them," she teased.

Christian frowned. "There were knitting needles in the drawer?"

She paused in her stitch. "Yes. Didn't you know it?"

"No." He smiled and her heart fluttered. "It might come as a surprise to you, my lady, but I don't knit."

She smiled back at him, then returned her attention to the little coat. "Perhaps your cousin left them here. Or your mother?"

The silence that followed was palpable. Sarah shifted uncomfortably in her seat as the awkwardness of the moment dragged on. She obviously shouldn't have mentioned his mother. They'd been having a happy exchange until that point. She searched her brain for something to say, some other topic to switch to and make things right.

Moments later, he stood, made his way over to the door, and retrieved his coat from the rack. "I must see to the horse."

Sarah nodded, but he didn't see her. He was out the door in a flash, the cold wind whipping into the room as he opened and shut the door as quickly as possible. She bit her lip and continued her work on the coat, but her mind was racing. Why had Christian been so unwilling to say anything about his mother? And it had to be his mother that was the sore subject. He'd seemed happy enough to discuss his cousin with her before.

Sarah sighed and glanced down at Fergus II. She'd left the rest of the wool she'd been using in the bedchamber. She stood to fetch it. Fergus II jumped up from his spot beneath the sofa and followed Sarah down the hall to the bedchamber. She entered the room slowly, pushing open the door. This was Christian's room. She'd usurped it. He hadn't said anything, but she'd figured it out the night before last when she'd opened the bedside drawer and noticed some of his personal effects. A copy of *Two Treatises of Government* by John Locke. A few coins. A small pocketknife. It was kind of him to allow her the use of his room. She hadn't had the nerve to mention it. Now she sat on the edge of the bed and opened the drawer again. It was awful of her to snoop through his belongings, but she suddenly had the desire to know more about this man. To understand him.

The book was still there, the coins, and the knife. This time she noticed a small envelope lying under the other items. She pulled it out and unfolded it. It contained a lock of dark blond hair. Next to it sat a small golden locket. She gingerly picked it up and popped it open. A tiny painting of a beautiful woman looked back at her. She squinted. The woman had blond hair and light blue eyes and was wearing a gown from the last century. Even in miniature, Sarah could see the resemblance. She was certain. It had to be Christian's mother.

"What happened to you?" she whispered to the locket.

The front door banged open just then and, guilt-ridden, Sarah dropped the locket back into the envelope, put the envelope back into the drawer, and shut it. Then she grabbed up the wool and hurried to the great room.

"So how do I become irresistible?" Christian asked, a smile on his face, as soon as he saw her.

Sarah laughed. Apparently he was back in a good mood. She was relieved. "I said elusive, not irresistible," she replied.

"Aren't they the same thing?" The teasing tone was back in his voice.

"Of course not."

"Why is it important for a gentleman to be elusive, then?" he asked as he shucked his boots and made his way over to sit in one of the chairs next to the sofa.

"It's not so much that you must seem elusive, really, it's more that you must not seem too available." Her knitting needles clicked together.

He rubbed the back of his neck. "But if I'm not available, why would I be looking for a wife?"

"No, *eligible* is quite different from *available*. All of the gentlemen the young ladies seem to swoon over act as if they can take or leave any *ton* party and may not even arrive at another one. That's why Almack's is the wrong place for you."

He laughed. "That's not difficult to pretend. I *can* take or leave any of the *ton* parties. Almack's included."

"Why is it that you can take or leave any of the *ton* parties?" she asked, truly interested.

"I've never enjoyed parties, really. Or going about in Society. I'd much rather be home, carving or reading or—"

She gave a mock gasp. "Mr. Forester. How can you say such blasphemous things? Why, in London, *Society* is everything."

He laughed at her obvious jest. "Which is why I've never been particularly popular in London. It's a pity I cannot marry a milkmaid in Scotland."

"You'd never find one in all this snow."

He grinned at that. "I'm willing to go back to London next Season. One last time. I'm committed to finally finding a willing wife."

"I think you're overcomplicating it. To be seen as elusive, you merely need to act as if you're uninterested in any particular female. It's quite simple, really."

"Didn't you tell me that females want to feel singled out, special?"

"Of course. But that's only *after* they've captured your attention. They want to feel as if it was a bit of a challenge at first. As if you might *not* ask them to dance."

He rubbed a hand over one eye. "That makes no sense."

"It makes perfect sense. That which is easily gained is often neglected."

"Very well. So I should strut around these *ton* events acting as if I don't fancy anyone in particular. Then what?"

"Ask a few ladies to dance. Talk to them. See who garners your attention."

"And once I'm properly attentive?"

"Ask her to dance again the next time you see her." Sarah put the kettle on to make tea. It had already become their nightly ritual.

"That seems to be a roundabout way of going about it," he said.

She pulled the canister that held the leaves from the cabinet. "It's courtship."

"It's inefficient."

"I know of no other way. You cannot ask a lady you admire to dance more than once or twice at any given ball. It would be unseemly."

Joining her, Christian pulled the teacups from the cupboard. She momentarily marveled at how he seemed to feel as comfortable around her as she did around him. She'd never felt this way with another person. Had he? Not even Cook allowed her this level of freedom at home. Wouldn't it be wonderful to be with someone who didn't constantly remind her of appearances and propriety?

"Unseemly?" he said. "I suppose the good news is that I haven't done so before, and any lady I have asked to dance more than once invariably turns me down."

Sarah put a hand on her hip and eyed him over the canister. "Why?"

"As I said before, it seems to me that most of the young

ladies I've taken an interest in have already set their sights on another man."

Sarah pulled the kettle off the hearth with a towel wrapped around the handle and set it on the counter. "You must take her attention away from the other man."

"That's easier said than done." Christian picked up the kettle and poured the water over the leaves.

"Of course it is. But I'd say a lady who isn't interested enough in you to be distracted by you when another man is around, probably isn't your best match."

He contemplated that for a moment. "Hmm. You may be right, Lady Sarah."

"Of course I'm right. I've been taught about all of these details since I was a child." She sighed. "I wish I hadn't been, but it's mostly all I know."

He pushed her teacup toward her. "So only two dances, eh?"

She picked it up. "If you do ask her three times, expect her to say no."

"If I asked you to dance three times, would you say no?"

"Of course." She winked at him over the rim of her cup.

"My dancing is adequate?" he asked.

"Yes."

"My repartee witty?"

"Absolutely." She took a sip of tea.

"My clothing will be up to snuff once I make a visit to the shops you've kindly pointed out to me."

"You cannot go wrong with them."

"And my beard, sadly, will be gone by the time I return to London."

"I wouldn't be so sad about it," Sarah mumbled, taking another sip.

"Should I mention I live with a well-dressed dog?"

She nearly spit out her tea. Her lips curled into a catlike smile. "It cannot hurt. Though please don't tell anyone who made Fergus his wardrobe."

"Don't worry. I won't."

She set down her teacup and made her way to the sofa, where she picked up the little coat she'd been knitting earlier. "By the by, will you come hold him while I fit him?"

"A fitting for a dog?" Christian sounded skeptical at best.

"How else will I be able to tell if I've allowed for enough room in the chest?"

Christian shook his head but stood from his seat, moved over to the sofa, sat next to Sarah, and scooped up the dog from the rug.

Fergus II seemed nothing but pleased to be receiving such attention. He turned his head and licked Christian's nose. Sarah smiled. She slipped the opening over the dog's head and arranged the bit of wool she'd already knitted over the dog's shoulders, or whatever the doggy equivalent of shoulders was. Her hand brushed against Christian's, and a jolt went through her body.

She glanced up into his eyes. He was looking at her.

She dropped her ball of yarn and the dog jumped off the sofa.

Christian leaned closer, his mesmerizing eyes never leaving hers. His lips hovered over hers.

He was going to kiss her. And she wanted him to. Oh, how she wanted him. She leaned forward. Waiting. Waiting.

"I've been meaning to ask you something," she murmured against his cheek.

"Anything." His breath was a hot brand against her lips.

"Did you really have a pistol that first night?"

"Yes."

Just before his lips touched hers, the front door burst open and Mr. Fergus came barreling through it in a snowy heap of plaid.

CHAPTER THIRTEEN

Sarah leaped up from the sofa and ran to the man whose overcoat was completely white with snow. Fergus II ran toward his master, too, barking. Mr. Fergus was nearly frozen. Bundled up in a huge coat with mittens and a scarf, his face bright red, lips pale blue, he was shuddering uncontrollably.

"How in the world did you make it?" Sarah asked, horrified, shutting the front door against the high wind and swirling snow.

"Bring him over to the fire," Christian called to Sarah.

Sarah ushered the shivering man over. Mr. Fergus was obviously alone. "Where's Mrs. Goatsocks?" Sarah asked in a shaking voice, fearing the worst.

"She had to stay behind at the doctor's house," Mr. Fergus managed through chattering teeth.

Breathing a sigh of relief that the news was not worse, Sarah sat the man down in front of the fire. Then she ran to the bedchamber to pull the extra quilts off the bed. She came back quickly, dragging them behind her, and bundled him up even more. Meanwhile, Christian pulled bricks out of the fire and placed them near Mr. Fergus's feet. Sarah concentrated on making the old man comfortable. There would be plenty of time to ask him about Mrs. Goatsocks later.

Once Mr. Fergus was adequately bundled up, Sarah set the kettle on again to make him tea while Christian continued to place bricks in the fire, pulling them out with tongs to set them by the older man's feet as soon as they were heated. Twenty minutes later, a normal color was slowly returning to Mr. Fergus's face and his lips were no longer blue. Fergus II was snuggled on his lap, obviously pleased to have his owner back.

"Thank ye kindly," Mr. Fergus said to Sarah as he sipped the tea she'd made him. "And thank ye, Master Christian."

Christian nodded. "I'm glad to see you in one piece, Fergus."

"You're more than welcome, Mr. Fergus," Sarah said. "Please, can you tell me what happened to Mrs. Goatsocks?"

"That woman is a handful," Mr. Fergus said, shaking his head and settling back against the sofa. He resettled the dog in his lap, too. "But I don't wish bad luck on anyone, especially not this time of year. Turns out her ankle was more than twisted. She broke the thing."

Sarah gasped. "No!" She put a hand to her throat.

Christian winced.

"Yes," Mr. Fergus continued. "The doctor wrapped it up tight and told her she had ta keep ta bed and not move it so much as a pace until it's good and healed. A month or more."

Sarah sat back on her heels, stunned. The wind had seemingly been knocked from her chest. "She's not coming back?"

"She carried on something fierce, I must tell ye, after

the good doctor broke the news ta her. Said she planned to crawl back here ta ye on her hands and knees if she had ta."

"Oh, my goodness." Sarah put her hand to her mouth. "That sounds like something Mrs. Goatsocks would say."

"Took both the doctor and his wife ta convince her ta stay. In the end, I think she only agreed because she tried ta walk on that blasted ankle of hers and she couldn't. Only succeeded in making it worse."

Sarah shook her head sadly. "Poor Mrs. Goatsocks."

"She tried ta bribe me, she did. Asked me if I might procure a sled and *pull* her up here." Mr. Fergus chuckled. "Never heard such an outlandish request."

"Oh, dear," Sarah said. "What did you say?"

"I told her there weren't enough coin in the kingdom and she'd be frozen ta death afore we made it halfway. Finally, I convinced her that I would come back and see ta ye. Bring ye to her if ye wished."

"Oh, that is kind of you, Mr. Fergus." Sarah swallowed and calmly folded her hands. This was a pickle, no question about it. She supposed she'd wait until the weather didn't pose a threat to Mr. Fergus's health and then take him up on his offer to accompany him to the doctor's house. She would just have to stay with Mrs. Goatsocks until her ankle healed. It would be the death of her reputation, no doubt, but what choice did she have? She couldn't leave her trusted friend and servant to fend for herself.

At the moment, however, she simply didn't want Mr. Fergus to worry about her. The poor man had been through enough on her account. "We'll figure out something," she said, patting his hand through the mass of blankets.

They sat around talking for another half hour or so. Christian had a score of questions about Mr. Fergus's journey. Sarah tried valiantly to keep the panic from rising in her chest while the caretaker told them the story of how he'd made it back to them through the tremendous amount of snow. Truly a marvelous feat. Sarah gave him another cup of tea, this time laced liberally with whiskey. She splashed a bit in her own cup as well. The old man smiled at her when she returned to the sofa and handed him his drink.

"Thank you for braving the snow to come to my rescue, Mr. Fergus. I greatly appreciate it."

Christian glanced up at her, an inscrutable look on his face. Was she surprising him again with her warm thanks for a servant? She tried not to think about how close she'd come to allowing him to kiss her. To kissing him back!

"I knew ye would be worried sick, me lady," Mr. Fergus said, closing his eyes for a moment. "I couldn't leave ye alone up here no longer. I didna know if Master Christian had made it before the storm. Besides, Mrs. Goatsocks was near beside herself thinking of ye alone up here. She insisted I leave her and come back for ye immediately."

"That was kind of you, but you needn't have risked your life for my sake. Besides, I had Fergus Two here, didn't I?"

Mr. Fergus sighed and pulled his hand from the mass of blankets. He set his empty cup on the table next to the sofa. "Aye, that ye did. Thank ye for taking such good care of the pup. I see he's got a new coat. Can't say as how I ever figured he needed one before now, but I suppose he's happy enough ta have it."

Sarah smiled sheepishly. "I was a bit bored while I was alone."

Mr. Fergus's wrinkled face broke into a smile. "I was worried about ye, truly I was. But if I'd known Master

Christian had made it here ta be with ye, I might not have been so troubled. He is a kind master and a most respected gentleman."

Sarah and Christian glanced at each other over Mr. Fergus's head. Neither of them shared the story of how she'd pulled a broadsword on him when they'd met. They tacitly agreed. That was a story for another time.

Soon Fergus was snoring and Christian pulled the old man's legs onto the sofa and placed a pillow gently under his head. Sarah moved away to make room. It was kind of Christian to treat his servant so well. She'd never seen Lord Branford so much as acknowledge his own.

Christian put his fingers to his lips to indicate to Sarah to be quiet, then he nodded in the direction of the bedchambers. She followed him down the corridor. Fergus II, clearly playing favorites, remained curled up on the sofa with his master, his snores interspersed with the man's.

Sarah and Christian stopped in between the doors to their respective bedchambers. They spoke in whispers.

"I'm such a bother to have brought poor Mrs. Goatsocks this far, up into the snow where she fell and broke her ankle. Poor woman. All because of me and my idiotic decisions. I feel absolutely terrible."

Christian glanced back toward the great room to ensure Mr. Fergus remained asleep. "Mrs. Goatsocks is a grown woman. She made her own choice to come with you."

"Only because she knew if I went without a chaperone, I'd no longer be allowed in polite Society."

"Still, don't blame yourself. You couldn't have known she would break her ankle."

"You heard Mr. Fergus. She may have to stay a month or more. I should write Mother and tell her the truth. Tell her that I'm not coming back for a long while and . . . Oh,

God. No one will believe it. No one will believe me. My reputation is entirely ruined and I have no one to blame for it but myself."

Christian crossed his arms over his chest and looked down at her. "What if I told you I have an idea?"

CHAPTER FOURTEEN

"An idea?" Sarah whispered, also glancing back toward the great room to ensure they weren't speaking too loudly.

"Yes," Christian replied.

"Whatever can you mean?"

"You've been helping *me*. In return, I will do everything in my power to help you reenter Society with as little scandal as possible."

Sarah pressed her back against the wall and hung her head. She tried not to remember how close she'd come to kissing this man earlier. In addition to her other sins, she was now well on her way to turning into a shameless hoyden. "How in heaven's name do you believe you might be able to accomplish such a thing?"

Christian ran a hand through his hair. "I've been thinking of ways we could get you back into London, back into Society, without anyone being any the wiser."

Her head snapped up, hope undoubtedly pinned to her features. "You've thought of something?"

"No." Christian chuckled. "I'm not that inventive. But I know someone who has a certain, shall I say, knack for this sort of thing. You haven't met my friends. They are ladies with sterling reputations and they are both inventive and a bit mad, which is precisely the combination we're in need of at present if I don't mistake my guess. If it takes an unmarried young woman to make a bachelor into the catch of the Season, it takes a respectable matron to do away with a potential scandal."

Sarah blinked. "Knack? Who has a knack for such things?"

"Lucy."

Sarah's eyes nearly bugged from her skull. "Your friend Lucy?"

"Yes."

"I don't know. She'd have to be awfully clever to fix *this*." She flourished her hand in the air, indicating the cabin.

"I'm positive she will, and if you'll just allow me to write to her and tell her the circumstances, I'm certain she'll come up with something perfect."

Sarah contemplated the matter for a moment. "She's good at this sort of thing?"

Christian nodded. "Excellent at it. You could say her plots are one of her most accomplished skills. She's quite remarkable, I assure you."

Sarah felt a momentary pang of jealousy. Who was this lady whom Christian obviously thought so highly of? Whom he had even tried to court once, if unsuccessfully?

"I suppose I have no other choice. I must throw myself on the mercy of your friend," Sarah said with a resolute nod. "And I thank you for it."

"Don't worry. I'll ride out as soon as I can to get a letter in the post. If the snow lets up, it shouldn't take longer than a few days to get a letter to Lucy. We'll meet her back in England."

Sarah's eyes widened with fright. "I can't leave Mrs. Goatsocks."

"We'll think of something. Once the snow stops, I'll go to speak to Mrs. Goatsocks."

"You said we'll meet Lucy in England. Surely you don't mean London?"

"No. Not London," he assured her. "Don't worry. Leave the details to me."

She lifted her chin and met his gaze. "Thank you for being so kind to me, Christian. You are a very good friend indeed."

Friend. The word hung in the air between them. But Christian knew as well as she did, they were both remembering their almost kiss.

"Good night." Sarah ducked into the bedchamber and shut the door behind her. She hopped into bed, pulled the quilt over her head, and drifted to sleep imagining what Christian looked like beneath his beard.

CHAPTER FIFTEEN

The next morning it had stopped snowing, but great amounts of the stuff remained piled high under the bright sun. Christian braved the enormous snow hills to travel into town to post his letter to Lucy Hunt. It had taken a great deal of convincing, however, to keep Sarah from coming with him. She desperately wanted to see her chaperone, but after Christian demonstrated that one of the snowdrifts outside the lodge came up nearly to his waist (and he was much taller than her), she finally relented.

Christian left Oberon in the barn. He didn't want to risk the horse hurting himself or becoming stuck in a drift. He tied snowshoes to the bottoms of his boots and trudged down the hill to town. The journey was long and tiring, and Christian spent the entire span trying to forget that he'd spent the better part of the night tossing and turning, thinking of the kiss he'd nearly shared with Sarah. That hadn't exactly been the action of a *friend,* had it? But he could already tell, his relationship with Sarah was going to end up the same way all his other relationships with women did. He'd volunteered to help Sarah get back to Society, back to her *intended*. He mustn't forget that the lady was spoken for. And he needed to get her back to London safely before he did something they would both regret. Yes. He was turning squarely into Sarah's *friend*. And that was exactly as it should be.

After posting the letter to Lucy, Christian stopped by the doctor's house to pay a visit to Mrs. Goatsocks.

It had also taken him no insignificant amount of time this morning to convince Sarah that leaving Mrs. Goatsocks with the doctor and traveling to England with him to meet his friends was, in fact, in Sarah's best interest. He promised her that he would personally see to it that Mrs. Goatsocks was provided adequate transportation to return to London as soon as she was able. Sarah had agreed on one condition: that he received Mrs. Goatsocks's blessing. That was just what he intended to do at the doctor's house.

Dr. MacTavish ushered Christian into the drawing room, where the patient sat on a sofa with her ankle propped up on a pile of pillows. She was fully dressed in her proper attire, a dark gown, dark stockings, and white collar. She even had a shoe on her good foot. Her back was ramrod straight and her chin was raised a bit. In her fifties, the lady had graying-brown hair, a plump build, and frown lines etched deeply on either side of her mouth. Mrs. Goatsocks stared at Christian so intensely with her dark, penetrating eyes that he wondered if she would indeed bestow her blessing once he informed her of the plan.

"Who are you?" she asked as soon as Christian stepped into the room, his hat in his hands.

"This is the viscount, madame," Dr. MacTavish explained. The thin, balding man seemed to be full of nerves. His eyes darted back and forth anxiously and he appeared to be sweating profusely. Christian suspected he'd never had an English viscount in his drawing room before.

"The Viscount of what?" Mrs. Goatsocks asked. Christian had the distinct impression that she would have pulled out a quizzing glass to examine him with had she had access to one.

"Viscount Berkeley," the doctor explained. "He's got a hunting lodge nearby."

"Master Christian," Christian added. He immediately saw the chaperone's eyes flare.

"I'd like to speak with the viscount alone, if you don't mind," Mrs. Goatsocks said to the doctor.

Dr. MacTavish nodded and bowed and wiped the sweat from his brow. He left the room quickly, no doubt pleased to not have to stay and play host to a viscount and a proper English lady.

Once they were alone, Mrs. Goatsocks narrowed her eyes on Christian. "I'm certain you'll understand that the doctor knows nothing of Lady Sarah's presence in this area, and for reasons that should be obvious, I intend to keep it that way. Mr. Fergus was quite accommodating on that score and I hope you will be also."

She clearly wasn't asking. She was telling.

Christian wasn't in the habit of taking orders from servants, but for Sarah's sake, he would suffer this woman's brusqueness. "Suffice it to say our interests lie in the same direction, and that is what is best for Lady Sarah," Christian said, bowing to the woman.

A bit of tension left the corners of her eyes. She looked him up and down. "Berkeley, eh? Mr. Fergus failed to mention you're a *viscount*." She paused and looked up at the ceiling, as if trying to recall something. "Berkeley. Estate in Northumbria. Generous income. Fine if unremarkable reputation. More handsome than I'd expected, but the beard is questionable."

"You know your *Debrett's*," Christian said, inclining his head and stepping closer to her.

She settled her folded hands over her middle. "It's part of my duty to know *Debrett's*."

Christian stopped a few paces away from the sofa and braced his feet apart. "Would you be surprised to learn that Lady Sarah didn't know who I was?"

Mrs. Goatsocks blinked only once. "Lady Sarah is young and doesn't pay much attention to things like titles. She's more interested in whether a person is kind and good than what his title is."

"Yes. I've learned that about her."

"It's *my* duty to worry about titles," the chaperone continued.

"Like that of the Marquess of Branford?"

"Precisely." Her nose lifted higher into the air.

"And what do you think of the marquess as a match for Lady Sarah?"

"I think what I am paid to think, which is that the marquess is exactly the match Lady Sarah's parents had hoped for her."

Christian eyed the woman up and down. Like any good servant, she wasn't about to gossip about her charge or the family that employed her. The lady didn't move in the slightest. The only clue that she was indeed alive was the occasional blinking of her eyes. He understood why Sarah said she'd never broken a rule. With this formidable matron looking after her, no wonder she was so proper. Which made it all the more interesting that she'd run away and that the venerable chaperone had followed her.

"Is Sarah well?" Mrs. Goatsocks asked.

Christian held his hat near his hip. "Yes, and she sends her regrets for the state of your ankle."

"It's not her fault." Her voice was flat, emotionless.

"She blames herself," Christian said.

"That's because she's a kind girl." Ah, a bit of emotion had sneaked through there. The chaperone obviously admired her charge.

"But you haven't come just to tell me that Lady Sarah is in good health, have you?"

"No." Christian could already discern that coming out with it was the best way to handle a woman as straightforward as Mrs. Goatsocks seemed to be. "I've come to tell you that I intend to help Lady Sarah get back to London with as little incident as possible. I believe it's in her best interest if she and I leave as soon as possible and not wait for your ankle to heal."

The frown lines around Mrs. Goatsocks's mouth deepened, but her voice was perfectly calm and clear. The lady was obviously not one to display histrionics. "How will it look if she returns to London with no chaperone?"

"I intend to employ my friends Lucy and Cassandra to help. We're leaving tomorrow for Northumbria to meet them."

Mrs. Goatsocks's eyebrows arched. "Lucy and Cassandra? Do you mean the Duchess of Claringdon and the Countess of Swifdon?"

Christian had to smile at that. He'd been right about her. The lady did know her *Debrett's*. "Yes, they are my friends. They'll help and be discreet, I assure you."

"You've got some illustrious friends, Viscount."

Christian inclined his head toward her. Mrs. Goatsocks certainly knew who was who in London Society. This was also the woman who hadn't allowed an eighteen-year-old to run off alone and instead had risked her own safety and comfort to go with her. And he had a question for her.

"Why didn't you talk her out of it?"

Mrs. Goatsocks's face remained completely blank. "Talk who out of what?"

"Talk Lady Sarah out of leaving London?"

Mrs. Goatsocks's gaze flickered slightly. It was the only crack in her otherwise impenetrable armor. "How do you know I didn't try to talk her out of it?"

"I get the distinct impression that you can be quite stubborn when you set your mind to something, and I doubt greatly that yours wouldn't be a match for Lady Sarah's stubbornness."

The chaperone pursed her lips. "You can tell that after having spent less than a quarter hour in my presence?"

Christian inclined his head again. "Am I wrong?"

A few seconds ticked by before Mrs. Goatsocks said evenly, "You are not."

Christian allowed the hint of a smile to touch his lips. He liked this Mrs. Goatsocks. Liked her immensely. "Then I'll ask again. Why didn't you talk her out of it?"

Mrs. Goatsocks flicked an imaginary piece of lint from the waist of her plum-colored gown. "You're astute, my lord, I'll give you that. Suffice it to say I didn't disagree with her reasons for leaving. But I am employed by the Earl of Highfield as a chaperone, and I'd be derelict in my duties if I were to allow his only daughter to run off to Scotland unattended."

"Lady Sarah speaks highly of you."

"And I, her. She is a special young lady."

"I am here to ask for your blessing for my taking Lady Sarah to Northumbria to meet the Duchess of Claringdon. Do you give it?"

Mrs. Goatsocks lifted her chin a bit higher. "Something tells me that you'll take her there regardless of whether I give my blessing."

Christian scratched the back of his neck. "Lady Sarah values your approval a great deal. She asked me to secure it. She doesn't want to leave you here."

Mrs. Goatsocks straightened her already straight shoulders. She stared across the room into the fireplace.

"I am not happy that my charge is no longer my charge. But I am taken ill and cannot adequately perform my duties. Lady Sarah's reputation is of the utmost importance to me. Knowing that she will be traveling alone with a gentleman concerns me, but if you say your friends are meeting you and they will be tasked with her chaperonage once they arrive, I might be persuaded. . . ."

"You have my word," Christian said.

"Very well. I see little other choice. I suppose I don't have to ask you for your discretion in this matter."

"Lady Sarah has done me a good turn. I owe her my allegiance."

The chaperone merely raised her eyebrows at that. "Very well, then. You have my blessing. You may inform Lady Sarah as much. But first allow me to apprise you of how sorely you will regret it if you do anything untoward or indecent to Her Ladyship. You shall have *me* to contend with. Do I make myself clear?"

Christian bowed, hiding his smile. No doubt this woman had made many a young swain cower in his boots. "You have my word as a gentleman on that score as well. She will be treated with nothing but my absolute respect and admiration."

"See to it that she is," Mrs. Goatsocks said imperiously. The effect was a bit ruined, however, by her wincing at the movement of her ankle on the sofa.

"Depending upon what Lucy Hunt decides is best, we might have to adjust your travel plans later, but for the time being, you'll remain here. We'll write to you as soon as we settle on a course of action."

"So, the duchess is in charge of this plan, is she?"

"Do you know her?" Christian asked.

"Not personally, of course, but I daresay everyone knows *of* her."

Christian hid his smile behind his fist as he raised the

back of his hand to his mouth. "Trust me when I tell you she is quite good at such things. If anyone can, Lucy will come up with the best way to attempt to return Sarah to London with as little scandal and gossip as possible."

The chaperone's face was a mask. He had no idea of her feelings until she said, "I'm trusting you, Viscount. Do not let me down."

"I won't." Christian turned to leave, but Mrs. Goatsocks's voice stopped him.

"How are Mr. Fergus and that dog of his?"

Christian turned back. "Fergus Two is now the happy owner of two woolen coats and a new toy made for him by Lady Sarah."

"Is he?" Mrs. Goatsocks raised both eyebrows.

If Christian didn't know any better, he might suspect the matron was *smiling*. "Yes."

"And *Mr.* Fergus?"

"He made his way back safely. He was quite worried about Lady Sarah's well-being."

"As he should have been. I'm pleased to hear he's safe."

Christian turned again to leave.

"How was the stew?"

He turned back, confusion marring his brow. "The stew?"

"Did you return in time to partake of the stew Lady Sarah made?"

Christian put his hat back atop his head and tipped the brim. "Yes. As a matter of fact I did, and it was delicious."

A tiny smile made an appearance on Mrs. Goatsocks's lips. "Please tell Lady Sarah I said . . . good luck."

Christian bowed to her again and took his leave. He paid the doctor handsomely for his trouble, asked the man to send any future bills incurred on Mrs. Goatsocks's behalf to him, and told him to let him know when she was ready to return to London.

"Will you stay to luncheon, my lord?" Dr. MacTavish asked, his upper lip already sheened with a fine sweat since returning to Christian's company.

"No. Thank you. I cannot stay. I must get back. I'm leaving for Northumbria immediately."

CHAPTER SIXTEEN

Sarah tried not to, but she couldn't help watching out the window expectantly for any sign of Christian's return. Had he made it to town safely? Had he managed to get his letter into the post? Had he found Mrs. Goatsocks? Was she well? Was she angry with Sarah? Had she given her blessing for their trip back to England?

Sarah paced to and fro in front of the door, Fergus II on her heels. Christian had told her a bit about the letter he'd written. In it, apparently he'd asked his friends to meet him at an undisclosed location in Northumbria. Sarah had little idea of what or who was in Northumbria, but she'd already thrown herself on the mercy of this kind man and his lady friends and she had few other options. Christian was so confident that his friends would heed his request that he informed Sarah they should begin their journey south as soon as possible. Lucy and Cass would meet them at their destination.

Sarah had spent the better part of her morning—when she wasn't pacing or looking out the window for him—writing a letter of her own to Mrs. Goatsocks. She'd needed more time to write it, so she hadn't attempted to send it with Christian that morning. In the letter, she'd informed her chaperone that she was fine and was with Mr. Christian Forester and going to Northumbria to meet his friends, who just might have a solution to her troubles, and she'd write again as soon as she was able. She regretted that she must leave the poor woman in Scotland, and she sent along enough money to ensure Mrs. Goatsocks had enough with which to travel back to London.

Christian returned in the midafternoon, and Sarah breathed a sigh of relief. She rushed to the door and pulled it open. Christian was standing there with a bundle under his arm, looking rugged and handsome in his wool coat and boots and hat.

"How was she?" Sarah blurted.

"First things first." Christian stepped into the house, shut the door behind him, and handed her the bundle. He removed his coat while she took the bundle to the table and opened it.

"Why, it's . . . it's cream . . . and sugar!" she exclaimed happily, holding up the small bottle of cream in one hand and the little bag of sugar lumps in the other.

"I thought you would enjoy some proper tea," he said with a laugh.

"Oh, I certainly would." She spun in a happy circle, Fergus II barking and nipping at her heels. "Thank you so much!"

Christian shucked his books and went over to the fire to warm his hands while Sarah made tea. He proceeded to tell her about his visit with Mrs. Goatsocks while she drank the most delicious cup of tea she'd had in days.

"She approves?" Sarah finally asked when he'd come to the end of the story.

"I don't know if I'd say that, but she did give her blessing. She wants the best for you."

Sarah fought the tears that stung the backs of her eyes. "I know she does. I only wish I was worthy of her friendship."

He reached across the table and squeezed her hand. Sarah felt the heat of it spread up her arm.

"Don't worry," he said. "You're going to be all right, Lady Sarah Highgate."

Sarah returned his gaze and managed a smile. "I'm lucky to have a friend like you."

Fortunately, by the next morning the snow was melting. And while the drifts were still high on the hilltop, Christian said they would get down to town and hire a coach to take them to England. Before they left, Sarah went to the barn to deliver her letter to Mr. Fergus. The old man took it with a questioning look on his face.

"Will you please give this to Mrs. Goatsocks?" Sarah asked. "The next time you go to town, I mean. Please don't make a special trip."

Mr. Fergus opened his coat and slid the letter into his pocket. "Aye, milady. I promise."

"Thank you." Sarah closed her eyes and expelled a breath. "Thank you for everything, Mr. Fergus. I'm sure I don't know what we would have done if you hadn't taken us in that night."

"Ye've nothing ta thank me for, lass."

"Of course I do. You could have refused us shelter that first night. You could have tossed us into the snow for wolves to eat."

"Och, now, I wouldn't do such a thing ta the wolves. That Mrs. Goatsocks looks none too tasty."

Sarah had to laugh at that. "I hope she didn't cause you too much trouble."

"She's shrill and a bit mad, I say. But nothing I couldn't handle. She is certainly loyal ta ye, lass, if ye don't mind me saying."

"I know, Mr. Fergus. She is a dear friend."

"I'll miss ye around here, lass. And I daresay Fergus will, too." He stared down at the dog who sat at his feet.

Fergus II, wearing his little red coat, pawed the ground next to Sarah and whined.

"I'm certain you'll make do without me," Sarah said to the dog. "You're properly outfitted now and have your toy."

"Aye," Mr. Fergus replied. "Thanks ta ye, I have the bonniest dog in Scotland. All the other dogs are certain ta admire his coats."

Sarah leaned down and scratched the dog's chin. "I should hope so."

"Ye're off ta Northumbria, eh?" Mr. Fergus asked.

"Yes. That's where we're going according to Mr. Forester. I'm not entirely certain why."

Mr. Fergus turned back to the pile of wood he'd been chopping. "Master Christian's estate is there. I've no doubt that's where he's headed," he said over his shoulder.

Sarah froze. "Estate?"

"Aye, Berkeley Hall."

"Berkeley Hall?" All she could do was blink.

The old man propped up the next bit of wood to split. "'Tis been in the family for generations. A fine place 'tis, though I've only been there once meself."

A dozen thoughts scattered through Sarah's brain. She couldn't focus on one in particular. Finally, she muttered, "Berkeley Hall? As in *Viscount* Berkeley?"

"Aye," Mr. Fergus said, raising the ax above his head to strike the wood. "Of course. After all, Master Christian is the viscount."

CHAPTER SEVENTEEN

It was two days' journey to Northumbria, and the coach Christian rented for Sarah's benefit was none too comfortable. He knew she was being bounced about unmercifully inside. Not to mention it smelled a bit of must and of something else Christian didn't want to examine too closely. But Sarah never complained once.

"My apologies, but it was the best I could do under the circumstances," Christian said, gesturing toward the ramshackle conveyance that rested outside an inn where they had stopped for lunch. The driver didn't look much better than his vehicle. He was a half-drunken man who slurred his speech and was wrapped in an understandably copious number of blankets that smelled a great deal of horse.

"It could be a good thing," Christian explained when Sarah first saw the slovenly coachman. "Perhaps he won't remember us."

The story was that they were a newly married couple traveling together. Christian rode his own horse next to the coach most of the time, but when they stopped for a meal halfway through the day, they had their first chance to talk.

Sarah dunked a flaky crust of bread into the beef soup the innkeeper had given her. "When were you going to tell me you're a viscount?" she asked sweetly.

Christian choked on the piece of carrot he'd been ingesting. He pounded his chest with his fist to clear his throat. "Wh-what?"

"You heard me."

"Fergus told you?"

"Yes, Mr. Fergus told me. He told me that we're going to your *estate* in Northumbria. I assumed we were meeting at some place one of your friends lived."

Christian didn't meet her eyes. "It's just a house and a bit of land."

"I don't understand why you wouldn't tell me such a thing."

Christian shrugged. "It didn't seem important."

"We were discussing your eligibility at length." She glanced over her shoulder as she whispered this, obviously so the drunken driver (who was even at present drinking in the corner of the inn) wouldn't overhear. The man seemed to be more interested in his ale and his lunch than anything Christian and Sarah were discussing, however.

"What does my being a viscount have to do with my eligibility?" Christian asked.

Sarah dunked another bit of bread into her soup. "You cannot possibly be serious."

"I don't want a wife who wants me for my title," Christian whispered.

"Of course not, but I daresay you'll have more ladies to choose from given that you *do* happen to have a title."

Christian took another bite of his soup and swallowed. "Mrs. Goatsocks told me you weren't preoccupied by ti-

tles. Is she wrong?" He couldn't help feeling a bit of a
sting from her words. It was obvious that even now that
she realized just how eligible he was, he was still her
friend. But he mentally chided himself for even having
that thought. Sarah was engaged. Engaged to a marquess.
And a marquess trumped a viscount.

Sarah's eyes widened and she looked positively affronted. "Preoccupied by them, no. But we do live in a
Society where they make a difference."

Another bite of soup. "I wanted you to help me whether
I was a viscount or not."

She arched a brow. "You were testing me?"

He lowered his voice even further. "When you were
brandishing a broadsword at me, you seemed to be quite
proud of the fact that you were an earl's daughter. I think
you might understand why I wasn't interested in rushing
to bandy about my title."

Sarah actually raised her voice a little, clearly per-
turbed. "That is understandable, I suppose. But afterward, when I was teaching you, helping you, you never
saw fit to mention it?"

"By then it just seemed . . . indelicate." He braced an
elbow on the table.

"So, what? We were just going to pull up to your estate and I'd find out as soon as all the servants began calling you 'my lord'?"

Christian rubbed the back of his neck. It did seem a
bit silly now that she pointed it out. "Something like that."

"And you say *women* are incomprehensible." Sarah
eyed him over the rim of her own glass of ale.

Christian had to smile at that. "I believe we're even."

She shook her head at him and returned her attention
to her bread and soup. "Anything else you're not telling me,
my lord?"

* * *

The next morning, Sarah got her first glimpse of the "house and bit of land" that was Berkeley Hall. They drove through giant gates that led past a sweeping expanse of land that was covered with a light snow. The trees had lost all their leaves, but Sarah could imagine how glorious it must look in the summer. The ride up to the main house from the gates took twenty minutes, and they passed a frozen lake, more barren trees, and a sprinkling of outbuildings before they came to the estate.

The house was set back, nestled among even more trees, with two large wings on either side of a huge main portion with great Gothic windows and pillars and a wide, curving drive.

The coach came to a stop in front of the massive home, and when Christian opened the door and took her hand for her to alight, she grinned at him. "Just a house and a bit of land, eh?"

He shrugged. "Come meet Mrs. Hamilton."

Mrs. Hamilton, Sarah soon learned, was the housekeeper. A short, plump woman in her middle years, she had a huge smile on her face the moment her master escorted Sarah across the threshold.

"Oh, Master Christian! Master Christian, you've done it at last. You've brought home a wife, and I must say she's the most beautiful thing I've ever seen! Though I daresay we should be able to outfit a viscountess in better clothing than what she's got on."

Sarah blushed from her roots to her toes while Christian shushed the woman. "Mrs. Hamilton, please come into the drawing room, and I'll explain."

The butler, Mr. Oswald, a tall, imposing, middle-aged man with streaks of gray at his temples, followed them.

"This is Lady Sarah Highgate," Christian explained quickly. "And I must ask both of you for your discretion.

Lady Sarah became lost on her way through Scotland and I'm simply escorting her back to England. My friends are coming to see her back to London, but we are not married. Now, I know I can count on both of you to keep this to yourselves and to ensure the rest of the staff doesn't gossip about our guest."

Both servants nodded solemnly, though Mrs. Hamilton looked so disappointed that Sarah thought she might cry.

"Don't worry," Christian said. "Lady Sarah here has been giving me advice on how I might go about finding my future bride. She was the belle of the Season last year."

Mrs. Hamilton tried to smile at that, but her heart clearly wasn't in it.

"You can count on me, my lord," Mr. Oswald said, giving a formal bow.

"Good. I'd like to keep Lady Sarah's presence here as unobtrusive as possible. Please assign the most discreet housemaid to attend to her."

"I'll attend to her myself, my lord," Mrs. Hamilton said, tucking her set of keys into the sash around her waist.

"Thank you. Perhaps that's best," Christian replied.

Sarah smiled at the housekeeper. "Thank you very much, Mrs. Hamilton."

Christian gave the housekeeper a warning glance. "Absolutely no one else can know she's here."

CHAPTER EIGHTEEN

"Would you care to see my house?" Christian said after Sarah had joined him in the upstairs drawing room that afternoon. She'd taken a nap and put on fresh clothing that Mrs. Hamilton had provided for her, a gown that had been borrowed from one of the maids at the hall. It was soft and clean and white, and Sarah felt refreshed after her long, bumpy ride in the coach.

"I've given most of the servants the afternoon off," Christian explained. "So we should have some privacy while I give you a tour."

Sarah smiled at him brightly. "I would love to see your house." She stood and took his hand and he led her into the corridor.

"We might as well begin with this floor since we're already here. There are twenty-seven bedrooms altogether, but most of the ones for guests are on this floor."

Twenty-seven bedrooms? A house and a bit of land indeed.

"I hope you're enjoying the room I chose for you."

"You chose it? For me?" Her voice nearly broke. She

was remembering the kiss they'd never shared. The thought made her throat tight.

"Yes," he said softly.

"And the lilies that were sitting on my bedside table?"

"I thought you would like them because of your perfume."

The man had noticed the scent of her perfume? The lump in her throat grew larger.

He led her down the grand staircase across the wide expanse of the marble-floored foyer and into another corridor lined with scores of Berkeley family portraits.

"You know, I feel completely foolish remembering how you asked me if I recognized the name Viscount Berkeley."

"What would you say if I told you Mrs. Goatsocks recognized my name immediately?"

"I would say I'm not a bit surprised. Mrs. Goatsocks has *Debrett's* memorized. I just don't know how you and I never met before."

"I was probably at Almack's and you were somewhere much more fashionable," he said, sliding his hands into his pockets.

Why did Sarah wish they had met? Why was it so important to her? It wasn't as if she wouldn't have become engaged to Lord Branford regardless. No. It was useless thinking about the what-ifs. If they'd met in London, Christian probably wouldn't have ever spoken to her for fear of stuttering, and . . . Oh, it didn't matter now, did it?

"What's next?" she asked him, gesturing to the next room and fighting the tears that unexpectedly stung her eyes.

Christian was a marvelous tour guide. He spent the afternoon showing her his house. He led her into not one but two ballrooms, the expansive library, and rooms and rooms full of additional Berkeley family portraits.

When they reached the exquisite conservatory, Sarah sucked in her breath. "I've never seen a more beautiful place," she said, turning around and around in the lush, flower-filled room. "Your house is beautiful, Lord Berkeley."

He walked up next to where she stood sniffing a lilac. "Thank you, my lady. But I do hope you'll continue to call me Christian. In private." He winked at her.

"Of course." She stood and turned abruptly, nearly knocking into him.

He grabbed her elbow to steady her. He didn't let go when she found her footing again. She stared up into his eyes. It was wrong for a score of reasons, but she was willing him to kiss her. Here in the heady-scented, humid conservatory.

"Sarah," he whispered.

She closed her eyes.

He leaned down and brushed her ear with his lips. He slid a violet that he'd plucked nearby behind her ear. "I want to kiss you. You don't know how much I want to kiss you. But . . ." He straightened to his full height and stepped back. "You're engaged to another man."

"I know." She nearly sobbed. "I know." She clutched her skirts and ran from the room.

That night, Sarah sat in the glorious bedchamber that Mrs. Hamilton had escorted her to soon after her arrival. The room that Christian had apparently chosen for her personally. It was decorated in soft blues and silver. The fresh lilies (no doubt from the viscount's conservatory) sat in crystal vases on the delicate white writing desk and the bedside table. The bed itself was a beautiful cherry four-poster, and the linens spread over it were soft and fresh and clean. Sarah hadn't realized how much she'd missed such luxury while she'd been hidden away in Scotland. Not that patchwork quilts didn't hold a certain appeal, but this bedchamber was positively glorious. Now she was hidden away in Northumbria, she thought with a wry smile, but the furnishings were a sight better.

She sat on a tufted stool in front of the dressing table, slowly pulling the pins from her dark hair and thinking about all the things that had happened in the last several days. Why in the world had Christian decided to keep his title a secret from her for all this time? Did he truly think she was preoccupied with such things? She wasn't the one who had decided to marry Lord Branford for his title. That had been her parents' doing. She had, however, seemed pompous when she'd informed Christian regally that she was the daughter of an earl. But at the time, she'd been certain that rape or murder might have been his intention. No. She didn't blame him for not telling her at first, but later . . . later, when they'd talked together, laughed together, waltzed together, played chess. Why hadn't he told her any of those times? She sighed. She supposed it didn't matter. She knew now, and it certainly did nothing but add to his appeal on the marriage mart, which was her part of their bargain, wasn't it? Helping him find a wife. Though she couldn't help wondering for the hundredth time why he was still unmarried if he was as handsome and well connected and kind and witty as he was and a viscount to boot. Not that *her* parents would accept a title as lowly as viscount. No. No. *Their* daughter must marry *up*. But many a young lady on the marriage mart would be happy to have him. So why was he still unmarried? Was it truly because he became every lady's *friend*? She felt anything but friendly feelings toward him. Well, that wasn't true, exactly. He *was* her friend. But did one want to madly kiss one's *friend*? She sincerely doubted it.

Her behavior in the conservatory had been wanton and shocking. She'd nearly begged him to kiss her. He'd known it. Known it enough to tell her why he couldn't. And damn her, she'd wanted him to do it even after he'd explained why he couldn't. The man was completely honorable through and through. He wouldn't kiss another man's betrothed. She shouldn't have wanted him to. That's why she'd left. Fled, actually. Like a coward. It was as if she couldn't stand another moment in his presence being tempted by him. She'd asked to have her dinner served in her room. And had hidden from him here. She needed time and space. She would face him tomorrow. His friends would arrive then. Hopefully they would have a plan to help her and she could get back to London, where she belonged.

There was a soft knock at the door and Sarah's heart leaped into her throat. The chances of it being Christian were slim, of course, but she couldn't help admitting to herself that she wished it was him. "Come in," she called weakly, her throat dry.

The door opened and Mrs. Hamilton stepped inside. The housekeeper quickly closed the door behind her.

Sarah let out her pent-up breath. Was it a sigh of relief or disappointment? "Good evening, Mrs. Hamilton," she said, smiling at the woman through the looking glass.

"Good evening, my lady," Mrs. Hamilton said, moving toward her. "I came ta help ye prepare for bed."

"Thank you very much."

Mrs. Hamilton crossed the plush rug to stand behind Sarah. First, she helped Sarah pull the last of the pins from her hair, and then the housekeeper picked up a silver-handled brush from the dressing table and began to stroke it through her hair.

"What do you think of Berkeley Hall, my lady?" Mrs. Hamilton asked, beaming at her in the looking glass.

"It's absolutely gorgeous," Sarah replied. "Superbly decorated with fine furnishings and perfectly kept." Lord

Berkeley was an interesting man. Handsome, kind, and friendly. Living up here all alone and wanting nothing more than someone to share it with. Sarah's heart ached for him.

"It is gorgeous, isn't it," the housekeeper said with obvious pride. "Been in the family for nine generations. My own family has been in service to the Berkeleys for four."

"That's quite impressive," Sarah said.

"You have beautiful hair, my lady, if you don't mind me saying so," Mrs. Hamilton murmured as she continued to brush Sarah's hair.

"I'm so sorry to be a bother to you," Sarah said. "My own maid is . . . was . . . indisposed."

"Don't ye worry about that."

"Also . . . I find I'm quite without my normal wardrobe." Sarah blushed.

"No matter about that either. If His Lordship says ye are to be here quietlike, I won't tell a soul or repeat anything I know about any of this. Ye can be certain about that."

"Thank you." Sarah turned and laid her hand on the housekeeper's. "I've only known you less than a day, Mrs. Hamilton, but somehow I feel I can trust you."

Mrs. Hamilton smiled at that. "I've known the master since he was a babe and there's no finer man. If he tells me ye're in trouble and need his help, I don't ask questions. I merely want ta help."

"That's kind of you." Sarah turned back around and smiled at the older woman's reflection in the looking glass. "What was Master Christian like as a child? I simply cannot picture him as a small boy."

A look of joy flourished across the housekeeper's face. "Oh, he was the cutest little towheaded thing ye'd ever like ta see. The nicest boy. Always helping others. A bit shy, mind ye, but so kind and thoughtful. Never acting lordly or arrogant like some of these baby blue bloods tend ta. No offense, my lady."

"None taken," Sarah replied with a laugh. "And that sounds like him."

"He was so sweet and happy. He and his cousin Harriet were inseparable. She lives in Bath now. A married lady is Harriet."

"He told me about her. He said she nearly burned down her doll house and he rebuilt it."

"Yes, he did. He spent nearly his entire summer home from Eton rebuilding that thing. Harriet loved him so for it."

Sarah glanced down at the top of the dressing table. "He has no brothers or sisters?"

"No."

Sarah glanced up again and met the housekeeper's gaze in the mirror. "What were his parents like?" Sarah hesitated only a moment before asking, "Is his mother still living?"

An unmistakably sad look passed over Mrs. Hamilton's face. "No. Neither of them is living. The old lord died nearly ten years ago now. A bad heart. And Her Ladyship, why, she died when Master Christian was just a young boy. Not yet five years old."

Sarah gasped. "Oh, no. How awful."

"'Twas a sad, sad time here, ta be sure, my lady."

Sarah cleared her throat. "What happened to her?"

Mrs. Hamilton shook her head again. "Fever. It was dreadful that year. His Lordship came down with it, too. He recovered. We took young Master Christian away so he wouldn't get sick. He never had a chance ta say goodbye ta his mama. Even when she was in the throes of it and we knew it wasn't likely that she'd live, she refused ta have him brought back so she could say good-bye ta him. She didn't want to take the chance that he might catch it. She probably saved his life. But the poor boy didn't understand where she'd gone. Ran all over the house looking for her. Calling for her."

Tears stung Sarah's eyes. She swallowed hard. "That's dreadful. . . . And his father? Did you know him?"

"I did." Mrs. Hamilton shook her head. "And my mama told me never ta speak ill o' the dead. So that's all I have ta say about that man. Never gave Master Christian a bit of rest, did he. Demanded so much from him. Too much, if ye ask me. But that's all I'll say on the matter."

"I understand." Sarah wasn't about to break Christian's confidence and tell the woman that she'd already heard a bit about how awful his father had been, but Mrs. Hamilton's words confirmed her impression of the former viscount.

Mrs. Hamilton heaved a sigh. "The master's grown up with such a good sense of humor and always quick ta laugh. But don't let him fool you. He's known pain, he has. I just wish he could find a young lady and settle down. That's why when I saw ye last night . . . well, ye know I thought . . . hoped, ye was the new lady of the house."

Sarah glanced away. "The fact is that I'm . . . engaged to be married to someone else."

Mrs. Hamilton sighed once more. "A pity, my lady. A pity. But I must say that your young man, whoever he is, is quite fortunate."

Sarah nodded slowly. "Thank you. I'm certain Lord Berkeley will find someone who suits him just fine."

"*If* he goes ta town next Season. He said he was thinking of staying here next year." Another sad head shake from Mrs. Hamilton.

Sarah brightened and smiled at the woman. "He told me he intends to come to London. I've given him some advice."

"I'm glad ta hear it, my lady. I've been afraid he may be near ta giving up."

Mrs. Hamilton had finished brushing Sarah's hair, and Sarah stood and made her way over toward the bed. "Don't worry. I have every hope for him next Season. And I shall be there to help him."

Mrs. Hamilton sighed again loud and long. "I hope it'll work, my lady. I can't wait till I hear the pitter patter of little feet in this house again."

"I shall do my best to help him," Sarah said, swallowing the unexpected lump in her throat. "Because I am his friend."

CHAPTER NINETEEN

A grand traveling coach arrived midway through the next morning. Two gorgeous ladies—one with black hair, one with blond—alighted from the conveyance. The black-haired lady wore a gown of bright emerald silk. Sarah could see the hem peeping out from under her coat. The blond lady had on a lavender gown with a beautiful silver coat over it. Sarah watched, fascinated, through an upstairs window as Lord Berkeley marched out across the icy gravel to meet them in the biting wind.

The ladies and their trunks were deposited in their rooms in short order, and the two of them made their way back down to the drawing room to meet Christian. Sarah stole quietly behind them. She listened at the door to the drawing room in front of the house while Lord Berkeley spoke with them.

"Dear God, Berkeley, when is the last time you've shaved?"

Sarah winced. Clearly Lucy (if that was indeed who was speaking) wasn't one for subtlety.

"I've been a bit preoccupied of late," Christian replied.

"And my valet went to visit friends in York. He wasn't expecting me."

"Yes, well, as to your 'preoccupation,' all you said in your letter was that you needed my help restoring the name of a young woman who was under your care," the same female voice said.

"That's right, Lucy," came Christian's voice.

"That's precious little to go by," Lucy replied. "Couldn't you have expounded a bit? Besides, Cass and I nearly died of anticipation. Who is it?"

"I've sent up a note," Christian said. "Mrs. Hamilton should be bringing her down any moment."

Sarah jumped. It was clearly time to stop listening at doors and make her appearance. Just then, Mrs. Hamilton arrived at her side. "Go on, then," the housekeeper prompted. "Mustn't keep Her Grace waiting."

Sarah gulped, and her eyes widened. "Her Grace?"

"Yes, Lucy Hunt, the Duchess of Claringdon."

"You mean to tell me the Duchess of Claringdon is in that room?" The Duchess of Claringdon was the epitome of style and grace as far as the *ton* was concerned. Young, beautiful, dashing. With a war-hero husband and a set of the most fashionable friends, she was a darling of the Quality. *She* was Christian's friend Lucy. Sarah could wring his neck for not mentioning it before.

"Yes, along with the Countess of Swifdon."

Ah, yes. Cassandra was the countess's first name. And rumor had it that she and the duchess were thick as thieves. Now it all made perfect sense.

Very well. No use hovering outside the door like a timid little mouse. If these great ladies had traveled all this way to help her, Mrs. Hamilton was right. She mustn't keep them waiting. Sarah quietly pushed open the door and stepped into the room. "Your Grace," she said in a quiet voice, looking at the duchess. "My lady," she said, turning her attention to the countess.

Both beautiful ladies in their grand skirts turned immediately and gave her a once-over. She'd never felt more out of place in her maid's clothing. She could tell right away they recognized her, too.

The countess gasped.

The duchess's eyebrows shot up. "Berkeley, you mean to tell me you've had Lady Sarah Highgate, the subject of some of the most intense gossip London's ever heard, with you this entire time?"

Sarah bit her lip. *Oh, no. The gossip was already bad. This plan was hopeless.*

"No," Christian replied. "Not this entire time."

The duchess nodded to Sarah. "We've met, but only briefly. Good to see you again, Lady Sarah. I simply cannot wait to hear this story."

"Yes," the countess said as Oswald brought in tea. The countess crossed to Sarah and squeezed her hand reassuringly. "You must be scared half out of your wits, you poor dear. Please tell us everything."

"Thank you, Lady Cassandra. It's good to see you both," Sarah replied tentatively. "I regret that we are meeting again under such inauspicious circumstances."

"Never mind that, dear. Come. Sit down. We're here to help." Lucy patted a spot next to her on the sofa. Sarah quickly made her way over to it and sat. A bit of the tension left her shoulders. She felt strangely comforted knowing these two ladies had left London and traveled here expressly to help her. Well, actually they were here to help Christian, but by association, her, and she was grateful to have their help at present. She settled into her seat.

The duchess was a gorgeous woman, with black curly hair and two different-colored eyes (one blue, the other green). The countess was perhaps even more beautiful, with soft honey-colored hair and bright cornflower-blue eyes. They both looked at her with great kindness and interest as she began to speak.

A half hour later, after the story had been thoroughly told and every question answered, Christian said, "So, as you can see, poor Lady Sarah here is in quite a bind. We need your scheming, Lucy, to get her out of it."

"I don't care for the word *scheming*," the duchess replied, but she had a smile on her face as she said it.

"It sounds like something Jane would say," the countess said.

"It does, doesn't it?" the duchess replied.

"Who is Jane, if I may ask, Your Grace?" Sarah ventured.

The duchess blinked at her. "Well, first of all, if we're to be friends, you must call me Lucy, not Your Grace. And of course we're to be friends, because any friend of Berkeley's is a friend of mine."

"The same goes for me," the countess added. "Please call me Cass."

Sarah nodded hesitantly. "And you must call me Sarah."

"A pleasure," both ladies said simultaneously, smiling at her widely.

Lucy and Cass were certainly friendly. Sarah immediately realized why Lord Berkeley was such good friends with them. They were easy to like.

"To answer your question," Lucy continued, "Jane is our very dear friend who is usually in league with us in all our so-called schemes, though she's a bit less enthusiastic about them than we are. You would know her as Mrs. Garrett Upton. Mr. Upton, of course, is my first cousin and the heir to my father's earldom."

"Ah, yes, I remember the name now," Sarah said.

"Jane would be here," Lucy said, "but she's settled in Bath for the winter to read."

"Who goes to Bath to read?" Christian asked.

"Precisely my point," Lucy continued. "But she says she gets fewer callers there in the winter than in London and she prefers it that way."

Christian laughed.

Sarah cleared her throat. "Lord Berkeley says you're quite good at coming up with . . . plots."

"She's excellent at it," Cass said, patting Lucy on the hand, a proud look on her face.

"I hope so, because since Mrs. Goatsocks is incapacitated, I have no chaperone. You mentioned gossip. Tell me the truth. I fear I am quite ruined. It's true, isn't it?"

"Nonsense," Lucy replied. "Nothing is impossible. Even the most egregious gossip can be made to seem like stuff and nonsense with the correct plan in place." She stood up and paced over to the fireplace, a twinkle in her eye. "You're not ruined at all."

Sarah expelled her breath, a rush of relief flooding through her. "I'm not."

"No." Lucy was clearly warming to her subject. "Of course not. Because you've had another chaperone this entire time."

Sarah furrowed her brow. "I have?"

"She has?" Cass echoed.

"She has?" Lord Berkeley asked.

"Yes," Lucy replied. "Until recently, this chaperone has been retired to the north. She's exceedingly proper and would never allow a charge of hers to do anything untoward. She also comes with excellent references. She's come out of retirement, and you're her first charge since."

"Her first . . . ?" Sarah pursed her lips, completely baffled.

Lucy flourished a hand in the air and grinned at the three of them. "Her name is Mrs. Bunbury."

CHAPTER TWENTY

"Brilliant!" Christian declared.

Both he and Cass knew that Mrs. Bunbury was fictitious. But she was, however, a fictitious *chaperone,* so the fact that she was "coming out of retirement" with Sarah as her charge made a certain amount of sense.

"Oh, Lucy, that *is* brilliant," Cass said, clapping her hands. "It's absolutely perfect."

"I don't understand," Sarah said, shaking her head. "Who is Mrs. Bunbury?"

Christian cleared his throat. "Mrs. Bunbury is a nonexistent chaperone whom Lucy invented and hired for Jane Upton."

Sarah looked at all of them as if they'd lost their minds. "Now I really don't understand."

Cass smoothed her hands down her silken lavender skirts. "When Jane came to my wedding in the country, she wanted to escape her mother, so she and Lucy invented a chaperone and named her Mrs. Bunbury. The woman never managed to be in the same room with Jane's mother, of course. She'd always just left moments before."

Sarah bit her lip. "I don't mean to be rude, but that sounds absolutely preposterous."

"Oh, but of course it's preposterous," Lucy said with a smile. "As so many of my plots are."

Christian could tell that Sarah was quickly losing faith in their saviors. "Perhaps you could explain what you have in mind in more detail, Lucy."

"With pleasure." Lucy paced back and forth in front of the fireplace, the twinkle remaining in her eye. "Here's what I've been thinking. Jane has been in Bath this entire time and rarely attends social functions because she'd rather be reading. She has also been known to employ Mrs. Bunbury. I shall return to London immediately and start the rumor that Sarah has been in Bath with Jane since she left London. You haven't told anyone anything that might contradict such a story, have you, Sarah?"

Sarah shook her head. "No. The only thing that I wrote in the letter I left for my mother is that I had to leave."

"That's perfect, then," Lucy said with a nod that caused one of her black curls to pop loose from her coiffure and bounce along her forehead. "I will say that I've just come from Bath, where I visited Jane and discovered you, Sarah."

She nodded toward Christian. "You and Sarah will travel to Bath via the western route and you shall deliver Sarah to Janie. I will inform Lady Sarah's parents of the story and no one will be the wiser."

"I'm not certain about that," Sarah said, worrying her hands together in her lap.

"Why not?"

"My mother will ask a lot of questions. She'll want to know all the details."

Lucy patted her coiffure. "Don't worry about that. Leave it to me. I will visit your mother, retrieve your clothing, and explain everything. Believe me, if your mother wishes to avoid a scandal, she'll help me."

"Where will everyone think Mrs. Goatsocks has been?" Sarah asked.

"Oh, yes, you mentioned her, didn't you?" she said to Christian. "Poor woman, I do hope her ankle is healing properly."

"Focus, Lucy," Cass nudged.

"Yes, of course," Lucy said. "Mrs. Goatsocks has been in Scotland visiting her sister."

"But she doesn't have a—," Sarah began.

"Believe me when I tell you that no one will know or care about such a detail. Why, I made up an entire branch of Mrs. Bunbury's family tree and no one asked a single question about it."

Sarah bit her lip. "Are you quite certain—"

Christian gave Sarah a reassuring nod. "Lucy will handle it. You must trust her."

Sarah nodded back. "Very well."

"In the meantime, I've brought you some clothing of mine that you may wear for your journey to Bath," Lucy said. "Berkeley told me you were dressed as a maid. My clothing may not fit exactly but close enough."

Sarah nodded again. "Thank you, Your Grace."

Christian watched Sarah closely. He could tell she was worried. Was she beginning to panic? He knew the feeling too well. He must help reassure her. She had to see that this was the only choice.

Lucy continued her explanation. "After I speak to Lady Highfield, Sarah will arrive in London with Jane days later. We'll all simply pretend it's been nothing more than one great big silly misunderstanding."

"A misunderstanding?" Sarah scrunched up her nose. "You truly believe that will work?"

"Oh, my dear," Cass said, patting Sarah's hand again. "You obviously don't know our Lucy."

CHAPTER TWENTY-ONE

Minutes later, Sarah retired to her bedchamber to rest. Christian stood and watched her leave the room, hoping she wasn't too discomfited by the discussion with Lucy and Cass. No doubt the poor young woman needed to lie down and think about all the outlandish things she'd just heard.

As soon as Sarah had gone, he turned to his friends. "You two can be a lot to take in at first. I wanted her to know I trust you."

"Don't worry about a thing, Berkeley," Lucy replied. "You know my plots always work out in the end."

He resumed his seat. "Yes. That's why I summoned you. Thank you for coming, by the by."

"Anything for you, my friend," Lucy said from her perch on the sofa, a genuine smile on her face.

"Now, you must tell us, how in heaven's name did you get wrapped up in this?" Cass asked, settling her lavender skirts around her.

"Sarah told you. She mistook my hunting lodge for her father's and then—"

"We heard all of that," Lucy replied. "But certainly you weren't obligated to escort her back to England and summon your friends to help. How did *that* happen?"

Christian scrubbed a hand through his hair. "I felt sorry for her."

Lucy arched a brow. "Sorry for her? Really? I couldn't help but notice she's quite beautiful, too. Did *that* have anything to do with it?"

Christian crossed to the sideboard and poured himself a drink.

"And now you're drinking?" Lucy said. "I don't think I've seen you have more than a spot of whiskey or a glass of champagne the entire time I've known you."

He splashed brandy into a glass. "Care for some?" he offered his guests.

They both declined.

Christian carried the glass back to his chair and sipped the drink slowly.

Lucy smoothed one dark eyebrow with a fingertip. "You didn't answer me, Viscount. Has Lady Sarah's beauty anything to do with your sudden interest in her?"

Christian leaned his head against the back of the chair. "You know me, Your Grace. Always the loyal friend to any damsel in distress."

"Yes, what you did for Alexandra and Owen was exceedingly kind of you," Cass said, referring to her brother. "They're engaged now. Thank you."

Christian raised his glass. "Glad to hear it. Always a pleasure to help a beautiful lady find the man of her dreams. But at least in this case, Sarah's actually been helping me, too."

Lucy's jaw dropped open. "Pardon?"

"Yes, while we were snowed in together, she gave me some advice on how to go about finding a wife," Christian said.

"Snowed in together? I'll leave that be for now." Lucy put her fists to her hips. "But Berkeley, if you wanted help finding a wife, why didn't you ask *me*?"

Christian laughed and took another sip of brandy. "Perhaps because you and I have never been snowed in together. Funny what you'll admit when you have days alone with someone. By the by, I am counting on your discretion with that information, the snowed-in bit. No one knows about it except Fergus, Mrs. Goatsocks, and a dog."

"Absolutely," Cass offered loyally.

Lucy sniffed. "I still don't see why you never asked me."

Christian took another sip of brandy. "Apparently, Sarah's the belle of the last Season. She's engaged to the most eligible bachelor. I thought she might know a thing or two about the current crop of ladies on the marriage mart."

"It's true, Lucy," Cass said. "She is younger than we are. I daresay she knows quite a bit."

"Besides," Christian continued, "Sarah says the way to get the unmarried ladies to notice you is to capture the eye of the most popular unmarried lady. Matrons won't do."

Lucy laughed outright at that. "Well, I can't say she's wrong about that. And she *was* the belle of the Season. It was *such* a scandal when she left. Of course if I'd known she would end up with you, I would have kept quiet, but I fear I participated in the gossip and conjecture."

Cass sighed. "It's a pity that lovely Lady Sarah must marry Lord Branford if she doesn't love him. Perhaps her parents will listen to reason after she informs them why she left so precipitously."

"First things first," Lucy replied. "We must get Sarah back to London and convince everyone that absolutely nothing scandalous happened."

"I suppose you're right," Cass agreed.

Christian twirled the brown liquid in his glass. "There's only one problem with the current plan."

"Which is?" Lucy asked.

"I promised Mrs. Goatsocks that the moment you two arrived, you would be officially chaperoning Lady Sarah."

"Oh!" Cass exclaimed.

"I doubt Mrs. Goatsocks—I like that name, by the by—would mind if she remains in your company a bit longer, Berkeley. You did promise the lady you would do everything you could to restore her to her family in London while causing the least amount of gossip, didn't you?"

"Yes," he agreed.

"If she were here now, Mrs. Goatsocks would see the logic in this plan and agree with me."

"Oh, Lucy, you're always so confident," Cass said.

"We don't have time to write to the woman," Lucy continued. "But believe me when I tell you, she'd agree with me. Besides, Sarah is officially in Mrs. Bunbury's care in Bath at the moment, at any rate. She's not unchaperoned at all."

Cass pulled her fur shrug closer around her shoulders. "Oh, Lucy, I do so adore how you think."

Christian shook his head. "I doubt even the Prince Regent could disagree with you once you set about making your point, Lucy."

Cass bit her lip. "But a misunderstanding? You really think telling everyone that will work, Lucy?"

Lucy crossed her arms over her chest. "You're talking to the same person who has hidden behind bushes and thrown my voice so that my future husband would think I was speaking for you, Cass."

"You're also talking to the same person who invented a fictitious person and then proceeded to conduct a house party in her honor and convinced half the *ton* to attend," Christian added.

"How could I forget?" Cass replied. "Since *I* was the one pretending to be that fictitious person."

"I, for one, trust you completely, of course," Christian said to Lucy.

Lucy reached over and patted him on the arm. "That's why I like you so well, Berkeley. You've always had faith in me."

Christian lifted his glass again. "Your schemes tend to work. There's evidence. Of course if this one works, Sarah will still be back in London, engaged to Lord Branford."

Lucy smiled and her different-colored eyes sparkled. "Why don't I leave that little problem for *you* to solve, Berkeley?"

CHAPTER TWENTY-TWO

There was little time to waste. The very next morning, two traveling chaises set out in different directions from Berkeley Hall. The one containing Sarah (who was filled with nerves) and Lord Berkeley (who had still not shaved) traveled via the western road to Bath. The other coach containing a confident Lucy and a hopeful Cass traveled via the southern road to London. Each had a distinct mission to accomplish.

Lucy had written a letter to Jane that she'd handed to Sarah just before they departed. "See that Jane receives this as soon as you arrive. It explains everything."

Sarah was sorely tempted to read it. She didn't, of course, but kept it sealed in her pocket. Lucy's clothing was a bit tight and short on her, but it would do better than a maid's dress. She didn't want to arrive on Jane Upton's doorstep in Bath looking squalid, letter or no. Sarah had given the maid's washed and pressed clothing to Lucy to return to the poor maid at her mother's house in London. Lucy had told Sarah not to worry about a thing, and Cass had given her a warm, friendly, encouraging hug.

Mrs. Hamilton had provided each set of passengers with a basket of food, additional blankets, and hot bricks with which to warm their feet until their first stop. They would get new bricks at each inn along the way. The rented hack from Scotland had been well paid and sent back north, so this time Sarah and Lord Berkeley traveled in one of the viscount's coaches.

"Take care, my lady," Mrs. Hamilton whispered to Sarah as she alighted into the well-sprung vehicle.

An odd lump formed in Sarah's throat. It made her inexpressibly sad to think she would never see Mrs. Hamilton again. "Thank you for everything," she replied, squeezing the woman's hand.

The ride was bumpy, cold, and long. They stopped only to change horses, to eat, and to use the convenience. Lucy had stressed that the faster they could get Sarah back to London by way of Bath, the sooner the gossip about her would die down. Lucy and Cass wouldn't be stopping at night either.

Christian sat across from Sarah, his beard growing longer each day. They slept fitfully off and on. She curled up on the forward-facing seat, tucked her legs beneath her, and attempted to rest despite the near constant jolting of the carriage. Christian must have been even more uncomfortable with his long legs squeezed into such a small space. He leaned against the wall of the coach and tried to doze that way, but she doubted he was able to, as evidenced by the increasingly dark shadows under his eyes.

The lump that had formed in Sarah's throat when she'd been saying good-bye to Mrs. Hamilton remained throughout the journey. It was so kind of Lord Berkeley and his two friends, so very kind of them to help her, a woman they knew little of and had no reason to help. During the day while they were awake, Christian attempted to make her laugh and keep her entertained with stories about his trip to the Continent after he'd left university and the foibles of his friends in London.

"And then there was the time Garrett Upton and I were nearly expelled from Eton," Christian said after they'd returned to the coach from eating a meal at an inn.

"I cannot possibly believe that," she replied with a laugh. "You? Nearly expelled?"

"I haven't always done the right thing," Christian replied.

Sarah had to look away. She was thinking of how he'd done the right thing in the conservatory when he hadn't kissed her. He had to be thinking about it, too.

She turned back to face him. There was something she had to say to him. "I can never repay you, you know—" Her voice caught at the end of the sentence.

His crystal-blue eyes held her gaze. "You don't have to, you know."

Tears stung her eyes. Bother. "I've never known anyone so kind."

He rubbed his forehead. "Didn't I mention my reputation as someone who helps damsels in distress?"

"I'm sorry, Lord Berkeley," she whispered, fighting away the tears.

The hint of a smile touched his firm lips. "I thought we were long past the point where you call me Lord Berkeley."

"Yes. Of course." She needed to change the subject, to banish the unwanted tears. She alighted on the first thing that came to mind. "Speaking of titles, however, I still don't understand why you didn't see fit to tell me your friends Lucy and Cass were a duchess and a countess."

"You didn't know I was a viscount. I thought you might wonder why I was keeping such company."

"I would have wondered, but that's not the point. You should have told me you were a viscount as well."

"I didn't tell you because when I first met you, you were trying to convince me of how a *gentleman* would behave in London."

She winced. "I was quite awful, wasn't I?"

"I don't know. I have to admit I was a bit impressed with your fearlessness. I've never had a lady attempt to brandish a sword at me before."

She laughed. "I wasn't fearless at all. I was scared witless. I had no idea you were Master Christian. I actually told myself you were another person who'd happened on the house by accident."

"Thought you might have to fight me for your claim, eh?"

She laughed again. "I thought perhaps you were a bandit."

"I'm impressed with your bravery. You were ready to fiercely protect yourself. Another young lady might have been hiding or weeping."

"I'm not much of a weeper, I suppose."

He grinned at that. "Meanwhile, I had no idea who was sleeping in my bed."

"I'm sorry if I frightened you, too."

"Nothing to worry about. I was more annoyed, actually, that someone had made themselves at home in my house."

"Why didn't you tell me you were a viscount after that?"

He shrugged. "It didn't seem relevant, really."

"Mrs. Hamilton is lovely," she added, wanting to change the subject again. Why had she even brought up his title yet again?

"Yes, sometimes she treats me as if she were my mother."

The lump was back in Sarah's throat. "She said your mother died when you were a child. I'm very sorry."

He shook his head and turned to look out the window. He narrowed his eyes on something in the distance. "That was a long time ago."

"But no doubt it's still painful for you to—"

"You should get some rest. We'll be in Bath by nightfall."

Sarah nodded, still struggling to swallow the lump. He obviously didn't want to discuss his mother. She pulled the blankets to her neck and settled against the side of the coach. She closed her eyes, hoping she hadn't dredged up painful memories for this man who'd been nothing but kind to her.

Her fitful dreams were filled with Berkeley family portraits and the image of Christian's mother's face staring back at her from the locket.

They did indeed make it to Bath by nightfall. The sun had just set as they made their way up the cobbled streets of the hill town. Sarah was thankful that they would be making their appearance under cover of night. There would be fewer people to potentially see her. They'd already decided to drive up to the back of Mr. Upton's house. Sarah had given the coachman the letter from Lucy and asked him to deliver it to Jane Upton herself. As soon as the coach pulled to a stop behind the house, the man leaped down, scurried up to the back door, and rapped on it three times.

The door soon opened, and after some discussion between the coachman and whichever servant had opened the door, there was a bit of waiting while the letter was obviously delivered to Jane.

Sarah sat up straight in the coach, her knees bouncing, nerves flooding through every bit of her body. Would Jane Upton accept her or think her friend Lucy had sent a hoyden to her door? Would Lucy's outrageous plan even have a chance of working?

"You've nothing to worry about," Christian said. "Jane will take excellent care of you. She's quite nice."

"I've no doubt," Sarah replied, knees still bouncing. "But I cannot help my nerves."

"I understand," Christian replied. He reached over and gave her hand a reassuring squeeze, settling her bouncing knees. Sarah didn't look at him. Instead, she concentrated on regulating her breathing, but she allowed him to hold her hand. It felt so warm. So warm and strong and nice. So reassuring. No one had ever made her feel so safe before. Certainly not her parents. All they'd ever done was add to her anxiety.

Several minutes later, the coachman returned and rapped on the door to the coach. Christian opened the window, and a rush of cold air filtered through it, making Sarah shudder. His hand squeezed hers more tightly.

"The missus says to come in, me lady," the coachman announced, flicking up the collar on his wool coat.

Sarah gulped and nodded. This was it. The coach door opened, and after the stairs had been let down, the coachman took her hand and led her down. Two of Jane Upton's footmen were already unloading her trunk (filled with Lucy's clothing and some of Sarah's undergarments) from the back of the coach. She turned to Christian, who remained in the coach. "Aren't you coming?"

He shook his head and Sarah's stomach plummeted.

"No," he replied. "This is where I must leave you. It wouldn't do for us to be seen together. You'll be much safer in the company of only the ladies from now on."

Sarah nodded and swallowed. Of course. That made perfect sense. Why hadn't she realized this would be the case? She should have said more, thanked him more. Now there was no time.

"Thank you," she blurted. "Thank you for everything, my lord."

She held out a hand to him, and he took it and kissed it, sending a rush of heat up her arm. "Best of luck to you, Lady Sarah."

She searched his shadowed face. "When you come to London, for the Season . . . I'll be there. I'll help."

His bright smile would visit her in her dreams. "Ah, yes. To turn me into a *legend*. Isn't that the plan?"

All she could do was nod.

"I fear I'll need all the help I can get." Christian gestured to the coachman to indicate that he was ready to leave.

More words, words like *I'll never forget you,* hovered on Sarah's lips, but she couldn't bring herself to say them. *Someday, some lady is going to be a very lucky wife indeed.* But she couldn't say those words either. Instead, she stepped back, stood in the alleyway, and watched as the coachman pushed up the stairs, slammed the door, and hopped back onto his perch. Then Lord Christian Berkeley's coach took off out of the alley and into the night.

CHAPTER TWENTY-THREE

Days later, Christian was back in Northumbria. He'd decided not to return to Scotland for reasons he couldn't quite determine and didn't care to examine too closely. He would spend the rest of the winter at his estate. There was always plenty of business to attend to, and this time he threw himself into his affairs with a single-minded determination that could only be the result of an attempt to block something (or someone) from his memory.

Mrs. Hamilton, of course, peppered him with questions about Sarah when they were alone, but he was able to brush them off and continue about his business. The winter was harsh, yet he spent it riding out to oversee his lands, meeting with his estate agent, and speaking with a variety of his tenants. At night, when he'd returned to Berkeley Hall, he read or carved a pipe he'd begun working on. It was to be a wedding gift for Cass's brother, Owen. Damn fool had done the right thing and asked the lovely Lady Alex to marry him.

Christian also wrote a few letters to friends and did his best to forget about Sarah Highgate. She wasn't for him.

She was someone who relished Society, loved dancing, parties, balls. She was someone who was in her element in London Society. It made no sense that he'd been wildly attracted to her in the first place. He must put her out of his mind. He especially tried not to imagine what might be happening to her and her reputation in London. It didn't matter, did it? He'd done all he could do for her. She was in Lucy's hands now. Lucy's more than capable hands.

The first letter from Lucy arrived several weeks after his return to Northumbria. The first time he attempted to open it, Christian dropped the blasted thing out of nervousness. He scooped it up off the rug in his study and broke the seal with a brass letter opener.

Dearest Berkeley,

I do hope this letter finds you well and pleasantly settled for the winter. I am pleased to report that our darling Lady Sarah is happily back in the good graces of the fickle ton. *I daresay a few well-placed rumors begun by the right people are all that are necessary to turn this town on its ear. It's quite ridiculous, actually.*

I'm less happy to report that Sarah's wedding to Lord Branford is still planned. Sarah seems resigned to it, but I have my doubts how happy she is. Her mother proved to be exceedingly reasonable when confronted with my plan to return Sarah to her place in Society, but exceedingly less reasonable when told why her daughter had left to begin with. Seems the earl and countess are entirely intent upon the match. Parents can be so foolish at times. Please remind me of this when Derek and I have a child of marriageable age. But don't tell Jane I said it. No doubt she'll use it against me to great effect one day.

At any rate, I've spoken to Sarah at length on several occasions and she declares that she has no desire to defy her parents again. She's quite resigned to her fate. So, count yourself another win for helping a damsel in distress, my lord. You've got a sterling reputation. Alex and Owen's wedding is planned for Spring, as is Daphne and Rafe's. I do hope you'll make it back to town for the Season, if only to attend the weddings.

Yours sincerely, et cetera,
Lucy

P.S. I daresay you should destroy this communication as to obliterate any inkling that we had anything to do with Sarah's reentry into Society. Not to mention it seems extremely clandestine and spy-like and you know how much I've always wanted to be a spy. Alas, Rafe Cavendish has never agreed to properly train me. Perhaps I might work on his twin brother, Cade. Now there's *a man who has secrets.*

Christian expelled his breath. He read the letter once more before he folded it, crossed the thick Aubusson carpet to the fireplace, and tossed it inside. So it was done, then. Sarah was back in the *ton's* good graces and still engaged to her marquess. Christian should be happy for her. He was glad to have been of assistance. That was his forte, after all. Just like Lucy's uncanny ability to carry out outlandish plots. So why wasn't he happy for Sarah? Why had it felt as if he'd been punched in the gut when he'd read that her wedding was still being planned?

He scrubbed a hand across his face and tentatively fingered his shaggy beard, which for some reason he still couldn't bring himself to shave. Sarah had never seen him without it. He immediately cursed himself for the thought. What did that matter? He braced an arm against the fireplace mantel. He *would* be returning to London in the spring. It would be rude of him to miss the weddings of his friends. Sarah's wedding, however, might be a different case entirely. He wasn't certain he could attend that one. Which might well be a moot point, because he hardly expected to be invited. But he would be going to London in April. For the first time in his life, he was restless in the country. Almost . . . bored. It made no sense. He'd spent a lifetime wishing he could stay here or in Scotland indefinitely. His only business in London involved Parliament, his unsuccessful attempts at finding a wife, and occasional visits with friends. He'd never actually craved Society. Quite the opposite, actually.

But, yes. He'd be going to London in April, not only because of the weddings, but because the Season would be starting and he needed to be ready to employ what Sarah had taught him. With her help, if she was still up to it. He was done with being every lady's friend. It was high time he found a wife. He was going to be a legend, after all.

CHAPTER TWENTY-FOUR

Sarah peeped out of the curtain of her upstairs bedchamber, breathing a sigh of relief at the sight of Lord Branford's coach pulling away from the front of her father's house.

"I doubt he'll believe you are sick for much longer, Sarah," Meg said from her perch on the light green velvet slipper chair that rested near the window.

"Neither will Mother," Sarah groaned. "But they both seemed to believe it today and that is all that matters."

Sarah had been back in London for many weeks. After Lucy Hunt had spread her story, the fickle *ton* had appeared to believe it with nary a thought. Lord Branford had been among those who welcomed her back. He'd laughed about what a silly misunderstanding the entire thing had been and how he'd love to meet the venerable Mrs. Bunbury, who was so highly regarded by so many of the *ton*'s best families.

Sarah had long ago decided Lucy Hunt was a veritable genius. How the woman had managed to convince the entire of London Society that a woman who didn't even exist was one of the most sought-after chaperones in the kingdom was a feat Sarah couldn't begin to fathom. She was only glad that Lucy's genius had been working for her and not against.

However, there was still one problem. Ever since Sarah had returned, Lord Branford had been putting increasing pressure on her to name the date for their impending nuptials. Sarah had tried. Truly she had. Somehow during her time away, she'd convinced herself that perhaps her memory of Lord Branford was exaggerated. Perhaps he wasn't half as awful as she'd made him out to be. But soon after she saw him again and he began prattling on about himself, she remembered exactly why she hadn't been enthusiastic about marrying him in the first place. She still wasn't looking forward to it. But she would do her duty as countless generations of women in her family had done before her, as her mother liked to point out.

Do as you're told, Sarah. The words rang through her head on a daily (if not hourly) basis. She *would* do as she was told. But every time she considered an actual wedding date, the walls of whatever room she was in seemed to close in on her and she began to perspire profusely.

So instead of setting a wedding date, she'd pretended to be indisposed, like an awful little coward.

Adding to her misery were her memories of Christian. The quiet times they'd sat together in the cabin, not having to say a word to each other. The easy way they'd begun a nightly ritual of cleaning the dishes and making tea. Their chess game. Taking care of Fergus II together. And the look on Christian's face the last time she'd seen him, when he'd smiled at her so beautifully.

"I think you should cry off," Meg stated loyally, her bright gold ringlets bouncing.

"You know I can't do that," Sarah replied, letting the curtain drop and pacing back toward her bed.

"I know you don't *want* to. You're worried about your

reputation. I understand, truly I do. When you were gone, I insisted to anyone who would listen that you hadn't run off at all. I'd do anything for you, Sarah. And I'll continue to protect you if that's what you truly want, but take it from someone who has barely any reputation left. It's not half as bad as you think." Meg grinned at her.

That was one of the things Sarah liked best about her friend. Meg wasn't one to wallow in her unfortunate circumstances. Instead, she made light of them. Accepted them with nary a complaint.

"Do you think he's in London yet?" Sarah asked, sighing.

"Who?"

"Lord Berkeley." Sarah plucked absently at the sleeves of her gown.

Meg's eyes widened. "Oh, we're talking about Lord Berkeley now instead of Lord Branford?"

Sarah continued to pluck while she paced back and forth in front of the bed. "What if he's changed his mind? What if he's decided not to return to London for the Season after all?"

"Aren't you supposed to turn him into a legend?" Meg asked, standing and smoothing her pink skirts. She pulled open the curtain and glanced down at the street below.

"That was the plan. That's what we discussed. I'm still willing to keep my end of the bargain, of course, but what if . . ."

"What if what?" Meg asked, letting the curtain fall back into place.

"What if I'm unable to keep my end of the bargain? What if he's decided he no longer wants my help?"

"Why should that matter to *you*?" Meg asked, folding her arms across her chest and facing her friend.

"I would feel guilty if I didn't keep my end of the bargain. Terribly guilty, Meg."

"If he has decided he doesn't wish to be the most eligible bachelor of the Season any longer, I should think there's little you can do to persuade him otherwise."

"Yes, but . . . but . . ."

"Could it be possible that it's not guilt that's nagging at you, but the plain desire to *see* the man again?"

Sarah stopped pacing. She took a long, deep breath. She couldn't hide anything from Meg. Had never been able to. She *did* want to see Christian again. She desperately wanted to see him. Everywhere she went, she craned her neck and scanned the place, searching, always searching for him. But it had been weeks now and she'd yet to see him. She'd begun to fear he wasn't coming. "Perhaps he's decided not to try to use my advice after all. Perhaps he's decided to remain in the north and live a quiet, simple life of a bachelor."

Meg eyed her carefully, her hips turning from side to side. "Perhaps he has."

Sarah pressed her fingertips to her eyelids. "Oh, what's wrong with me, Meg? I've been telling myself it's because I want to help him. I spent a considerable amount of time and attention giving him advice. I owed it to him."

"You'd merely be gratified to see that he'd taken and used your advice to become the most sought-after gentleman in the *ton* this Season?"

"Something like that," Sarah murmured. But she knew deep down that she wanted to see him again because she . . . missed him. Missed his company. Missed his sense of humor. His quick smile. His wry jokes. His kindness.

"The Hollisters' ball is next month," Meg said. "If he's coming to town for the Season, he's sure to be there."

"I suppose." Sarah stopped pacing and braced her hand against the bedpost.

"The question is, can you hold off Lord Branford much longer?" Meg asked.

"I know I shouldn't, but . . ." Sarah bit her lip again.

Meg shook her head. "I simply cannot wait to meet this Lord Berkeley."

A knock sounded on her bedchamber door and Sarah hurried over to open it. It was Hart. Her brother strolled in wearing dark chocolate-brown breeches, a white shirt, a green waistcoat, and costly leather boots. He was busily consulting his gold pocket watch and didn't even bother to look up.

After Sarah closed the door behind him, he glanced at her. "Ah, so you aren't abed," he said with a laugh, leaning down to kiss her on the forehead.

"Don't you dare tell Mother!" Sarah warned.

"I wouldn't dream of it." Hart strolled farther into the room. "Miss Timmons," he said absently to Meg. Meg and Hart had known each other for years. Meg murmured a quick greeting and quietly sank back into the slipper chair.

Hart turned in a circle to face Sarah again. "I promised Mother I'd come and check on your health."

"Tell her I'm pale, and cold, and coughing. Mention the coughing," Sarah said, doing her best to fake a cough.

Hart smiled and shook his head. "You cannot hide from your betrothed forever, you know."

"You're one to talk." Sarah put her fists on her hips. "Mother and Father have been waiting for you to choose a bride for ages and yet you steadfastly refuse."

"Don't remind me. I received yet another speech from Father just this week on my refusal to perform my duty."

"How do you manage to get out of it?" Sarah asked.

"I just remind him that as long as he's alive, there is already a perfectly good heir. I don't think he likes to contemplate his own demise."

"That's not going to work forever, you know," Sarah mimicked.

"No. And neither is your fake illness." Hart braced his hands on his hips to mimic her.

Sarah smiled at him. "We're a pair, aren't we, dear brother?"

"Yes, now you'd best climb back into bed and do a better job at coughing. Mother may well choose to pay you a visit herself. She's determined to get you healthy before the Season begins in earnest. I heard her calling for Cook to make some chicken soup."

Sarah groaned. "Oh, dear."

"I must go," Hart announced. "I'm off to the clubs later and hope to be half in my cups beforehand." He gave Sarah a wicked grin. Contemplating his timepiece again, he strolled back toward the door. "Miss Timmons," he said, again not looking at her.

Meg murmured a good-bye.

Just as Hart's hand was on the door handle, pulling it open, Sarah called out, "Hart? Do you know a . . . Lord Berkeley?"

Hart paused. He dropped his watch back into his pocket and narrowed his eyes. "Berkeley? Yes, nice chap. Viscount, isn't he? The man did me a good turn at school once. Though he's much too respectable to carouse with the likes of me." Her brother winked at her. "What about him?"

"Oh, nothing. I just wondered if you'd . . . heard of him."

"Seems to me he's thick as thieves with Claringdon and Swifdon and their set. The only one from that group I tend to spend time with is Owen Monroe. Though now that he's settling down, that chap's become a downright bore."

Hart pulled open the door farther. "Feel better, dear sister." And then he was gone, his boots thumping down the corridor.

Meg sighed loud and long. "I still think you should cry off from Lord Branford."

Sarah whirled around to face her. "Why?"

"Because ever since you've returned from Scotland, the only man's name I've heard on your lips is Lord Christian Berkeley."

CHAPTER TWENTY-FIVE
London, April 1817

London was a different place entirely in the spring. The grass in the park was growing, baby birds were coming to life in the trees, and while the rain made for muddy ruts in the dirt roads, there was still a fresh energy to the town that was not there in the heat of the summer or the cold of winter when coal smoke clogged the air.

Christian ensconced himself in his town house on Upper Brook Street and set about making appointments with all the tradesmen Sarah had mentioned. First, he allowed his frustrated valet, Matthews, to shave him and cut his hair. The man seemed beyond pleased with his master's sudden desire to be well-groomed again. Matthews was even allowed to cut his hair particularly short, much shorter than he normally wore it. Close-cropped: That's what Sarah had told him was all the rage in London. "Yes, my lord, at once," the valet replied with a gleam in his eye, no doubt from relishing his duty.

Once he was freshly shorn, Christian embarked upon a shopping trip. He made his way to Hoby's for new boots and shoes, Weston's for new coats, Martin's for new shirts and cravats, and Yardley's for new hats. One by one he checked off the list that Sarah had prepared for him, ensuring that he was the best-dressed man in the *ton*. Or one of them, at any rate.

He even met Owen Monroe at the stores a time or two, and the stylish man gave him advice on what precisely to order and lessons on tying not only the mathematical knot, Sarah's favorite, but the l'Orientale and the mail coach as well. Once that tedious business was done, Christian waited for his purchases to arrive.

In the meantime, Lucy stopped by nearly every day to regale him with tales of the latest goings-on of the *ton*. He steadfastly refused to ask about Sarah.

"You're going to Daphne and Rafe's wedding next week, aren't you? It's to be in the country at Cass and Owen's parents' estate."

"Of course," Christian replied, reading the latest political news from the front page of *The Times* while Lucy sipped tea in Christian's drawing room. "I received my invitation weeks ago. I wouldn't miss it."

"And Alexandra and Owen's next month?" Lucy prodded.

"Yes, of course. I had a heavy hand in that one." He chuckled, turning the paper's page. "I'm greatly looking forward to it."

"What about Sarah's?" Lucy asked in a singsong voice.

Christian's hand arrested halfway to the teacup he'd been about to pick up.

"Will you attend that wedding?" Lucy asked. She was trying to keep her tone nonchalant, but Christian knew he was being closely watched.

"I haven't been invited," he replied evenly, spreading the newspaper open in front of his face.

"That's because it hasn't been scheduled yet. Rumor

has it the bride has been reticent to set a date," Lucy announced.

"Is that so?" Christian asked from behind his paper.

Lucy continued in the same singsong tone of voice. "You know that Sarah will be at the events of the Season."

Christian continued to feign interest in his paper, but he was no longer actually reading. "What does that have to do with anything?"

Lucy traced her fingertip around the edge of her teacup. "You'll be there, too. I just thought perhaps you might want to attempt to court Sarah yourself. Change her mind about marrying Branford."

Christian folded the paper hastily and slapped it against the tabletop. "That's preposterous."

"Not so preposterous," Lucy replied, dropping two extra sugar lumps into her cup.

Christian stood and paced toward the windows. "She's engaged to be married. The contracts have been signed. You know as well as I do that these things aren't just called off." Had Lucy lost her mind?

Lucy quietly stirred her tea, holding only the end of the silver spoon. "But I don't believe Sarah's happy with him. She ran away from him once, for heaven's sake."

"Women marry men they aren't particularly happy with all of the time. It's hardly out of the ordinary. You know that." He didn't stop pacing. What the hell was Lucy about, saying such outlandish things?

"Yes, but we *know* Sarah. She's our friend." Lucy's voice was calm. Far more calm than usual. That worried him.

"That makes no difference. She's clearly decided to go through with it."

"But she might well be persuaded to change her mind," Lucy replied. "I simply think—"

Christian clenched his jaw. "What in heaven's name makes you think she'd choose *me* over a marquess, at any rate? She was the belle of the Season last year. I'm the most forgettable man in the kingdom."

"You are not!"

"Oh, really? Shall I remind you of how well my other attempts at courtship have turned out?"

"That's only because you hadn't found the right lady yet."

Christian stopped and braced a hand against the wall. "And you believe Sarah is the right lady?"

Another petite stir of her tea. "I think she may be."

"A betrothed woman? You've really gone round the bend this time, Lucy."

"But you've told me yourself. You feel comfortable with her. You don't stutter in front of her. She likes dogs and has a dry sense of humor. Why, she even named her horse the exact same name as yours, for heaven's sake. And it's not a particularly *common* name. What more evidence do you need?"

The doorbell rang, interrupting their argument and Christian's regret that he'd confided so much in Lucy in the past weeks and over the winter in their correspondence. He hadn't remembered he'd told her all of that, actually.

The butler soon entered the drawing room. "Where would you like the boxes to be placed, my lord?"

Lucy arched a brow over the rim of her teacup. "Boxes?"

"The shipments from Yardley's, Hoby's, Weston's, and Martin's have arrived," the butler explained.

"Have them all brought up to my bedchamber. Matthews will see to them," Christian replied.

"New clothing, eh?" Lucy asked, after the butler had left the room to see to the disbursement of the goods.

"Yes, actually. An entirely new wardrobe."

Lucy smiled at that. "I see you've shaved, too. You look quite handsome, Christian. The new crop of lovelies this Season will be certain to notice you."

Christian stroked his smooth chin. "I'm happy to hear that. Because I'm going to the Hollisters' ball tomorrow night for the beginning of the Season and I intend to find myself a wife. One who is *not* already betrothed to another man."

CHAPTER TWENTY-SIX

Bother. Bother. Bother. Sarah was *not* enjoying her evening. Meg had spilled chocolate on her gown and had rushed off to the ladies' retiring room to see to it. That left Sarah standing near the refreshment table at the Hollisters' ball, listening to Lavinia Hobbs, the eldest daughter of the Duke of Huntley, take swipes at her.

"Well, of course, we all thought the worst," Lavinia was saying. "When you were gone so suddenly. Imagine our surprise when it turned out that you were merely rusticating in Bath with Mrs. Upton of all people."

Sarah sipped the tepid glass of ratafia she'd been cradling in her hand all evening. She'd long ago decided that saying as little as possible about her time away was the best course of action. Lavinia Hobbs was one of the few people who clearly didn't believe the story Lucy had concocted. Lavinia was detestable as usual, but even her hideous company was better than some others'. Namely, Sarah's betrothed's.

For the moment, Lord Branford didn't relish Lavinia Hobbs's company any more than anyone else did, so

Sarah was actually safe from him if she remained with the spinster. Snide comments were preferable to closing walls.

Sarah was about to suggest to Lavinia that she refill her ratafia glass and volunteer to undertake the task herself when a commotion by the entryway to the ballroom caught her attention.

"Who's there?" Sarah asked, craning her neck to see above the throng.

Lavinia waved a dismissive hand in the air. "No doubt some popular young lady who's just made her come-out. Every Season there's always someone new to make a fuss over. I hear this Season it's set to be Lady Claire Marchfield." Lady Lavinia's eyes narrowed to blue slits. "Don't be *too* disappointed that you're no longer the belle of the Season, Sarah. That distinction is always fleeting," Lavinia finished with a smirk.

"Oh, I'm not disappointed," Sarah replied. Good heavens, Lavinia probably couldn't keep herself from being rude even if she tried.

"Why would you be?" Lavinia sneered. "You've got Lord Branford, after all."

"Yes, lucky me," Sarah said under her breath.

Lavinia touched a hand behind her ear. "What was that?"

"Nothing." Sarah stood on her tiptoes, still trying to get a glimpse of whoever was causing a stir near the doorway.

"Viscount Berkeley," the Hollisters' butler intoned, and Sarah gasped and fell back to her heels.

"Viscount Berkeley?" Lavinia echoed, turning up her nose. "Viscount *Berkeley* cannot possibly be who that crowd is making such a fuss over."

Just then, Viscount Berkeley himself began to descend the long staircase that led down to the ballroom. Sarah glanced up at him and sucked in her breath again, this time for an entirely different reason.

It was Christian all right. He was there, in the flesh. But he'd shaved. And his hair was close-cropped, and oh, God, he looked positively divine. He was wearing startlingly black evening attire, a crisp white shirt, a perfectly starched snowy cravat that had been expertly tied in a mathematical knot with a bit of a jaunty kick to it, and perfect new shoes. His blond hair was slicked back. His crystal-blue eyes shone in the light of the candles from the chandeliers, and he laughed at something someone with him had said, revealing his bright, white, perfectly aligned teeth and a smile that made her heart ache with the memory of it.

Sarah pressed a hand to her belly. She'd never seen him looking like this. He looked rested, and clean, and . . . *excessively* handsome. He'd done it. He'd done what she'd suggested. He'd obviously been to Hoby's, and Weston's, Martin's, and Yardley's, for he was decked out in some of the finest clothing London had to offer. And he wore it all *very* well. No doubt he smelled like firewood. The thought made her go weak at the knees.

He was standing with Lady Alexandra Hobbs, Lavinia's younger, much nicer sister, and her betrothed, Lord Owen Monroe, Cassandra Swift's older brother, who was known to cut a dashing figure in town. They were his friends, however, so he wouldn't be shy with them. Wouldn't stutter in their presence.

"Good heavens, what the devil has happened to Lord Berkeley?" Lavinia said near her ear.

Sarah couldn't respond. Her throat had gone dry and her lips wouldn't form any words.

He'd obviously done quite a lot to change his appearance, but Sarah knew it would take more than that to turn him into the bachelor of the Season. The good looks and fine clothing were a fine start, but he needed reinforcements. Immediately.

She spotted Meg slowly wandering back from the ladies' retiring room. Sarah quickly excused herself to Lady Lavinia and hurried over to her friend.

Meg was dressed in a gown that had at one time been white, but after much use she'd been forced to dye it pink to hide a few of the stains. Tonight, a blob of chocolate had landed squarely on her bosom, and it seemed her efforts in the retiring room had served only to smear it.

"I'm hopeless," Meg said, her bright jade-green eyes sparkling and her dark blond curls bouncing as she stared down unhappily at her décolletage. She quickly lifted her head again, however, a wide smile on her face. That was another thing Sarah loved so much about her friend. Meg was irrepressibly happy, even with many reasons not to be. "Who is that who just came in?" Meg asked. "He's causing quite a stir."

"That is Lord Berkeley," Sarah replied, nodding toward Christian and his friends.

Meg's eyes turned as wide as tea saucers. "*Your* Lord Berkeley?"

"Well, he's not precisely mine, no. But if you mean the man I've been telling you about, then yes. *That* Lord Berkeley."

Meg turned and stood on tiptoes to get a better look. "Why, Sarah Highgate. You've been holding out on me. You told me he was handsome, but dear heavens, you failed to mention he looked like *that*."

"I've never seen him cleanly shaved before," Sarah answered lamely.

Meg swayed on her tiptoes. "I could swear I've met him before. The name was familiar, but I feel as if I would have remembered *him*."

"It looks as though he's taken some of my advice."

"Hoby's? Martin's? Yardley's?"

"And Weston's," Sarah replied.

"Very well." Meg straightened her shoulders. "What can we do to help this poor soul? I'm willing to sacrifice myself."

Sarah laughed at her friend's antics. They both knew that Meg was madly in love with Hart, but it never stopped her from jesting about other handsome gentlemen. Just as Sarah was destined to marry Branford, Hart needed to marry well. And a penniless daughter of a baron, whose father happened to be their father's sworn enemy, wasn't exactly future countess material. No matter how much Sarah loved her friend, she knew her parents would never approve the match. And Hart had never seemed to even notice poor Meg.

"He's looking quite fine," Sarah said, glancing back at Christian again. "But I know he'll need our help." She gestured for her friend to come closer. "Here's what I want you to do."

CHAPTER TWENTY-SEVEN

When a small woman with bright green eyes and a riot of blond curls atop her head came sidling up to Christian, at first he thought little of it. He was concentrating on keeping his breathing straight with so many pairs of eyes on him. He'd no idea what a difference a haircut and some clothing could make, but by God, so far everything that Sarah had told him was paying off in spades. His appearance here tonight was certainly the first time an entire ballroom full of people had turned to look at him.

Lucy had promised she'd remain by his side, but he knew at some point he would have to brave the masses and ask some of these ladies to dance. Speak to them, hopefully *sans* stutter. Blast. It had all seemed so much easier with Sarah in Scotland.

When the tiny pink-clad woman tapped him on the shoulder, he turned to look at her with a frown. Did he know her? She was a pretty little thing, but no, he didn't recognize her. "Yes?" he asked, blinking at her. For some reason, she didn't make him nervous either. Perhaps it was the smeared chocolate on her décolletage that set him at ease in her presence. She was too small and cute to make him nervous. She reminded him of a kitten.

"I'm Meg Timmons," she informed him. "Lady Sarah sent me."

Sarah sent her? No wonder this young woman didn't make him nervous. He glanced around the room but didn't see Sarah. Where was she?

Lucy, who'd been keeping a close eye on him, leaned forward. "Ah, Miss Timmons. How lovely to see you. Do you know my friend Lord Berkeley?"

"I do not," Meg replied, clearly relieved at Lucy's having performed the proper introductions.

"I'm certain Miss Timmons would like to dance. Wouldn't you, Miss Timmons?" Lucy continued.

"I would indeed," Miss Timmons replied with a curtsy.

Christian cleared his throat. Obviously Miss Timmons had been sent by Sarah to ease him into the ball. No doubt she'd witnessed the commotion his entrance had made. He had to smile to himself. Sarah was indeed intent upon keeping her end of the bargain after all these months.

"I'd be honored if you would dance with me," he said, entirely without stuttering. "If you would be so kind, Miss Timmons."

"I'd love it," Miss Timmons replied. Her smile was bright and infectious. He couldn't imagine any man stammering in her presence. Sarah had sent the perfect friend to help him. But he remembered what she had said about Meg being hopelessly in love with another man. Meg was here as an emissary only. She wasn't someone suitable to court.

He led the young woman to the dance floor and whirled her around in time to the music.

"How is your friend Lady Sarah?" he asked after they'd been around the floor once.

"She is doing quite well, my lord. In fact, she has a message for you."

"Does she?"

"Yes, she says to remember your dance in Scotland and to pretend you're there with her."

Christian's chest tightened. Sarah had remembered that he would be anxious and that his stutter would return in a crowd full of ladies. Especially ladies he was meant to court. Another reason her choice of Meg to approach him was perfect.

"She also wants you to take note of that young woman standing in the group just near the refreshment table."

Christian glanced about to locate the group in question. There was a small blond woman standing in the middle of what appeared to be a dozen suitors. She was pretty and smiling and laughing, obviously holding court.

"That's Lady Claire Marchfield," Meg offered, nodding toward the young woman.

"Why am I to take notice of her?" Christian asked.

"Because she is the current belle of the new Season," Meg explained. "She is whom you need to impress if you're to become the most highly sought-after bachelor this year."

"She is, is she?" Christian's hands began to sweat just thinking of approaching the belle of the Season.

"Yes, and she does have beautiful gowns, I must admit," Meg said with a sigh. "Of course, I'm convinced she doesn't do idiotic things like drop chocolate on them."

Christian's heart tugged at the memory of Sarah explaining to him how Meg's clothes were old and outdated. He felt a sense of kindred with Meg. They were both the outcasts, apparently. Or had been in the past.

"Why didn't Lady Sarah come tell me this herself?" he couldn't help asking. He also didn't want to admit to himself that he wanted to see her. To know where she was.

Meg's irrepressible grin widened. "Because she's busy spreading the rumor that you're the most highly sought-after bachelor of the Season, of course."

CHAPTER TWENTY-EIGHT

By the time Sarah made her way across the ballroom to find Christian more than an hour later, two things had happened. First, the rumor that Christian was *the* bachelor of the Season had spread like wildfire, no doubt helped along in no small part by his stunning good looks and fine clothing. Second, Lady Claire had heard the rumor (truth be told, she'd been informed by Sarah herself) and had positioned herself in Christian's crowd. Her own group of admirers had followed her, as had all the other young ladies and their mothers vying to get a glimpse of the eligible viscount. When Sarah approached the group, it had turned into a veritable swarm of people.

She picked up her light blue skirts and pushed her way into the crowd, scanning the faces for Christian. Lucy Hunt was standing at one of his elbows, Lady Claire at the other. The girl had blond hair and blue eyes and an excessively pretty, round, pale face. A stab of something that felt far too much like jealousy ripped through Sarah's middle entirely unexpectedly. But she also felt pride. Pride for Christian.

He *was* doing it. Exactly as she'd taught him. He'd somehow managed to speak to Lady Claire, the new belle of the Season, and immediately be seen with her. The man was obviously a quick study.

Sarah desperately wanted to talk to him. She had no idea what she would say once she got there, but she found herself drawn to him like a moth to a flame.

She stood on the outskirts of his little group and watched while what seemed like scores of young women competed for an introduction to him. Lady Claire hovered next to his arm like a timid little bird.

Finally, Lady Alexandra saw Sarah and pulled her closer to Christian. "Lady Sarah, there you are. It's so good to see you."

Was it Sarah's imagination or did Christian's back stiffen when he heard her name? He was standing at right angles to her, speaking to one of the many ladies fluttering around him like so many pretty butterflies. She detected no stutter. She smiled.

"It's nice to see you, too, Lady Alexandra. Best wishes on your upcoming wedding. I was just speaking to your sister about it," Sarah replied.

Lady Alexandra's pretty brown eyes clouded. "Oh, I'm sorry to hear you've had to endure Lavinia's company." She soon brightened, however. "But thank you for the kind words. The same to you on your own impending nuptials."

Sarah stiffened this time. She tried to smile, but her lips were tight. "Thank you."

Christian turned then and his smile dazzled her. This close to her, he was even more handsome than he'd been far away. He didn't smell like firewood. Instead, he was wearing some sort of spicy cologne that made her senses reel.

"Lady Sarah, have you met my friend Lord Berkeley?" Alexandra asked in a sweet voice.

Sarah shook her head. Lucy had told her that she and Christian had agreed they should pretend not to have met if they saw each other in London this Season. When Lucy had explained the reason for it, Sarah had merely nodded and jerked her head away. She'd been plagued with thoughts of Christian all these months. Why? *Why?*

She told herself again and again that if only she were engaged to a man she admired and respected, she wouldn't spend her time thinking about someone else. It was shameful to do so. Shameful and wrong. God knew she'd spent enough nights tossing and turning in bed, trying to think of ways to banish Christian Forester from her mind, but nothing seemed to work. Lately, she'd been so preoccupied with the fear of having to pick a wedding date that the thoughts of Christian weren't as vivid as they had been when he'd first left her in Bath. But the sight of him here, now, sent them all rushing back to her in excruciating detail.

"A pleasure, Lady Sarah," Christian said, taking her hand and bowing over it. He'd saved her from having to say the lie outright herself. Oh, his gloves were fine, too. He must have stopped at the glovemakers as well.

"M-m-my lord," she intoned instead, curtsying to him as soon as he righted himself. Then she blushed scarlet for having stuttered the first word.

"Would you care to dance?" he asked smoothly, surprising her with the question.

"Thank you." She offered him her hand and noticed a small pout form on Lady Claire's face as she watched him take Sarah's arm and lead her to the dance floor.

A waltz began to play and Christian spun her into his arms.

"Did I hear you stutter when you greeted me?" he said with a teasing smile.

"Guilty," she admitted. "I must say, you look quite . . . quite . . . different from the last time I saw you."

His grin widened. "I should hope so. If I remember correctly, the last time you saw me, I was sporting several days' growth of beard and wearing coarse woolen trousers."

She eyed him up and down. "You went to Martin's, didn't you?"

"And Hoby's and Weston's and Yardley's."

"I could tell."

"What do you think?" They continued to spin around the dance floor. The man was an extremely graceful dancer. Just as she'd known he would be.

"I told you I could make you into a legend." The old lump was back in her throat.

"I don't know if I'd go *that* far yet."

"You seem quite popular, however. I saw the line of young ladies hoping for introductions to you tonight. Including Lady Claire."

"Yes, Meg delivered your message about Lady Claire being the belle of the Season."

"Well, she's *expected* to be the belle of the Season. She certainly appears popular. As do you."

"If I am popular, it's due to my proximity to you. And I have *you* to thank, of course."

"Nonsense," she replied. "I was only jesting."

"I suppose I have the rumors you've started to thank for my increased and sudden popularity?"

"It's nothing at all. Just a few well-placed comments in the right ears."

"I've never had so much attention before."

"I didn't hear you stutter once."

"I have you to thank for that as well," Christian replied. "Remembering our dance together in Scotland has proven exceedingly helpful."

Sarah bit the inside of her cheek. "I'm only glad I could be of help. You helped me so much last winter."

"How is Mrs. Goatsocks?" he asked.

Sarah lowered her voice, glancing around. "Her ankle is completely healed, the dear, but we told Mother that she'd left to visit her sister in Scotland. She's stayed up there all winter. Her letters have hinted that she's paid more than one visit to Mr. Fergus."

Christian whistled. "Is that so? Fergus's letters to me haven't mentioned anything about it."

"No doubt he's embarrassed. I have a feeling Mrs. Goatsocks has taken a fancy to the man."

"I daresay Mr. Fergus can handle himself." Christian spun Sarah around again. "How are you faring without a chaperone?"

"Well, Mrs. Bunbury had to stay in Bath, of course," she said with a sly smile. "So Mother has taken on the task for the time being. She says she never should have relinquished the role to begin with."

"Keeping a strict eye on you, is she?"

Sarah nodded, staring blankly into his cravat. Why did he have to smell so very good?

"How are you, Sarah?" he asked in a tender voice that made her throat ache.

Tears burned her eyes. "I'm . . . f-fine."

"You don't sound fine."

She shook her head and lifted her chin, forcing herself to paste a smile on her face. "I'm perfectly fine."

He squeezed her hands. "Your engagement?"

"Is proceeding as planned." *Bother.* She could hear the unmistakable note of melancholy in her own voice.

"I'm sorry to hear that. For your sake," he hastened to add.

"I must do what they say. I've little choice. What am I to do, run away again?" She gave a halfhearted laugh.

"I'm certain Fergus Two misses you," he said.

The tears stung harder. *Bother. Bother. Bother.* "I was

given a chance that few young ladies are. A second chance. A clean slate. A restored reputation. I know how valuable that is."

"That's quite a string of reasons you've come up with. But are you happy?"

She couldn't look at him. She forced the words through her dry lips. "I'm content."

"Fine." He glanced away over her head, looking off into the crowd as if he could tell their conversation was no longer honest.

The dance soon came to an end and Christian escorted her back to the group of people they'd been standing in. Lady Claire moved closer to him, obviously hoping for the next dance.

"I'll just leave you to your new friends," Sarah said, picking up her skirts and turning.

His hand was still on her arm. His voice was a whisper at her ear so the others wouldn't hear. "I could always use friends," he murmured. "That's what we are, Sarah, aren't we? Friends?"

"Yes," she whispered back, biting the inside of her cheek to keep from crying. "We're friends, Christian. Just friends."

That night, when she climbed into her bed, Sarah could feel the walls closing in around her.

CHAPTER TWENTY-NINE

The next afternoon, Christian arrived at the town house of the Earl of Marchland wearing an entire set of his new clothing, including his fine boots, his hair freshly cropped again, a smile pasted on his face, and holding a bouquet of flowers for Lady Claire. The girl seemed lovely and sweet enough, but she tended to giggle too much and he was beginning to think she might be a bit silly. What did he expect from an eighteen-year-old? But then he thought of Sarah and how she was only nineteen now. She'd had a birthday this spring, according to Lucy. But she'd never seemed silly to him.

Sarah.

Seeing her last night had been both better and worse than he'd expected. Better because he'd clearly done something right to have the belle of the Season somewhat interested in him. He was proud to show Sarah that he'd readily employed everything she'd been so generous to teach him. He'd even managed to ask for a favor. Though it had been deuced uncomfortable doing so. He'd asked Lady Alexandra to help. Alex had readily agreed and quickly was yet another voice whispering it about that Christian was considered *the catch* of the Season.

Lucy was right. Society was strange and fickle. The right well-timed rumor whispered by the right well-heeled person could be quite convincing. However, seeing Sarah again—even in his own much more popular state—had been a bit like looking directly at the sun too long. She was even more beautiful than he remembered, her dark hair piled high atop her head, a few tendrils left to brush her shoulders. She'd been wearing a light blue gown with a fitted bodice, and she still smelled like lilies. It made his mouth water. Worst of all, she was still steadfastly engaged to Branford. Christian had watched her after their dance—not when she was looking, of course, but he'd been unable to help himself—and he'd noticed she hadn't danced so much as once with her estimable future husband. Branford had been holding court at the far end of the room, a group of ladies and gentlemen hanging upon his every word. No doubt exactly the way the marquess liked it.

Sarah had spent the better part of her evening laughing and talking with Meg Timmons near the refreshment table. It was good to see Sarah laugh. She'd seemed upset when he'd asked her how she was during their dance. But she clearly enjoyed Society and parties and was quickly back in her element, dancing with several young men and laughing with her friend. Christian had asked Lady Claire to dance a second time, just as Sarah had advised him. Lady Claire had been only too willing to do so, and his apparent success in that quarter led to his arrival upon her doorstep today with a handful of violets.

Lady Claire seemed happy to see him and had surprised him by ignoring the half score of other suitors who had arrived before him—most with roses, he noted with some irony—and asking Christian to take her riding in the park. Christian had considered the request for a moment and then decided that the only thing more ill-mannered than taking the focus of so much attention away to ride in the park would be to *refuse* to do so, especially when the young woman had requested it so prettily. Besides, this was exactly what he'd always wanted, wasn't it? The attention of a perfectly suitable, unattached lady who was looking for a husband? What the devil was he waiting for?

They'd barely made it onto Rotten Row in his sleek new curricle before Christian sorely regretted his decision, however. It seemed Lord Branford and Sarah had also decided to go riding in the park.

Christian noticed the chaise first, flashy, overly ornate, the crest of the marquess boldly outlined in gold leaf upon the side. Then Christian's gaze shot to the two occupants who sat perched on the high seat. The marquess looked like a peacock basking in the glow of the imagined admiration of everyone in the park. Sarah, however, looked . . . bored. Her face was tight, her eyes were blank, and she didn't appear to be listening to a word the marquess said.

As Christian's curricle approached theirs, Lady Claire squealed, "Oh, there's the Marquess of Branford and Lady Sarah Highgate. They were *quite* the *last* Season's most celebrated couple, you know."

"You don't say?" Christian drawled just as the marquess's chaise pulled to a stop beside his.

"Eh there, Berkeley, seems it's been an age since I last saw you," Branford announced. He pulled a pinch of snuff from out of his embroidered sleeve and sniffed it.

Christian let his gaze travel over the marquess. He'd never really considered the man before, but now he tried to see him as a woman might. A woman who was engaged to him. The man had a quickly thinning patch of blond hair atop his head. A rather decided nose. Thin lips and a puffed-out chest, though whether by anatomy or by intention, Christian couldn't be certain. The marquess wore a heavily embroidered waistcoat, an overly fussy cravat, and a bright blue velvet coat. It was peacock blue. Fitting.

He also managed to carry an excessive number of accessories, including a top hat, a brass-tipped cane, an eyeglass, and of course his oft used snuffbox. In a word, the man was a dandy, something Monroe had explained to Christian one day while they'd been picking out shirts at Martin's. Branford's boots, however, did indeed look as if they were the work of Hoby, the master boot maker.

"I've been in the country all winter," Christian replied, forcing himself to stop his inventory of the marquess.

Christian's gaze met Sarah's and he saw a flicker of something in her eye. Humor? Interest? Both?

"Eh, what fun is that? Hiding in the countryside," Branford replied. "London's full of the amusements, don't you know."

"So I've heard," Christian replied.

"I *quite* agree," Lady Claire surprisingly piped up from beside him.

Christian turned to look at her, then back at the marquess. "Do you know Lady Claire Marchfield?" He drew a hand toward his companion.

"I don't know. Have we met?" Branford demanded of a flustered Lady Claire.

The young woman immediately began to stammer. "I . . . oh, well, n-no, my lord. I don't *quite* believe we have met."

Branford waggled his eyebrows at her. "Then we have not," he insisted. "For I daresay you'd recall if we had."

"Y-yes, of course," Lady Claire replied. *"Quite."*

Christian could have sworn Sarah rolled her eyes at

that. He gave her a knowing look. She hid her smile behind her gloved hand.

"Do you know each other?" he asked Sarah, gesturing to Lady Claire again.

"Oh, yes, we've met. *Quite.* Lady Sarah attended the come-out ceremony and was such a dear to give some of us advice this year."

"That was kind of you, my dear," Branford said. "A good reflection on the Branford name, I daresay."

"We're not married yet," Sarah murmured.

Branford looked disgruntled, but he quickly changed the subject. "Have you met the future marchioness?" he asked Christian.

"Yes, we . . . Lady Alexandra Hobbs introduced us last night."

Sarah shot him a knowing look this time. He ignored it.

"And as she's to be your marchioness, I believe congratulations are in order," Christian said, turning his attention back toward the marquess. "For your wedding."

"Oh, yes," Lady Claire squealed, clapping her hands. "*Quite.* You are to be married soon, aren't you?"

"Not soon enough," the marquess said, his tone disgruntled as well.

Sarah promptly blushed.

"Lady Sarah has yet to set a date," the marquess continued.

"Surely there's no rush," Sarah replied. She kept her eyes trained on her hands, which were now folded tidily in her lap.

"I'd like to marry before the snow flies again." The marquess laughed heartily at his own jest.

"Oh, *quite.* Certainly you'll be married before then," Lady Claire exclaimed, blinking in confusion at Sarah.

"There is much to be considered," Sarah replied noncommittally, glancing back over toward them while the marquess frowned.

"I, for one, *quite* cannot wait until *my* wedding day." Lady Claire blushed prettily, gazing up at Christian from beneath long lashes.

Christian's eye caught Sarah's, and this time she waggled her eyebrows at him.

Christian was spared from replying to Lady Claire's loaded statement, however, by a scream that rang out across the park. The four of them swiveled their heads to see what had happened. The scream was promptly followed by a loud splash. A young lady's horse had thrown her into the Serpentine.

Springing into action, Christian tossed the reins to Lady Claire and leaped from his coach, sprinting over to the luckless young woman, who was sputtering helplessly in the water, her yellow flowered skirts obviously dragging her down. Christian ripped off his hat and coat and tossed them to the bank but dove in with the rest of his clothing in place. With long strokes, he swam out to the middle of the lake and firmly grabbed the sobbing young woman.

"Put your arms around my neck," he demanded.

Thankfully, the woman complied and he swam back to the bank with her clinging to him, her nose pressed to his shoulder. By the time they reached the shore, a sizable crowd had formed and in it stood Lady Sarah and the marquess. A quick glance told Christian that Lady Claire was still sitting in his curricle, though she was craning her neck to see what had happened.

Christian ensured the young lady he'd saved was delivered safely to her mother. The woman cried and both of them thanked him profusely.

"No thanks are necessary," Christian said. "I'm only glad I was able to help."

"Yes, yes," came the marquess's booming voice. "I certainly would have rescued her myself, but you've no idea how costly these boots are. Not to mention my coat." He lovingly brushed a hand against the velvet blue.

Everyone looked at Christian's obviously expensive and obviously ruined clothing.

"That was kind of you," Sarah said quietly. She glanced at him and looked away. Christian looked down to see that his shirtfront was plastered against his wet chest. He plucked at it, trying to separate it from his body.

"Yes," Branford said, oblivious to Sarah's reaction at the sight of Christian's muscled chest. "Kind indeed. Berkeley, you must come to my house tonight for a dinner party I'm hosting. God knows once the talk of your heroics here today reaches the rest of *ton,* you'll be the most highly sought-after dinner guest in London, and I pride myself on having the most sought-after guests at my parties."

Christian slicked back his wet hair with his fingers. "I don't think—"

"Nonsense," the marquess interrupted. "Of course you will. Bring that delightful Lady Claire with you. Ten o'clock. See you then."

Sarah had apparently retrieved his hat and coat from the bank on the way over. He hadn't noticed her holding them before. She took a step forward and pressed them into his hands.

"See you tonight," she whispered.

CHAPTER THIRTY

"Did you hear that Lord *Berkeley* is coming tonight?"

Sarah smiled to herself. She must have heard that same question from every single woman milling around Lord Branford's drawing room waiting to go in to dinner. All anyone could talk about was Lord Christian Berkeley. And it wasn't because of his heroics in the park this afternoon. No. That act had merely *added* to his appeal. Viscount Berkeley, it seemed, had somehow been egregiously over-looked in years past, but now he was in London, sporting a new wardrobe, new boots, a new haircut, and a new curri-cle and looking quite fine. And did you see the expert tie of his cravat? Why, the viscount had always been rich and handsome, but now he was somehow looking even *more* rich and *more* handsome than ever before. Rumor had it that he was considered *the catch* of the Season.

They'd done it. The two of them. Christian was as popular as he could want to be. Sarah had fulfilled her end of the bargain and was inordinately pleased with herself.

But there was one highly unexpected side effect of their success. It had been excruciating watching Christian in the park today sitting in his curricle next to Lady Claire. Jealousy had clawed at Sarah. Unwelcome, unwanted jealousy. How could she make it go away? She hadn't the faintest idea. It was so like Christian to leap into a lake to help a woman in need. It hadn't helped anything to see him emerge from the water with his shirt plastered to the front of him. It reminded her of how very . . . *muscled* the man was. She'd seen his chest briefly in Scotland, but now it was all she could think about. That ninny Branford had said he hadn't tried to rescue the poor young woman because of the price of his boots. Yes, heaven forfend he should risk a pair of expensive shoes to save someone's life.

Sarah had dressed for the dinner party tonight with infinite care. A week ago, she hadn't given a toss about Lord Branford's party, but as soon as she knew Christian would be there she'd asked her maid to twine her hair around her head in an especially fetching fashion. She chose to wear her favorite gown, a sparkling silvery-white one with a wide red bow, and matching silver shoes. A ruby necklace finished the ensemble, and she'd felt quite smart standing in front of the looking glass before she'd left for the party.

Now she was standing next to the marquess, getting ready to be escorted in to dinner, when Christian entered the room. He was accompanied by Lady Claire and her mother. That lady was looking quite pleased with herself for her daughter's arrival with the most talked-about bachelor of the Season. Not to mention that she was attending the dinner party of the *former* most popular bachelor. But *why* did it bother Sarah? She'd wanted this for him. For goodness' sake, she'd *recommended* Lady Claire to him. Sarah should be nothing but pleased to see him making headway in his suit with the young woman.

Sarah barely had time to nod a greeting to Christian from across the room before they all were trotted in to dinner, but she soon realized that Branford had seen to it that Christian was seated directly across from them.

"Didn't catch a cold from your adventure earlier, did you, Berkeley?" Branford said as soon as they'd sat and the wine was being poured.

"Not yet. However, I did ruin an excellent pair of boots."

"Egad." Branford shook his head sadly. "A pity."

"I don't know how you could have possibly been so brave, my lord," Lady Claire offered from Christian's right side. Her mother was sitting farther down the table. "It was *quite* harrowing to watch, I assure you."

"Nothing brave about it at all," Christian replied, taking a healthy sip of wine.

"I beg to differ, my lord," Lady Claire replied, her eyes downcast. "You were terribly brave. Why, I nearly swooned."

Christian glanced up to see Sarah unmistakably roll her eyes.

"Yes, well, I nearly saved someone once . . . ," Branford was saying, and Christian rolled his eyes at that. Sarah kicked him lightly under the table, and he kicked her back.

Lady Claire looked back and forth between Christian and Sarah and redoubled her efforts to engage Christian in conversation.

"Lord Berkeley, will you be attending the Rutherfords' ball tomorrow evening?" Lady Claire asked.

"I will indeed," Christian replied.

"Oh, wonderful, for I shall be there, too," Lady Claire replied with a bright smile.

"Oh, goody," Sarah drawled. She picked up her wineglass and took a deep draught.

"Will you be attending the Rutherfords' ball as well, then, Lady Sarah?" Christian ventured.

"Yes," she replied simply.

"It's too bad I cannot accompany you, my dear," the marquess said. "I have been invited to Carlton House, and one simply does not turn down an invitation from the *prince*." This was said in an overly loud voice to ensure that most of the occupants at the table heard it.

"I wouldn't know," Christian replied, tasting the watercress soup that a footman had placed in front of him. A memory flashed through his mind of Sarah's stew and the laughter they'd shared in Scotland.

"Never been to Prinny's?" the marquess asked, obviously pleased to have something to pontificate about.

"Never," Christian replied.

"Yes, well, his dinner parties are *legendary*. I mustn't eat too much tonight in preparation, I daresay."

"Perhaps you should save your conversation for tomorrow evening as well," Sarah said. When Lady Claire gave her a horrified look, Sarah hastened to add, "You wouldn't want your voice to be hoarse for conversation with His Royal Highness."

The marquess nodded. "Sage advice, my dear. Quite sage." He promptly stopped talking, taking small spoonfuls of his soup.

Sarah took another large drink of wine, draining her glass. A footman rushed to refill it, and she thanked him prettily. Then she turned her attention to Lady Claire.

"How are you finding the events of the Season, Lady Claire?"

"Oh, I find I am *quite* enjoying myself so far," Lady Claire replied, taking a dainty taste of her soup. Somehow Christian couldn't imagine the delicate Lady Claire making stew and knitting a dog's sweater in the middle of a snowstorm in Scotland.

"And the gentlemen, how are you finding them?" Sarah continued.

Lady Claire's pale cheeks turned bright pink, and she glanced up hesitantly at Christian. "Everyone has been *quite* lovely and *quite* accommodating so far. I'm *quite* in awe of the number of callers I've had."

"Quite," Sarah echoed, drinking more.

"Claire, do not brag. It is not seemly," her mother said from a few seats away.

"Yes, Mother," Lady Claire replied, her cheeks still pink.

Sarah lowered her voice. "You've had a great many suitors, have you?"

Claire glanced down the table nervously to ensure her mother wouldn't hear. "A dozen today alone," she whispered back. "Including Lord Berkeley here."

Christian winced.

"Ah, you paid a call on Lady Claire today?" Sarah asked him.

"Yes, actually. That's how we came to be riding in the park together."

"He brought me the most lovely flowers," Lady Claire gushed, beaming at Christian.

"Not roses, surely?" Sarah said, taking yet another drink of wine.

Lady Claire shook her head, her blond ringlets bouncing. "No. Violets. *Quite* the most lovely bouquet of violets."

"A fine choice," Sarah replied, sitting back in her chair and taking another long draught of wine.

The next several courses were served while an increasingly drunken Sarah peppered Lady Claire with a series of questions about her suitors and her marital prospects. Christian tried not to listen while he spoke with another gentleman across the table about the current crop of horseflesh at Tattersall's. Meanwhile, Lord Branford spoke only a few words from time to time, obviously having taken to heart his intended's advice about saving his voice for conversation with the Prince Regent on the morrow. He did, however, take every opportunity to paw at Sarah, touching her hand and shoulder with a frequency that made Christian's gut clench. It was all *quite* ridiculous and was punctuated by Lady Claire's incessant use of the word *quite*.

Finally, after an excruciatingly long dessert course had been completed, the marquess pushed back his chair, indicating that the meal had come to an end. "Don't let's be formal tonight," Branford said. "I find I don't want to be long separated from my betrothed. Let's take our drinks in the drawing room with the ladies this time, gentlemen."

Christian said a brief prayer of thanks to the heavens for being spared the marquess's concentrated company.

The entire group stood and headed to one of the drawing rooms at the front of the town house, where Branford promptly situated himself upon the sofa in the middle of the room and pulled Sarah down to sit next to him. Lady Claire and her mother hovered nearby. Lady Claire's mother seemed intent upon asking the marquess all about the Prince Regent.

Christian took a seat at the far end of the room and gladly accepted a glass of port from a footman who was serving them from a silver salver. He surveyed the group in front of him, wondering how long Lady Claire and her mother would want to remain. Dinner had been torturous. Watching Branford paw at Sarah and Sarah's uncomfortable response. Listening to Lady Claire drone on in *quite* the most excessive fashion he'd ever heard. And watching Sarah slowly drink herself into oblivion. Was Branford more palatable to her when she was half-foxed? Christian couldn't watch it any longer. He steadfastly kept his gaze off of her but couldn't help but notice when Sarah's mother called her over. The two ladies exchanged a few obviously terse words in the corner before Sarah returned to Branford's side, a disgruntled look on her face.

Christian had been sipping his port and halfheartedly examining a book about ancient Rome that he'd found on the table next to his seat when he looked up to see that Sarah had slipped away from the marquess's court and was slowly making her way over to him. Christian watched her approach. She swayed a bit on her feet, but her wineglass was still clutched firmly in her gloved hand.

She came to stand a few paces in front of him. "Interested in ancient Rome?" she asked, raising her glass to him in a silent salute.

"Immensely," he said, sliding the book back into place on the table. He watched her carefully, hoping she didn't tip over.

She took a seat on the bench near the window not far from his chair and swung her legs in front of her.

"Bored of your intended's company so soon?" Christian nodded toward the group she'd just left. He glanced over to see Sarah's mother staring at her with daggers in her eyes.

"I'm weary of counting the number of times Lady Claire said *quite*," Sarah replied with a tight smile.

"More than a dozen?"

"More than two dozen." She lifted her glass to her lips before pausing to say, "I'm pleased to see you aren't suffering any ill effects from the lake today."

He nodded toward his feet. "Other than my new boots?"

"Rescuing another damsel in distress?" she asked in a slightly slurred voice.

Christian shrugged. "It seems I have a knack for it."

"Also seems as if you've found a young lady." Sarah glanced back toward where Lady Claire sat listening attentively to Branford's tales.

"Who? Lady Claire?" Christian asked, crossing his booted foot over his knee.

Sarah took another sip of wine. "Yes, Lady Claire. I seem to recall she was in your company at the Hollisters' ball as well."

"Was she?" Christian drawled. He didn't know what to make of this Sarah, this slightly drunken, seemingly jealous Sarah.

Her eyes narrowed on him. "You know she was."

"I suppose my new clothing and aspect have been good for something. You said yourself she's considered the belle of the Season."

"She is," Sarah said curtly, turning her head to stare at Lady Claire.

"As I said the other night, I have you to thank for my success," Christian offered.

Sarah didn't seem pleased to hear it. Her mouth was tight, drawn. "You didn't bring her roses."

"No."

Sarah glanced away. She twisted her wineglass around in her hand. "I adore violets."

"No doubt Branford can afford a great many violets." Christian didn't know why he said it. Why couldn't he let it go? Why did he always have to bring the conversation back to Branford?

Sarah half laughed, half snorted. "He brings roses when he remembers to bring anything."

"Ah, so that's where your dislike of roses comes from."

She waved her empty gloved hand in the air. "Roses are so . . . unimaginative."

Christian studied his port. "Yes, I believe you said that once before. How imaginative are violets?"

"Judging from Lady Claire's reaction, I'd say they are *quite* imaginative and *quite* welcome."

"Careful, Sarah. If I didn't know any better, I'd think

you were jealous." The words were out of his mouth before he had a chance to examine them. He nearly winced. He shouldn't have said that, either.

She sputtered and coughed. "Me? Jealous?"

"You may want to lower your voice," he warned. A few of the other guests had glanced over at them. Sarah's mother looked ready to pounce upon them.

"Me? Jealous?" she hissed in a whisper, leaning toward him.

"Yes, perhaps."

"Of Lady Claire?" she huffed, and took another sip of wine.

Christian stood. "I'm not certain you're in a state where you should be having this conversation. I think you're a bit worse for wine this evening. May I?" He gestured to her glass. She reluctantly handed it to him.

Christian delivered both the wineglass and his half-full glass of port to the nearest footman. "Bring Lady Sarah a glass of water, please," he instructed the footman.

Sarah bowed her head and rubbed her temples. "Perhaps you're right. A glass of water sounds like exactly what I need."

"I must gather Lady Claire and her mother and go," Christian said. "I fear I've worn out my welcome. Branford doesn't seem to enjoy my speaking privately to his future marchioness." He nodded to the marquess, who remained on the sofa. The man was definitely watching them now with a more than interested look on his face. "You should get back to him," Christian said.

Sarah stood and took a deep breath. She began to walk away but turned and asked over her shoulder, "Are you jealous of the marquess?"

Christian inclined his head toward her. But he whispered so she couldn't hear, "More than you can know."

CHAPTER THIRTY-ONE

The Rutherfords' ballroom was ablaze with the light of a thousand candles twinkling in the chandeliers that hung from the enormous frescoed ceiling. Sarah and Meg had been standing next to Lady Alexandra Hobbs for the last twenty minutes. Sarah was asking after the details of Lady Alex's upcoming wedding.

"I simply cannot wait," Alex said, beaming. She glanced across the ballroom toward where her bridegroom, Lord Owen Monroe, stood in a group of gentlemen. The look the two exchanged made Sarah feel as if she were intruding upon a private moment. A pang of regret twisted in her heart. She would never know such devotion. Such love.

"How did you know?" Sarah asked suddenly, the words flying past her lips.

Alex blinked at her. "How did I know what?"

Sarah cleared her throat. "How did you know that Lord Owen was the right man for you?"

Meg leaned closer to hear, too.

Alex smiled softly and a faraway look came into her eyes. "I've loved him since I was fifteen years old."

"I know the feeling," Meg mumbled.

Sarah tilted her head to the side. "Really? Fifteen?" she said to Alex.

"Yes," Alex continued. "I saw him under my window at a party my parents had at their country house. He was defending a stable boy against a couple of older bucks who were making fun of the child. I fell in love instantly."

"You just knew?" Sarah asked, leaning forward and biting her lip.

Alex nodded her dark head. "Yes, I just knew. Just like that."

"Sometimes you just know." Meg sighed again.

Sarah wrapped her arms around her middle. She'd always assumed that Meg was a special case, loving Hart so deeply for so long. But Lady Alex had confirmed it. Some people were lucky that way. Love just arrived under their window one night. But how exactly was one supposed to go about making such important decisions when one wasn't absolutely certain?

Sarah had stayed awake for hours last night, tossing and turning and thinking about what had happened at Branford's dinner party with Christian. She *had* had too much to drink last night; that much was certain. Her mother had lectured her the entire way home. Christian had once again done her a nice turn, taking away her wineglass and asking for a glass of water. She would have had the devil of a head this morning had he not seen to her. As it was, she didn't feel entirely right. Either way, she'd been unable to sleep. *Had* she been jealous of Lady Claire? It seemed silly, petty, beneath her. But she hadn't been able to stop asking the poor girl questions—and the way she'd blinked up at Christian and gone on and on about the violets . . . well, it had driven Sarah to drink, that's all. Not that she could blame poor Lady Claire for her own excessive behavior, but jealousy was an entirely foreign concept to Sarah. She'd had no idea that she was even capable of such an emotion. Had her ancestors felt this way? Betrothed to one man but jealous of another? It was entirely unpleasant. Or was she merely getting her emotions confused because of Branford's lack of appeal and his incessant insistence upon setting a wedding date? She had to find some way to be certain. She couldn't have been the first young lady with this problem, and she certainly wouldn't be the last. Perhaps Lady Alexandra could provide her with some answers.

"Did your parents approve?" Sarah blurted to Alex.

"Pardon?" Alex's brown eyes blinked.

"Did they ever expect you to marry a different man?"

"Saaaraaah," Meg dragged out the word in a warning tone.

"No, it's quite all right." Alex laughed. "It was much worse than that, actually. They decided that *Lavinia* should marry Owen."

This time Sarah blinked. "Your sister?"

"Yes. It was all quite complicated, really, but worked out well in the end. Thanks to Lucy Hunt and Cassandra Swift and Lord Berkeley, actually."

Sarah kept her face blank. She was not supposed to know anything about Lucy and Cass and Christian's penchant for helping people. "Lord Berkeley?" she echoed in as nonchalant a voice as she could muster.

"What did Lord Berkeley do?" Meg echoed, obviously interested, too.

"He's a dear friend," Alex said. "I wouldn't be happily engaged to Owen if it weren't for him."

"Is that so?" It occurred to Sarah that although Christian had told her he'd helped Alex, she didn't actually know the details. Was the plot behind Alex's engagement as outlandish as the one Lucy Hunt had concocted to save Sarah?

"What exactly did he do to help you?" Sarah prompted.

Meg leaned forward again, her green eyes sparkling with curiosity.

Alex glanced back and forth over both shoulders, obviously to ensure they wouldn't be overheard. "Can you keep a secret?"

"Upon my honor," Sarah replied, crossing her fingers over her heart.

"Absolutely," Meg agreed.

"Well," Alex began, "Lucy and Cass decided that Owen wasn't coming up to scratch sufficiently. He kept trying to court Lavinia because his father threatened to cut off his allowance and disown him if he didn't. It was maddening because he and Lavinia obviously didn't care for each other a bit. But his father insisted and my parents insisted and, well, suffice it to say it was all a mess for quite some time."

"What did Lucy do?" Sarah asked.

Alex gave them a catlike smile and leaned even closer. "Lucy asked Lord Berkeley to pretend to be interested in me to give Owen some healthy competition."

Sarah widened her eyes. "And he agreed?"

"Yes, he's such a dear. A true friend." Alex nodded. She glanced across the ballroom to where Sarah was already only too aware of the fact that Christian was dancing with Lady Claire. "Which is why I'm so pleased to see how well he's doing this Season himself."

Sarah nodded solemnly. "He's quite popular, isn't he?"

Meg elbowed her.

Alex nodded again. "This Season they're saying he's a legend."

"Are they?" An inexplicable pain shot through Sarah's chest.

"Yes, and I couldn't be happier for him. I helped to fuel the rumors myself." She looked positively pleased with herself. "It's high time ladies took notice of him. He will be the most devoted husband in the world, I've no doubt. He deserves nothing more than to find the right young lady and settle down."

Meg began to speak. "He seems quite nice and—"

Sarah couldn't help herself. That ugly fiend jealousy reared its scaly little green head. "Do you think Lady Claire is the right young lady?" she blurted to Alex.

A troubled look came over Alex's face briefly. "I'm not at all sure. We must each of us decide who is right on our own, and I daresay Lord Berkeley will know when he finds his true love. But I certainly wish him well. Lady Claire seems a nice enough girl. Do you know her well?"

Sarah shook her head slowly back and forth. "No. But she does seem nice. *Quite* nice." Why had uttering those last words caused her such pain, as if she were chewing upon shards of glass?

"Can you believe," Alex continued, "that at one point my maid tried to tell me to cheer up? She thought I was sad because Lord Branford hadn't offered for me because you were so much more popular than I."

Sarah swallowed the lump in her throat. "Truly?"

"Yes. Of course, she didn't realize I was already madly in love with Owen or she wouldn't have said such a nonsensical thing." Alex patted her coiffure and lifted her champagne glass in silent salute. "At any rate, it's all worked out the way it was meant to, hasn't it? I'm happily engaged to Owen and you're happily engaged to Lord Branford." She beamed.

Meg pressed her lips together and gave Sarah a don't-say-a-word look.

Sarah couldn't return Alex's smile. "I assume your parents decided that Lavinia didn't have to marry first?"

Alex's smile turned conspiratorial. "The truth is, they didn't have much of a choice because it was so obvious that Owen and Lavinia would never suit. She did some awful things that I won't bore you with. Just think . . . someone's parents trying to force him into a match that would make him so obviously unhappy? I cannot imagine what Owen's parents were thinking."

"I hear that happens quite a lot." Tears stung the backs of Sarah's eyes. She clapped her hand over her mouth, suddenly certain she was going to cast up her accounts. She turned on her heel and fled out the nearby patio doors.

CHAPTER THIRTY-TWO

Christian saw Sarah run outside. Without a second thought, he ended his dance with Lady Claire, deposited her next to her mother on the sidelines, and hurriedly made his way toward Alex.

"I'm not certain what happened," Alex said, staring after the space Sarah had just occupied. "One moment we were happily chatting and the next—"

"I'll go see to her," Meg offered, turning toward the doors and lifting her skirts.

"No. I will." Christian didn't wait for agreement. He took long strides toward the patio doors before Alex or Meg had a chance to say another word.

When he got outside, he scanned the area. Sarah was standing near the far end of the empty veranda, her hands braced against the stone balustrade, her head leaned over the edge, breathing heavily. He made his way quickly but carefully over to her.

"Sarah, are you all right?"

At the sound of his voice, she turned and dropped her arms to her sides, her back against the balustrade. She had a wild look in her eyes and she was sucking in great gulps of air, her shoulders quaking.

"Sarah, tell me, are you all right?" Christian asked, moving even closer.

They were alone on the veranda for the moment, but he didn't dare touch her in case someone else came out.

Sarah placed a hand on her heaving chest. "I . . . I couldn't breathe. I had to get out of there."

Now that she was talking, Christian relaxed a bit. "I understand."

"It was the strangest feeling. As if the ballroom weren't big enough for me."

"The same thing has happened to me before, on more than one occasion."

She was calming down, her breathing becoming more shallow, her eyes returning to normal. "It has?" she asked, an incredulous note in her voice.

"Yes. Try breathing through your nose. Bend over as far as possible. You want your head near your knees if you can."

With her stays firmly in place, Sarah wasn't able to bend over that far, but breathing through her nose seemed to work and she was able to brace her hands on her knees. Moments later, her breathing was completely back to normal.

"Thank you," she murmured. "I feel much better now, and quite silly."

"You're not silly at all," he replied.

She placed a hand back on the balustrade. "I'm sorry to have caused such a fuss. I'm perfectly fine now."

He offered his arm. "Would you like me to escort you back inside? To your mother, perhaps?"

"No!"

He arched a brow.

"I'm sorry," she said more calmly. "I said that far more

forcefully than I meant to." She smoothed her coiffure with her hands. "What I meant to say is, I'd like to stay out here, in the air a bit longer, if I may."

Christian nodded. "I'll leave you, then."

"No." She said the word much more softly this time.

Their eyes met. They stood together, a few paces apart, in silence for a few moments. Christian remembered their time together in Scotland and the ease and comfort he'd always felt in her presence. They didn't have to speak to each other. Sarah was one of the few people he knew who didn't require talking, endless, constant talking.

A few more minutes passed and then Christian strode over to the balustrade and braced his forearms against it. "Why didn't Lord Branford take you with him to the prince's dinner party tonight?" He mentally cursed himself for bringing up that peacock Branford, but apparently he couldn't help himself.

Sarah sighed. "I don't know. I suppose it's because we aren't married yet."

"Missing him tonight, are you?" Damn again. Why did he say *that*?

Sarah turned on him, her eyes flashing. "You know I'm not."

"Yet you remain engaged to him." For the love of God. He *really* couldn't stop himself. Why was he being such an ass?

Her jaw was tight. "You know I have no choice."

Christian bowed his head toward his arms, which remained braced against the balustrade. The scent of lilies carried on the slight breeze. "You know what I want to know, Sarah?"

"What?" she whispered.

"Where is the girl who ran away?"

Sarah pushed away from the balustrade and Christian

turned to watch her. She pressed two fingers to her temple as if willing away a headache. "She got wise."

He pressed his back against the balustrade this time. "Is it wise to throw away your entire life on someone you don't love?" Christian didn't even know who he was any longer, asking these sorts of questions. And yet he *still* couldn't seem to stop himself.

She flung a hand in the air. "People do it all the time. You know that as well as I. Are you saying you love Lady Claire, for instance?"

His jaw was tight. "I haven't offered for Lady Claire."

"So you loved Lucy Hunt, then?"

"I didn't offer for her either," he shot back.

"But you wanted to."

Christian turned toward the balustrade again and cursed under his breath. "Are you going to marry him, Sarah? Truly? Is that what you want?"

She spoke slowly, deliberately, resignedly. Her voice floated behind him. "It's not what I want, but yes, I'm going to marry him."

That was it. His control snapped. Christian swiveled around, took two steps toward her, and pulled her roughly into his arms. His mouth came down quickly to savage hers. His tongue pressed inside and she melted against him. Her arms twined around his neck and he softened the kiss. Anyone could walk out and see them. She would be ruined. The scandal might be unparalleled, but at the moment Christian didn't bloody well care. He kissed her with all the pent-up longing and passion he felt for her. And she kissed him back.

Moments later he released her and she staggered back, pressing a gloved hand against her swollen lips. "Christian, I—"

"Tell me you're going to marry him. Tell me you feel

absolutely nothing for me. Tell me we're merely *friends*. Tell me, Sarah, tell me right now."

She drew a weak, shaky breath. "Don't do this, Christian."

"Tell me," he demanded, his voice shaking with anger.

She drew another breath, a deeper one this time, and her voice, when it came, was clear and determined. "I'm going to marry him. I'm sorry." She picked up her skirts and rushed across the veranda, through the double doors, and back into the ballroom. Christian watched her go, clenching his fist against his side, wanting to punch a hole through the bloody stone wall of the house.

Moments later, Lucy Hunt's face appeared through the French doors. She'd obviously seen Sarah flee. She looked at Christian and shook her head.

CHAPTER THIRTY-THREE

The Duchess of Claringdon's fine coach pulled to a stop outside of Sarah's father's home the next afternoon. The duchess herself, wearing a soft green pelisse and matching bonnet, emerged from the conveyance and made her way onto the street and up the front steps. Miss Meg Timmons accompanied her. Ten minutes later, the two ladies were sitting in the yellow drawing room having tea with Sarah.

Sarah had come to treasure her friendship with Lucy. Not only had the duchess been instrumental in saving Sarah's reputation, Lucy had a knack for listening and providing sound, if sometimes outrageous, advice. She had also proven kind to Meg. But the thing Sarah liked best about Lucy was that she was not judgmental. Sarah could say anything to Lucy and Lucy would understand. She didn't judge Sarah and she didn't judge Meg for being poor and having only two nice, if aged, gowns. As a result, Sarah had confided in Lucy on more than one occasion. But today, for some reason, Sarah dreaded the duchess's questions. Sarah had a sinking feeling she knew why Lucy had come.

"I brought Meg with me because I sense she, too, has a vested interest in this situation. And one can never have too many friends helping her."

Meg merely nodded and took a sip of tea.

"Situation?" Sarah echoed, nervous.

"How are you getting on, Sarah?" Lucy asked as she plucked off her gloves.

Sarah pushed a dark curl behind her ear. "Fine. I'm perfectly fine."

"She's not fine," Meg announced.

Lucy arched a brow over her blue eye. "I can tell. No one who is fine uses the word *fine*. *Fine* is a decidedly tepid description of oneself. Therefore, allow me to ask you in another manner," she said to Sarah. "Have you set a wedding date yet?"

Sarah sighed loud and long. Then she dropped her head into her hands. "Oh, Lucy, not you too. I have enough trouble sidestepping Mother and Lord Branford when they ask."

Lucy let her gloves drop to her lap. "Ah, that answer tells me everything I need to know."

Sarah lifted her head and shook it. "What? How?"

"You're putting it off," Lucy declared.

Sarah glanced down at her slippers and stared unseeing at the pattern on the rug beneath them. "There's much to be considered."

"She's putting it off," Meg agreed.

Lucy tsked Sarah and flourished an elegant hand in the air. "Your mother will take care of the considerations. You've a household of servants at your disposal as well. You are indeed putting it off."

"I am not. I—"

Lucy leaned over and put a hand on Sarah's, forcing Sarah to look at her.

"I saw you and Berkeley last night," Lucy said softly.

A flash of fear shot through Sarah's chest. Had the duchess seen them kiss? "And?"

"And obviously something was wrong. I saw you run into the house. You looked quite upset. When I went to see whom you'd been speaking to, Berkeley was standing there."

Sarah couldn't very well ask if she'd seen anything else. "Did anyone else notice?"

"Not that I could tell. Except perhaps Meg and Alex."

Sarah breathed a sigh of relief. "Thank heavens."

"I knew," Meg announced. "But I did what I could to keep the other guests away from the patio. I *may* have started a rumor that there was a swarm of bees out there."

"Meg, you did not!" Sarah put her hands to her hips.

"Ingenious, Miss Timmons." Lucy touched a hand to her coiffure. Then she settled her hands back in her lap and addressed Sarah. "I'm going to tell you something you may not want to hear. I suggest you prepare yourself."

Sarah groaned. "Oh, Lucy, no, please."

Meg sat sipping her tea, obviously hanging on Lucy's every word as if she were an opera singer and Meg in the audience at a command performance.

"You two are obviously perfect for each other," Lucy said to Sarah with a determined nod.

"Who?" Sarah said, pushing her slipper against the rug, not meeting Lucy's eyes.

"Don't play dumb with me, miss. I know how truly intelligent you are. You and Berkeley, of course."

"You're right," Sarah murmured. "I didn't want to hear that."

Lucy squeezed her gloves in her hand. "I'm sorry, but someone had to say it out loud. It is the burden and the curse of the blunt person to always have to be the one to vocalize such things."

Meg nodded.

"How do you know we're so right for each other?" Sarah continued.

Lucy smoothed a brow with a fingertip. "Because Berkeley told me, of course."

Sarah gulped. "He said that?"

"No. He said you both laugh at the same things, you both are plagued with attacks of the nerves, and you both share a sense of humor, among other things."

"Yes, but—," Sarah began.

"Need I mention the horse's name?"

"Oh . . . that." Sarah bit her lip.

"Yes, that."

"Oberon," Meg whispered, nodding. "*Such* an obvious sign."

Lucy sighed. "What I don't understand is why you two are being so pigheaded about declaring your intentions for each other."

Sarah lifted her chin and faced her friend. "Lucy, I appreciate everything you've done for me, truly I have, but—"

Lucy waved a dismissive hand in the air. "But you couldn't possibly disappoint your parents and break off your engagement, et cetera, et cetera. I've heard such patronizing tones before, too."

"But that's precisely right." Sarah folded her hands in her lap and blinked at the duchess. "I cannot possibly disappoint my parents and—"

"I told you she was going to say this, Lucy," Meg interjected, still sipping tea.

Lucy straightened her shoulders and forced Sarah to meet her eyes. "Meg says that Alex told you the story of how Owen was supposed to be engaged to her sister."

Sarah nodded hesitantly. Lucy obviously had decided

to try a different tactic altogether. Just what was her friend getting at? "Yes, Alex told me that last night."

"If *that* debacle could be called off, I daresay your parents can stand you crying off from the Marquess of Branford."

Sarah pushed her shoe against the pattern of the rug again. "You don't understand. The marquess is friendly with the Prince Regent, of all people, not to mention the *princesses,* even the queen. Father and Mother would never stand the blow to their reputation were they to insult the marquess in such a public way."

Lucy was studying her fingernails now. "Something tells me Lord Branford's self-regard could well withstand such a blow."

"I've absolutely no doubt whatsoever," Meg added.

Sarah rubbed her temples. "*He* might withstand it, but Mother and Father would never forgive me." How could her friends not understand the horrible predicament she was in?

"But they're forcing you into an unhappy marriage," Lucy said.

"Unhappy marriages happen every day," Sarah replied.

Lucy slapped her gloves against her thigh. "My goodness, your parents have conditioned you well. You're quite obedient. But obedience doesn't always equate to happiness, and that is what I care about at the moment. Your happiness and Berkeley's. Can't you see how perfect you are together? You actually *care* for each other. I can tell. I can see it in your eyes. And his. For example, I've never seen him rush off from a dance before to follow a lady out onto a patio. He's clearly smitten with you. And if I don't mistake my guess, you are equally smitten with him."

"She's smitten," Meg said.

Sarah gave Meg a condemning glare. "He's a dear *friend*." But even as she said it, the words he'd spoken to her last night on the veranda punctured her heart. *Tell me you feel absolutely nothing for me. Tell me we're merely friends.*

"Stop it." Lucy slapped her glove against her knee this time. "I know he's more than a friend."

"He is," Meg agreed.

Sarah's voice was measured, as calm as she could make it. Ignoring Meg, she merely said, "I don't want this to come between you and me, Your Grace."

"Ah, enough of that 'Your Grace' business. I consider you a friend, Sarah, and I've no wish to upset you. I'm simply trying to get you to see reason. I don't think you fully understand how miserable you will be married to a man you don't love."

"Thank you for your concern, Lucy, but I—"

Lucy held up a hand. "You're one of the most stubborn chits I know. Did anyone else ever tell you that?"

"She's stubborn all right," Meg agreed, pushing a blond curl away from her forehead.

"Yes, both Meg and Mrs. Goatsocks like to inform me of that on a regular basis," Sarah replied with a long-suffering sigh.

"Meg and Mrs. Goatsocks are correct." Lucy stood and began to pull on her gloves again. "Very well, Sarah, you've left me little choice. We must fight this battle on another front entirely."

Meg stood to leave, too.

Sarah watched them go, more than a bit afraid of what exactly Lucy Hunt had meant by that last statement.

CHAPTER THIRTY-FOUR

Lucy Hunt marched unannounced into Christian's breakfast room the next morning, drawing off her expensive kid gloves, a decided frown on her face. "You're not going to let Sarah marry that ninny Branford, are you?"

Christian nearly choked on the piece of melon he'd been eating. "Good morning to you, too."

"This is serious, Christian. She's perfectly miserable."

I'm perfectly miserable, too. "I'm not certain how you'd expect me to have any say in the matter."

"Ask her to marry you."

This time, Christian nearly spit out his coffee. He set down his cup to be safe. Lucy had no idea what she was asking of him. Especially not after what had happened on the veranda with Sarah at the Rutherfords'. But he suspected his friend hadn't seen the kissing part. Which proved there was a God as far as Christian was concerned. Still, Lucy could be adamant when she made up her mind about something. He must handle her carefully this morning, nonchalance being the order of the day.

He pretended to study his newspaper. "The last time I

checked, the lady was engaged to another man. I may not have the most exquisite manners in the kingdom, but I know proposing to a betrothed woman is frowned upon."

Lucy brandished her gloves in the air. "Oh, Christian, you're being so thickheaded. She's obviously miserable with him and perfect for you."

He let the paper drop and gave her his best impression of a bored look. "What do you suggest, Lucy? That I pick her up, toss her over my shoulder, and cart her off to Scotland to elope?"

Lucy's eyes widened. She stepped toward him. "Why, that's an excellent idea!"

Christian rolled his eyes and turned back to the paper. "You cannot be serious. I was jesting."

"Perhaps if we *tell* her we plan to cart her off . . . you know, so as not to unduly frighten her." Lucy tapped a finger against her cheek, obviously contemplating the matter.

Christian refused to look up. "No, Lucy, no more schemes. She's made up her mind."

Lucy moved forward and braced both hands against the back of one of the chairs that sat around the table, forcing Christian's gaze to return to her. "She doesn't understand the consequences. She's young and her parents are unreasonable."

Christian pressed a palm against his right eye. "And not likely to look with favor upon a son-in-law who absconds with their daughter."

"She's been putting off the wedding," Lucy said in a singsong voice.

Christian stiffened. He couldn't help himself. "Did she tell you that? That she's putting it off on purpose?"

"She told me some nonsense about how there are things to consider, whatever that means. But she hasn't set a date despite her mother's insistence as well as Lord Branford's.

What does that tell you?" Lucy stamped her foot on the wooden floor.

"It tells me it's none of my blasted business." Christian wasn't about to tell Lucy how he knew that Sarah wasn't interested in him or at least that she had no intention of calling off the wedding in favor of him. His meddling friend would just have to take his word for it this time.

"But I saw the way she looked at you the other night, Christian," Lucy pleaded. "She's already more than half in love with you."

Christian stood and tossed both the paper and his napkin onto the table. "Lucy, I've always appreciated your penchant for matchmaking, but heretofore it's been done between two parties who were not already attached. This time you go too far. You must stand down."

Lucy plunked her hands on her hips. "Tell me you aren't half in love with her, Christian. If you can honestly tell me that, I'll stand down."

Christian slammed his palm on the table. "It's too late, Lucy. Even *you* can't fix this."

"But—"

Christian clenched his jaw. "Lucy, I'm warning you. Stay the hell out of it." He turned on his heel and strode away, leaving Lucy Hunt standing alone in his breakfast room.

CHAPTER THIRTY-FIVE

Later that afternoon, Cass and Jane arrived at Lucy's doorstep for their weekly visit. The tea had been served and Jane was halfway through her second tea cake when Lucy, heaping lumps of sugar into her cup, announced, "Ladies, we must do something to help Berkeley and Sarah."

Cass glanced up from her own cup, her pretty forehead marred by a frown. "What? Why?"

Lucy stirred in the sugar. "Because they need our help, of course. Berkeley desperately needs it. I can tell."

Jane politely swallowed her bit of cake before speaking. "What in heaven's name makes you think that?"

Lucy turned toward her friend. "Because he swore at me, Jane. He told me to stay the *hell* out of it. If those aren't the words of someone crying out for help, I don't know what are."

Jane shook her head. "I can't imagine what it's like living inside your head, Lucy."

Lucy flourished her spoon in the air. "I don't know

what you mean, Janie. Everything in my head makes perfect sense to me."

"I agree with Lucy," Cass offered. "I've never seen Lord Berkeley so agitated. He ended his dance with Lady Claire immediately to rush after Lady Sarah when she left the ballroom. I think he cares for her a great deal."

"But isn't she engaged to Lord Branford?" Jane asked, helping herself to another tea cake.

"Yes," Lucy said, tasting her tea for the proper excessive amount of sugar.

"And?" Jane prompted.

"And that's obviously one reason they need our help. She's in quite a pickle," Lucy replied, dropping in one final lump.

"Did she *ask* for your help?" Jane prodded.

"No," Lucy confessed, stirring the last lump into the cup. Her spoon made little dinging noises against the china.

"Did she *hint* that she wanted your help?" Jane continued.

"No," Lucy repeated, then lifted her cup and took a satisfied sip.

"Has Lord Berkeley done *either* of those things?" Jane prodded.

"Not in so many words." Lucy flourished the spoon again.

Jane rubbed the spot between her eyes with two fingers. "Then why in heaven's name would you think either of them wants your help?"

"I didn't say they *want* our help," Lucy replied. "I said they *need* our help. Quite different. I'm certain you'll agree."

Cass sipped her tea. "Let's hear her out, Janie. What are you planning, Lucy?"

Lucy set the spoon on her saucer. "Nothing too drastic. Don't worry."

Cass let out a relieved breath and set down her teacup to stir in more cream.

"We simply must do something to stop the wedding, that's all," Lucy continued in a calm voice.

Cass's eyes widened in alarm and her silver spoon clanked inside of the cup, abandoned.

A tea cake arrested halfway to her mouth, Jane Upton groaned. "How are we supposed to do *that*?"

"We must do *something*," Cass replied, obviously recovering herself. She continued to stir her tea. "Lord Berkeley has helped so many of us. Now it's our turn to help him."

"Finally, someone else is seeing reason," Lucy said, eyeing both her friends over the rim of her teacup, a catlike grin pinned upon her gamine face.

"What do you suggest we do, Lucy?" Cass asked. "How can we stop the wedding?"

"As usual, I want no part of this," Jane announced, taking yet another bite of cake.

"We must procure an invitation," Lucy said. "I'll need your help for that, Cass."

Cass blinked. "An invitation to what?"

"Why, an invitation for Lady Sarah to attend Daphne's wedding, of course."

CHAPTER THIRTY-SIX
*Surrey, the country house of
the Earl and Countess of Moreland*

Christian had been at Daphne Swift's wedding house party for a full five hours before he became aware that he was under surveillance.

He'd been happy, damn glad, to get out of London for a few days, away from Lady Claire, who was *quite* grating on his nerves, and away from the hordes of young ladies who seemed intent upon stopping him to talk in the park, and on Bond Street, and at any other bloody place he went. Had he really ever wished to be sought after? Why? It was a bloody nuisance. But most of all, he was glad to be out of London so that he wouldn't be tempted to pay a call on Sarah.

Damn Lucy and her mad schemes. She'd actually tried to convince him that if he declared himself to Sarah, something might come of it, change, be different. But that was madness. A signed marriage contract didn't suddenly disappear, and even if Sarah herself decided to cry off, it would cause a huge scandal, which was exactly what they'd worked so diligently to avoid last winter. No. Absolutely no good could come from entertaining Lucy

Hunt's outlandish idea. Besides, Christian knew for a fact that it wouldn't work. He'd bloody well kissed Sarah, after all, kissed her right there on the veranda at the Rutherfords' ball. If that hadn't been a declaration, what was? Sarah had turned right around and declared her intention to marry Branford no matter what. It was over. Done. There was nothing more to say.

But those few moments haunted him. Those few moments when she was in his arms, tasting like sunlight, her arms wrapped tightly around his neck, her mouth open and wanting and willing. In those few moments he'd known, he'd felt it. She wanted him. And he would never be able to forget.

He shook his head to rid it of such unhelpful thoughts. He'd come to the country to see his friends marry, but he'd also come to clear his head. Relax. Reconsider things. Get a different perspective on the whole marriage mart. The problem was that now that he was traipsing about in a country garden in the middle of the day, fresh air abounding, his head seemed less clear than ever.

First, there was Lady Claire to consider. He'd spent a good portion of the ride to Surrey considering that perhaps the girl wasn't as annoying as he recalled. Perhaps her silliness would lessen as she aged. Perhaps she'd eventually stop using the word *quite* with such alarming frequency. He'd finally decided it was no use. She wasn't his sort, no matter how interested in him she seemed to be. How was that for irony? A year ago he would have given his right arm to have a young woman as lovely and sweet as Lady Claire seemed to be hanging upon his every word. Now he just found her cloying. What the hell was wrong with him?

He scrubbed his hands through his hair. It didn't matter. Lady Claire wasn't the only other female in Society besides Sarah. He'd simply reevaluate the current crop upon his return to town. Simple enough. For now he was intent upon thinking about nothing other than relaxation.

"Berkeley, good, man, there you are," his friend Garrett Upton called as he jogged out to where Christian was strolling through the garden.

"Upton, good to see you." Christian clasped Upton's hand as soon as the other man reached him.

"Seems Daphne and Rafe are finally getting married," Upton said in his usual jovial voice.

"Seems to be the case by the looks of it," Christian replied.

Upton didn't meet his eyes. "How are *your* marital prospects these days?"

That was when Christian knew. He was being watched. Lucy Hunt's web of spies extended throughout the town and into the country and was now apparent in the personage of his closest friend. In fact, Upton was the reason he'd met Lucy to begin with in Bath nearly two years ago, not long after Waterloo. He and Upton had attended school together, had known each other since they were boys. Upton had never, in all their years of friendship, asked him about his *marital prospects*.

Christian crossed his arms over his chest and eyed his friend warily. "Lucy sent you, didn't she?"

Upton's crack of laughter rang through the garden. "Don't look so alarmed. She's worried about you. You know, I met Lady Sarah when she stayed with Jane and me briefly in Bath, and she's quite a nice young woman. You—"

Christian's mind filled with a hazy cloud of rage. "By God, Upton, I'm warning you—" But Christian broke off as he looked up to see Lady Sarah herself, along with her mother, following Cass's mother, Lady Moreland, down a footpath in the garden. They were walking not twenty paces ahead down a lane at right angles to theirs, obviously receiving a tour of the grounds.

"What in the—?" Christian's jaw fell open. All he could do was stare.

Upton glanced at him and then at Sarah and back. "Speak of the devil. Didn't expect to see Lady Sarah here of all places. You all right, Berkeley?"

"No. I mean, yes. It's . . . it's fine. It's nothing. What were you saying?" He tried to drag his attention back to his friend. But Christian didn't hear a word Upton said. All he could think about was Sarah. He imagined he could smell the scent of lilies on the breeze. What was she doing here? Did she know Daphne or Rafe? Well enough to attend their wedding? She hadn't mentioned she was coming. Had she seen him?

That question, at least, was quickly answered when Sarah glanced at him and immediately averted her eyes. Moments later she was gone, following Lady Moreland and her mother back into the house.

Christian had to go. He had to find out what she was doing here. "Excuse me a moment, won't you, Upton?"

"Going to greet Lady Sarah?" Upton asked with a wide grin.

"No," Christian ground out, already striding back toward the house. "I'm going to hunt down your cousin Lucy."

Hunting down Lucy Hunt was much easier said than done. Christian spent the better part of the afternoon attempting to locate the elusive duchess. By teatime he was convinced she was avoiding him. Every time he found someone he was certain would know where she was, that person managed to have a convenient and suspicious lapse of memory.

"I believe I saw her in the conservatory," Cass offered.

"I only know she's not in the library," Jane announced.

"I could have sworn she told me she was going riding," her husband, Claringdon, informed him.

A half hour before dinner, Christian finally spotted her, coming around a corner in one of the downstairs corridors. "Lucy," he called. She quickly turned to retreat in the opposite direction.

"Oh, no, you don't." He set off after her, nearly running down the marble hallway and skidding to a halt once he'd reached the corner.

Lucy had made it halfway down the other side and was busily looking about, obviously for someplace to hide.

"Stop!"

She whirled around and gave him an innocent look, as if she hadn't been trying to elude him at all.

"Berkeley, there you are," she said prettily, pushing a dark curl behind her ear.

He arched a brow. "Don't pretend you haven't been hiding from me."

They walked toward each other and met in the middle of the corridor.

"I don't know what you mean." Lucy pushed the same errant curl back into her coiffure. She didn't meet his eyes.

"Yes, you do." He gave her a look dripping with skepticism.

More blinking innocence. "Did you have something to *say* to me, Berkeley?"

"Yes, I have something to say to you. Why is Lady Sarah here?"

Lucy had perfected her innocent face; he'd give her that. "What? Lady Sarah is here? Why, I didn't—"

"Don't pretend," he drawled. "You know as well as I do that she's here, and I want to know *why*."

Lucy sighed. "Why does it matter why she's here?"

He crossed his arms over his chest. "Did you or did you not have a hand in inviting her here?"

Lucy crossed her arms over her chest, too. "The question is . . . now that she's here, what are you going to do about it?"

Christian's arms dropped to his sides. "What the hell does that mean?"

"Speak with her. Alone. Admit you have feelings for her. I can't believe it won't matter to her."

"Damn it, Lucy, I all but—"

Lucy whirled on him, her green skirts twirling about her ankles. "All but what? Have you admitted you care for her?"

"No." He cursed under his breath.

Lucy shrugged one shoulder. "Can you stay away from her, then, Berkeley?"

"Yes," Christian ground out through clenched teeth.

Maddeningly, Lucy studied her fingernails nonchalantly. "Very well, Viscount. Prove it."

CHAPTER THIRTY-SEVEN

Dinner had been served and consumed with gusto. Afterward, all of the guests had retreated to the drawing rooms and study to drink and play games. The sky was dark and the air cool when Christian went for another walk in the gardens. Thankfully, he was alone this time. But he was cursing himself unmercifully. It had taken him less than four hours. Less than four pathetic hours to admit that Lucy, that infernal meddler, had won. She was right. He couldn't stay away from Sarah. He hadn't seen her at dinner, but he had to speak to her. Alone.

A torchlight came bobbing toward him, and he soon recognized the form of Lord Owen Monroe heading his way. "Berkeley, there you are. I've been scouring the house for you."

"If Lucy sent you, I don't want—"

"Lucy? Why would Lucy send me?"

Christian's eyes narrowed on Monroe. "Why did you come?"

"My, you're suspicious tonight. I thought we patched things up between us back in Bath. Not to mention the shopping. Why, I've showed you how to tie a mathematical knot better than my valet. Doesn't that deserve some loyalty?"

Christian expelled his breath. He scrubbed a hand against the back of his neck. "We did patch things up. My apologies, Monroe. I'm just a bit . . . on edge this evening."

"Perfect, because it sounds as if you could use a drink, and that's precisely why I came looking for you. I want to talk to you if you have a moment. Care for a drink?"

"No." Christian usually wasn't so blunt, but tonight all he wanted to do was find Sarah and—

"Yes, you do. Come on. We'll go to the library. It's nearly empty. We can toss Jane Upton out."

Berkeley shook his head at Monroe's audacity. Something told him he wasn't going to win an argument with the man tonight. Besides, Christian couldn't exactly hunt down Lady Sarah and charge into her bedchamber. No matter how much he'd like to. "Very well. Lead the way."

Less than a quarter hour later, Christian was sitting in the otherwise empty library with a glass of port in his hand, watching as Monroe lit a cheroot.

"Father's got some of the best wine in the country," Owen said, leaning back against the large leather chair in which he sat. He slung a long leg over the arm of the chair. Monroe was anything but proper.

"It was good of your parents to agree to have the wedding here," Christian said.

Monroe sucked on the end of the cheroot. "It was all Cass's doing. She adores Daphne. Nearly as much as she adores Daphne's brother, her husband." He chuckled.

"Cass is one of the kindest people I ever met," Christian replied. He spent a few silent moments contemplating the wine in his glass before he finally said, "Forgive my bluntness, but what did you want to speak with me about?"

Monroe took a long pull from his cheroot and blew the smoke into the air, making perfect rings. He remained splayed in a haphazard fashion across the chair. "I apologized for punching you when we were in Bath last autumn, Berkeley, but I wanted to tell you something else."

Christian nodded. "Which is?"

"That I owe you a great deal."

The hint of a smile touched Christian's lips. "You owe me nothing."

"On the contrary, I owe you everything—my happiness, at least. If you hadn't been willing to pretend you were interested in Alex to make me jealous, I might never have come to my senses and declared myself. I was a damned fool."

Christian took a long sip of port. Monroe was right. His father did have some damn fine wine. "As I said, you owe me nothing. It was all Lucy's idea."

Monroe's bark of laughter echoed off the wooden bookshelves in the room. "I don't doubt it, but you could have told her no."

Christian snorted. "Do you know how difficult it is to say no to Lucy?"

Another laugh from Monroe. "Actually, I do."

Christian's eyes narrowed on the other man. "Don't tell me, you lied to me. You're up to her bidding tonight after all, aren't you?"

"No. No. I'm not up to Lucy's bidding. However, I *may* have had a talk with Cass earlier."

Christian groaned. "Cass? Fine. You might as well come clean. What errand did Cass send you on?"

Monroe blew another set of smoke rings into the air. "No errand other than to remind you that you've helped many of us find love, and it's high time you accepted some help yourself."

Christian bowed his head. He was slowly being defeated by his own friends. It seemed the lot of them were conspiring against him. He expelled his breath. Very well. So be it. "How do you propose to help me?"

"Cass tells me that you want to speak with Sarah alone."

"I never said—"

Monroe arched a brow at him. "Do you want to speak to her alone or don't you?"

Christian rubbed his palm against his eye. "Bloody hell. Fine. Yes."

Monroe grinned at him. "Excellent. Tomorrow afternoon, two o'clock, there's a gamekeeper's cottage on the far northern edge of the property."

"How in the name of God—"

"Ah, ah, ah. Don't question my methods." He blew another set of smoke rings into the air. "Alex is helping with this, too. She's pleased as punch to have the opportunity to be of assistance to you after what you've done for our relationship. Leave everything to us."

"But—"

Monroe took a long sip of port. "The gamekeeper's cottage. Two o'clock."

CHAPTER THIRTY-EIGHT

Sarah had absolutely no idea why Alexandra Hobbs was so insistent on showing her the far reaches of the Monroe estate. She supposed the woman was overly fond of the place since she would be the lady here one day. It was a lovely property. But by the time she and Lord Owen and Lady Alex had hiked all the way out to the far northern border, Sarah was beginning to wonder why she'd agreed to this "little walk" in the first place.

Her inability to sleep had returned with vigor last night after seeing Christian in the gardens yesterday afternoon. She'd managed to convince her mother that she had a headache and was served dinner in bed last night, thereby avoiding the dining room and any conversations fraught with anxiety. But she would have to face him sooner or later. She was certain of it. And she'd known it. She'd known all along when she'd come to Surrey that she would see him. He'd mentioned the wedding to her last winter in Scotland. Daphne Swift and Rafe Cavendish were two of Christian's closest friends. She was the interloper here. She'd only come because her mother had insisted.

Apparently, the wedding of a daughter and sister of an earl to a newly minted war-hero viscount was a social boon as far as her mother was concerned.

Sarah had spent the entire ride here going over their next meeting in her mind. What would she say to him? What *could* she say to him? The last time they'd seen each other, she had been passionately kissing the man, then she'd run from him. Like a ninny. There weren't many things one *could* say after such an episode. Last night she'd been unable to come up with a single coherent thing to say to him. She'd agreed to go on this outing with Alex and Owen partly because she was a coward. If she left the house for a while, she'd have even less chance of running into Christian. But the outing had turned into a far greater adventure than she'd expected, and her feet ached.

"I really should be getting back," she called to her companions, slowing her pace. "Mother wants me to have one more fitting for the gown I'm wearing for the wedding tomorrow morning and—"

"Ah, look, there. The gamekeeper's cottage." Alex pointed to a small whitewashed house resting on a low rise ahead of them. "Isn't it quaint?"

"Very much so," Sarah replied, barely glancing at the small structure. "But I should—"

"Let's get a closer look." Lord Owen set off at a brisk pace across the wide expanse of grass toward the cottage. Alex quickly picked up her skirts and followed.

Sarah glanced back toward the main house. She couldn't very well traipse all the way back there alone. Her mother would wonder why she'd left her companions. No. She'd have to convince her friends that she needed to return.

"Wait for me," she called, reluctantly picking up her skirts and following them.

By the time the three of them made it to the front door

of the cottage, Sarah was out of breath and had a pebble in her slipper. Lord Owen was peering in a window, and Alex was studying the bright red flowers that spilled from the window planters.

"Is the gamekeeper in there?" Sarah asked, bracing a hand against the cottage wall in order to pluck off her slipper and shake out the errant pebble.

"Father isn't employing a gamekeeper at the moment," Lord Owen replied, still peering in the window.

Her shoe free of the small stone, Sarah joined Alex near the planters. "A pity for such a pretty little house to be empty."

"Let's go inside," Alex said, motioning toward the door.

Sarah's gaze flew to her friend's. "Oh, but we really should—"

"Go on." Lord Owen nodded. "I expect the door is unlocked."

Sarah glanced at the little red door. She was standing closest to it. She hesitated for a moment but eventually decided that the sooner they looked about the place, the sooner her friends would be willing to return to the main house. She might as well get this over with.

She grabbed the door handle and turned it. Lord Owen was right. The door was unlocked. She pushed it open and stepped inside. The room was pleasant and swept clean. A small table and chairs, an unlit hearth, two wooden chairs near the fireplace, a large feather bed in the corner. It smelled faintly of dust and wood. But overall it looked quite pretty and tidy.

She was about to turn around to motion her friends inside when a movement from the corner of the room caught her eye. She looked again. A man was standing there. She gasped.

The man turned to face her. It was . . . Christian. He

stood there in buckskin breeches, with a white shirt and cravat, a sapphire waistcoat, and black Hessians. His hair was slicked back and he was clean-shaven, as he had been since his return to town. The look on his face was unreadable, but his crystal-blue eyes met hers and fire leaped between them. Sarah braced a hand on the door frame. He was so handsome. She instantly wanted to touch him.

She took another step inside the room. Her breath caught in her throat. "What are you doing here?"

He slid his hands into his pockets. "I wanted to see you."

She shook her head. "To see *me*? But we—" She glanced behind her. No Alex and Lord Owen. The door was still open, but they weren't there.

She stepped back outside and looked back and forth. Gone.

She reentered the cottage, completely confused. "Where did they—"

"They've probably continued their walk. They said they would give us some privacy."

"Some priv . . ." Sarah's mouth fell open. "You planned this? With Lady Alex and Lord Owen?"

"Yes." Christian stepped closer to her. "I hope you're not angry."

She pushed the door shut behind her, to give herself a moment to think. How did she feel, exactly? How was she supposed to feel? He'd lured her here? For what reason? "No. I'm not angry. I . . . I don't know what to think."

He rested an arm against the fireplace mantel. "I didn't know you were coming to this wedding until I saw you yesterday in the garden."

Sarah untied her bonnet and pulled it from her head. She felt conspicuous suddenly, wearing it inside the cottage. Christian's hat was sitting on the table. "We received a late invitation. Mother readily accepted because Lord Branford was invited. Apparently he knew the former earl, Lady Daphne's father."

Christian's back stiffened. "Branford's here? I didn't see him at dinner."

She quickly shook her head. "He's not coming until tomorrow for the wedding itself. Seems the prince needs him at another dinner party this evening."

Christian arched a brow. "That sounds like Branford. Always interested in the most prestigious invitation."

Sarah tugged at the ribbons of her bonnet. "You didn't bring me here to talk about Lord Branford, did you, Christian?"

He shook his head. "No. I'm hoping you'll listen. For just a moment."

She took another step toward him. They were only a few paces apart. She tossed her hat onto the table beside his. He held out his hand to her and then let it fall back to his side. "Never mind. This was idiotic. I'm sorry I even thought of it. I should—"

She looked up at him. "Tell me. What did you want to say?"

He stared down at his boots. "Something that I doubt will make any difference."

She took a deep breath. "Say it, Christian."

He turned to face her. His gaze met hers. "What if I offered for you, Sarah? Would you cry off from Branford? Would you defy your parents?"

Tears filled her eyes. She couldn't believe it. Couldn't believe she was hearing these words. That he was actually saying them. "Oh, Christian."

He fell to one knee and pulled her hand into his grasp. "Marry me, Sarah. I'll save you from him."

Tears slipped down her cheeks. "Christian, I—"

He stood again quickly, cupped her cheeks in his hands,

and searched her face. "You can't tell me you love him. I know you can't."

She shook her head. "It's true. I can't."

"You don't want to marry him. I know you don't. You ran away to Scotland to avoid the man. You can't possibly want him."

She shook her head more vigorously, biting her lip. "I don't. I know I don't."

"Then marry me, Sarah. You'll never have to see him again."

"I don't know what to do. I'm so confused."

"Let me convince you." He pulled her into his arms and kissed her. His tongue plunged into her mouth and Sarah melted against him. Every thought in her head was telling her to stop him, to pull away, to say no, but she couldn't. She *wanted* to kiss him, had wanted to from the moment she saw him standing there next to the fireplace.

"Christian," she whispered fiercely, standing on tiptoe and wrapping her arms around his neck.

His mouth didn't leave hers. He kissed her until her lips were swollen. Then his mouth traced the line of her cheek, her jaw, his tongue dipped into her ear, and she shivered against him.

He picked her up in his arms and carried her the few steps over to the bed.

"Christian, we can't—"

"Just let me touch you. Only touch."

She nodded, her mind hazy with lust. She wanted him to touch her, too. Wanted it so badly that it was all she could think about. He pulled off his cravat, and his shirt was soon gone. There was that muscled abdomen again. She sat up and he worked on the back of her gown. He pulled down her stays, freeing her breasts to his hungry mouth. She traced his muscled chest with her fingers while his lips found her nipple and he sucked one and then the other. She held his head to her chest, wanting it never to end. Then his hand moved under her skirts, up her leg, and she shivered again as his fingers made their way inexorably toward the juncture between her thighs. She wanted his touch there most of all. She spread her legs and his fingers toyed with her. Oh, God, this was wrong, but she didn't want it to stop. Ever.

One finger slid inside of her and she closed her eyes and moaned. "Christian. Oh, Christian . . ."

"You're so wet, Sarah. So hot. So perfect."

His finger moved and she tossed her head back and forth against the pillow. She'd never felt anything like it before. His mouth was back on her nipple and pangs of heat and desire shot through her from her breast to the intimate spot between her legs where his finger touched her, so softly, so gently. So right.

She arched her back to bring her breast into even closer contact with his mouth. Then his mouth moved back up to her lips and he kissed her again and again, finally dragging his mouth across her cheek, back to her ear, then down to her neck, where he sucked her roughly.

All the while his finger was still playing with her, moving in and out in a forbidden rhythm that made her hips arch and twist to meet his thrusts. "Christian, I don't—"

"Shh. I only want to watch you." Then his thumb rubbed her in tiny circles in a spot between her legs she barely knew existed. She cried out and he kissed her again, swallowing her cries in his mouth.

The pressure between her legs built and expanded and Sarah wrapped her arms around his neck and kissed him fiercely one last time before waves of pleasure streaked through her entire body and she called out his name.

Christian pressed his forehead to hers, hard. His breathing was heavy. He was panting and he looked to be in pain. She kissed his temple and whispered in his ear, "What can I do? For you? To—"

"Nothing."

Her hand had reached for his waist, for the buttons on his breeches, but he captured her fingers, brought them up to his mouth, and kissed them.

"You're so beautiful, Sarah. So lovely when you—"

A knock at the door interrupted them. Alex's pretty voice floated through. "Sarah, we're back. Are you all right? We should probably return to the house now."

Sarah abruptly pulled away from Christian, her breathing still heavy, her heart pounding in her ears.

"Yes, yes. I'll be right there," she called back.

"We'll just wait out here," Alex replied.

Christian rolled over on the bed, his arms splayed. "Damn it."

Sarah scrambled up and frantically righted her clothing. "I don't know what to say."

He stood, too, and faced her. "Say you'll leave him. Say you'll marry me."

She shook her head. Tears filled her eyes. "I want to. I do. I truly do, but—"

"But what? What else is there? Why would you stay with him when you don't love him?"

"Are you saying *you* love me?" She searched his face. If he only said yes. He had to say yes.

He pushed himself up on one elbow and savagely scrubbed a hand through his hair. "Sarah, I—I want to marry you. We are obviously attracted to each other. I know you care for me more than you care for him."

Tentacles of ice clutched her heart. He couldn't say it. He didn't love her. She bit the inside of her cheek so hard she tasted blood. Then she turned, grabbed her bonnet, and raced out the door.

CHAPTER THIRTY-NINE

That night, after she'd prepared for bed and dismissed her maid, Sarah stood and stared out the window of her guest bedchamber into the inky night sky. She wrapped her arms across her middle. It had been like touching a little piece of heaven kissing Christian today, feeling Christian touch her in the intimate way he had. She would never be able to forget it. Not a moment of it.

But there was only one problem. He hadn't been able to tell her that he loved her. There might be passion between them, that much was obvious, but with her he was just doing what he always did, attempting to rescue a damsel in distress.

I'll save you from him. Those had been his words. Not *I love you madly and cannot live without you.* How would a marriage based on being rescued be any better than one based on a heartless contract? No. Even if the threat of scandal weren't hanging over her head, she refused to allow Christian to martyr himself for her. He'd already done so much to help her. She could ask no more of him.

She traced a finger along the windowpane. When she

was a little girl, she'd dreamed about her wedding day. In her dreams, a wonderful man who loved her was by her side. But her childhood dreams had been shattered long ago. By the time she was barely thirteen, she'd been told in no uncertain terms that her parents had other plans for her. Plans they'd had from the day she was born. They'd dressed her up like a doll and trotted her out into Society and intended to hand her off to the most socially advantageous bridegroom. She'd known it would happen. She'd been prepared for it, or thought she was. That's how it worked in their world. Why, she had half a score of friends who'd married last year while barely knowing their husbands, let alone being in love with them. She had been told since she was a girl that she must do as she was told. That's all there was to it. Fine. Meg seemed intent upon remaining unattached while she pined for Hart. But that was different. Meg didn't have a dowry. She didn't have a string of suitors lined up. She could afford to at least pretend to follow her heart. Sarah didn't have that luxury. She *must* do as she was told. She could *not* shame her parents.

Blast Lucy Hunt and her friends for making Sarah think she should ever expect anything more. All of them appeared to be madly in love with their spouses. But that wasn't the usual way of things in the *ton*. Their marriages were special. Different. Not everyone had such good fortune.

Sarah might not love Lord Branford and she had no illusions that he loved her, but he was well connected, rich, powerful, and not entirely bad looking. He wasn't cruel or a spendthrift or a lout. He seemed healthy enough and had decent teeth. He could be a much worse choice for a husband, after all. Once they were married, they probably wouldn't even spend much time in each other's company. Like most of the married couples in the *ton,* they would live quiet, happy, separate lives, especially after she did her duty and produced an heir or two. That's the way it was supposed to happen. It was quite tidy, actually.

The only untidy thing was her feeling for Christian. Why did she have to *want* him so? She thought about him, dreamed about him, lay awake at night imagining what it would be like to be with him, have a life with him. The worst part was, she already knew a little how it would be. Their time together in Scotland had taught her.

A soft knock at her door interrupted her thoughts. She turned toward the sound. "Come in."

The door opened and her mother stepped inside. "I was hoping I'd catch you before you fell asleep."

"You did." Sarah left the window and made her way over to the bed, where she sat down on the edge. Her mother joined her, a worried look on her face.

"What is it, Mother?"

Her mother folded her hands in her lap. "I was going to wait to tell you this until after we returned to London, but I think it's best you know now."

Panic rose in Sarah's chest. "Know what?"

"Your father spoke to Lord Branford. They decided the wedding should be sooner than later. The men have agreed that you'll marry in three weeks' time, as soon as the banns are read."

Sarah pressed a hand to her chest. She couldn't breathe. "As soon as the banns are read?"

"Yes, dear. There's no use putting it off any longer. I know you have your nerves, which is quite normal for a young bride. But there's nothing to worry about. I'll tell you everything you need to know and—"

"No, Mother, it's not that. It's—"

"What, dear?"

"I just . . ."

Her mother's face turned serious, harsh. "Sarah, I know you've been preoccupied by Lord Berkeley."

More panic. "What?"

"I saw the way you looked at him at the Hollisters' ball and the way you spoke to him at the marquess's dinner party. It's plain as day that you have feelings for him."

The tiniest bit of hope unfurled in Sarah's chest. "Mother, what if I wanted to . . . marry for love?"

"There is no such thing," her mother scoffed.

Hope died a quick death.

"But, I—"

"You'll marry Lord Branford, Sarah. Afterward, if you'd like to have a discreet affair with Lord Berkeley, by all means, do so. But for the love of God, wait until after you produce the heir. That's all I ask."

Sarah recoiled from her mother. It was as if she didn't even know the woman sitting next to her. Why had she thought for one moment that her mother might actually understand? Be sympathetic? Sarah hung her head. She would never ask Christian to have an affair with her. It was beneath him. Beneath her. It just proved that her mother didn't know her at all.

Her mother patted her hand. "Lord Branford has been good to wait all these months, especially after your unfortunate little escapade last winter. It's time you stopped being childish. Do as you're told, Sarah."

"Yes, Mother," she murmured. *Do as you're told, Sarah.* The words thundered in her ears until her head ached.

"It's not all bad. Just think, we can finish shopping for your trousseau as soon as we return to London. That should cheer you up."

No. Her mother didn't understand anything.

"Yes, Mother." Another stiff murmur.

Her mother patted her hand once more. "You've already begun fittings for your wedding gown. We'll simply increase the number of appointments each week."

"Yes, Mother." It was all she could say. Her afternoon with Christian played through her mind with excruciating detail. The parson's noose was tightening around her throat until she couldn't breathe.

"Everything will be all right, dear." Her mother stood and moved toward the door. "Now, get some sleep. Lord Branford will be here for the wedding tomorrow and you'll want to look fresh and rested for him."

"Yes, Mother."

The door closed behind her mother and Sarah's throat began to contract. The walls of the bedchamber were marching toward her. The room became smaller and smaller. Marry Lord Branford in three weeks' time. Marry Lord Branford in three weeks' time? Three weeks? It was too soon. She couldn't breathe. She pushed herself off the bed and raced to the door. She was wearing only her night rail and dressing gown, but it didn't matter. She had to get out of the tiny room. She wrenched open the door and fled down the corridor. Thankfully, it was dark and empty. She was running somewhere, to someone, even though she wouldn't admit it to herself. Alex had mentioned to her the location of Christian's room earlier when they'd been touring the house together. Lord Owen had pointed out his own room and said Lord Berkeley was right next door. At the time she'd thought it seemed like superfluous information, now she was thankful for it.

Sarah hurried down the corridor on bare feet, turned toward the bachelor wing of the house, and flew along that corridor, too. She had to see him. Had to tell him. She didn't know why. All she knew was that Christian was the only other person she'd ever met who had told her that he experienced the sensation of walls closing in around him also. He was the only person who could understand.

She nearly skidded to a stop in front of his door. Her breathing was so harsh, she feared she'd wake the entire row of bedchamber occupants. She knocked as softly as she dared, then placed her ear against the door to listen for any movement.

Several moments ticked by interminably before the door swung open and Christian stood there, soft linen breeches covering him from the waist down and absolutely nothing on his bare chest. His hair was a bit mussed, as if he'd been abed, but he looked so handsome that she nearly rushed in and kissed him. Instead, she swallowed hard.

He pushed a hand through his rumpled hair. "Sarah, what is it? What's wrong?"

"I had to get away from my room. I . . . I couldn't breathe. The walls were closing in." She dragged her nails across her arms.

He stuck out his head and glanced both ways down the corridor to ensure they were not seen, then he quickly pulled her inside his bedchamber. "It's not safe for you to be out there. If someone saw you, your reputation would be in ruins."

"I know. But, I had to tell someone. Tell you . . ."

"Tell me what?"

"I couldn't breathe, Christian. The walls . . . I can't . . ."

He pulled her by the hand to the bed, where he sat her down and placed his hands on her shoulders. "Lower your head toward your knees. Breathe."

She did as she was told, bending at the waist to move her head as close to her knees as possible. Without her stays, it was simple. He rubbed her back, his hand a hot brand through her dressing gown. She struggled to breathe, her head bowed, her hands in her hair.

"In through your nose, out through your mouth," he said quietly.

Several moments passed while her breathing calmed and he stroked her back. His hand moved up to her hair.

She tried to ignore how good it felt. She didn't want it to stop. Finally, she sat up again and drew in a shaky breath.

"Are you all right?" he asked.

"Yes." She nodded and tried not to look at his muscled bare chest. He was being so nice to her. He always was nice to her. Even after she'd cruelly rejected him this afternoon. Run from him.

"Can you tell me now what's wrong?" he asked.

She turned her body slightly toward his and met his gaze. "Father and Mother are moving up the wedding. It's to be in three weeks' time, as soon as the banns are read."

"I see. And that sent you into a panic?"

She nodded miserably, wanting to launch herself into his arms and hug him. Press her head to his chest and breathe in his spicy scent of wood smoke and cologne. "I only knew I had to see you, Christian. I had to . . ."

His gaze searched her face. "Had to what?"

She had no more words. She launched herself at him, her hands in his hair, her mouth meeting his in a fierce clash. He toppled over backward onto the mattress and she moved atop him, kissing him, matching her body to his. His hands moved into her hair, his tongue in her mouth. Then his hands moved down to her hips, her waist, and he positioned her atop him. His hands moved back up to tangle in her hair, which spilled over his shoulders in dark waves.

"Touch me, Christian. Please. Like you did this afternoon."

In an instant she was on her back, he was over her, and his hand moved along the edge of her dressing gown. He untied the knot at her waist and peeled the gown from her shoulders. She sat up to help him remove it and quickly tossed it aside. Then his hand was at the hem of her night rail and he pulled it up, off her. She lay there naked under his hot regard as his eyes roamed over her entire body. All she felt was pride. Pride and the desire to see him naked as well. His hand touched her bare ankle, moved up her lower leg, brushed over her calf, then her outer thigh. Then moved in between her legs. She shuddered and spread her hands over his bare chest, marveling as the muscles flexed at her touch.

"Show me how to make you feel the way you made me feel today."

"No." He shook his head.

"Please," she breathed against his open mouth. "I want to." She had a vague idea of what would make him feel good. She moved her hand down to his breeches and rubbed the hard outline of him underneath.

He groaned. "Sarah, I—"

"Let me touch you, Christian."

But he pulled her hand away and pinned it, along with the other, above her head on the mattress. Then he slowly lowered himself down her naked body. "You're beautiful, Sarah. Your body is perfect. Just the way I knew it would be."

"Touch me," she begged.

His mouth trailed down her neck, to her breasts. He sucked each one in turn before continuing his descent. He kissed her ribs and her flat belly, then moved down lower. *Lower.*

Sarah clamped her legs together and gasped when she realized what he was about to do. He'd let go of her hands and she was trying to push him away when his hot, wet tongue found the core of her and licked deeply in long, lush strokes that made her head fall back against the pillow. She twisted against him, wanting to move but not wanting it to stop.

"Oh, my God. Christian!"

"Shh." He drew a finger up to her mouth. She opened her lips and sucked on it while he continued to lick her in deep strokes that made her thighs tremble and her knees weak.

He found that perfect spot again and licked in tiny circles again and again until Sarah writhed and twisted against the bedsheets. One of his hands was braced against her hip. The other left her mouth and moved down to her nipple, playing with it until she arched her back against it. Then the most perfect feeling, the wave of lust that shot from her breast and the final delicious lick from his hot tongue on her sex, sent her over the edge. She cried out and he covered her mouth with his hand while sharp zings of pleasure rippled throughout her entire satisfied body.

This time, however, she was not going to be denied. She wanted to touch him, too. To see him. Make him feel the way he'd made her feel. She waited for the intense pleasure to recede from her body before she rose on one elbow and pressed him on his back. She kissed his mouth long and hard.

"We need to talk," he began, trying to sit up.

But she wasn't about to let him get away with it. "No. Shh." She pressed a finger over his mouth just as he'd done earlier to her.

"Take off your breeches," she demanded.

Lust flickered in his light eyes. "Sarah, you don't know—"

"I know exactly what I'm doing. I'm only going to touch you. Only touch."

Her hands found his waist and she set about pulling down his breeches. Christian moved his hand down to stop her.

"Don't stop me or I'll scream and the entire household will come running," she warned.

"You wouldn't dare." His eyes flashed at her.

"In the mood I'm in tonight, I absolutely would dare. Now take off your breeches or else."

Christian did as he was told. In his entire adult life, he couldn't remember anything as lust inducing as beautiful

Sarah ordering him about in bed. She wanted him to take off his breeches. He would comply. Not only because he wanted to know what she was going to do to him, but also because he believed her when he said she might well scream and bring the house down on them. He couldn't allow her reputation to suffer when she'd clearly come here so upset. He wasn't certain what she was capable of at the moment. But he—and his cock—desperately wanted to find out.

His breeches were gone in a matter of seconds. He finished unbuttoning them, ripped them off, and tossed them on the floor. Sarah kissed his mouth, his cheek, his jawline. She dipped her small tongue in his ear, and he nearly came off the bed. Then she moved lower and began peppering his bare chest with tiny kisses. He liked it. He liked it a lot.

Her soft hand moved down and closed around him and he clenched his jaw tight. Dear Jesus God. What was she doing to him? Touching, she'd said. Only touching. But he didn't know if he'd bloody well be able to stand it. He might just come in her hand like an untried lad. He bit the inside of his cheek and tried to think of something else. Perhaps something morbid. Sad. But what? What?

Then her hand began to move up and down and he couldn't think of anything else.

"Sarah, you shouldn't—"

"Shouldn't what? Do this?" She stroked his hot, heavy flesh.

"No," he groaned.

"What about this?" She stroked him in the opposite direction.

"No—" His voice was tortured. "Don't do that either."

"And this?" She squeezed her fist around him and he bit the inside of his cheek again, but this time for an entirely different reason. His hips lifted off the bed. "Please."

"If you don't want me to do that, I'm entirely certain

you won't want me to do this," she said, a catlike smile on her face, just before she bent her head, moved down, and covered the head of his cock with her sweet, lush mouth.

"Damn it." Christian's fingers tangled in her dark hair.

She lifted her head then and smiled at him. "Tell me what to do, Christian. Show me."

"No," he groaned. By God, he was on the torture rack. He'd obviously done something very bad—or very, very good—in life to deserve this.

"Very well," she said, still squeezing him in her hand. "Then tell me what *not* to do." There was a mischievous twinkle in her eye.

He ground his teeth together. "Don't . . . don't put your mouth on me again," he warned.

"Like this?" She moved her mouth back over him.

He ground his teeth tighter.

"Don't . . . do not move your mouth up and down," he groaned.

She did just that and his eyes rolled back in his head. He squeezed them shut, tight. But soon he opened them again, because oh, God, he wanted to *watch*.

"Whatever you do," he ground out, "don't rub your tongue against me while you move."

And she did. She did just that. She lowered her mouth again, taking him fully into her throat, and moved down, oh, so slowly. Then she moved up again, the entire time her tongue brushing against his ridges while Christian's head pressed desperately against the pillow.

Her mouth moved down, then up again, again and again, and his hips were helpless to follow the rhythm of her torturous mouth. All he knew in that moment was that if she stopped, he'd never be the same again. Hell, he wasn't going to be the same either way, but her mouth on him was the most unholy torture he'd ever experienced.

She popped her wet mouth off his cock and blinked up

at him innocently. He looked down at her over the plane of his abdomen, breathing so heavily that he couldn't talk. And he sure as hell couldn't think.

"What will happen?" she asked in the most artlessly seductive voice he'd ever heard. "If I keep doing this, Christian?" She was rubbing his cock up and down, kissing the tip of it, sucking it.

"Sarah—" His throat was dry. He was breathless. His hands fisted in the sheets on either side of his hips.

"Would it make you feel as good as you made me feel?" she asked, her tongue licking the head of his cock, driving him wild.

"I—" It was the only word he could manage to drag past his dry, cracked lips before her mouth descended over him again and her rough tongue rubbed him up and down unmercifully. Again and again and again.

Sweet Mother of God. The woman was going to kill him. They'd find his dead body in this bed in the morning. But it would be worth it. So bloody well worth it.

She pulled her mouth away once more. "Let's find out, shall we?" she teased.

Shall we, what? He couldn't think straight. What had she said? What did she mean?

"Let's find out what happens if I keep doing this," she said as if she'd read his mind, just before her mouth descended again and Christian's head fell back, twisting against the pillow.

She sucked him hard and his hips arched up. She rubbed her tongue up and down against him. If only it hadn't been so long since he'd been with a woman. If only it weren't *Sarah* sucking his cock as though she'd been born to do it. If only she weren't so bloody good at it. He grasped the back of her head and groaned just before he spilled his seed inside her hot, wet, delicious mouth.

Sarah didn't try to pull away. In fact, she kept sucking

him until the last of the shudders racked his body. It was good. Oh, so good. Then she leaned up on an elbow and smiled at him, obviously pleased with herself.

What did one say to a woman, an innocent no less, who had just . . . "You can spit—"

She wiped the back of her hand across her mouth. "Too late." Her lips glistened with him.

He watched in awe as she leaned up, her dark curls spilling over her perfect breasts, and kissed him fully on the mouth. "Now we're even," she said with a wide smile.

"I've never in my life experienced anything . . ." But his hoarse words trailed off, and instead he just pulled her into his arms. Her head rested on his chest, directly under his chin. He kissed the top of her head.

"What do we do now?" she asked, wrapping her arms around his shoulders.

His heart still pounded. "What do you want, Sarah?"

Sarah pulled away from him, leaned up on an elbow again, and stared down at his handsome face. Her heart was lodged firmly in her throat. The answer to the question she was about to ask would determine their entire future. "Do you love me, Christian? Can you say you love me?"

His face froze, as if time had stopped. The only sound for several seconds was her breathing. His had seemed to stop. He rolled away from her and stood up. He grabbed his breeches from the floor and pulled them on. He tugged at the waist of them and cursed savagely under his breath.

Sarah pulled the sheet up to cover her nakedness. Tears filled her eyes as she watched him pace away from her, fiercely scrubbing a hand through his hair. She didn't know exactly what reaction she'd expected, but it wasn't this. For some inexplicable reason, she'd told herself that perhaps when she'd asked him earlier at the cottage, he simply hadn't been ready. Hadn't been prepared. But he'd had all day to think about it. And he *still* couldn't say it? When he spoke, his words were measured, calm. "You said yourself that marriages don't have to be based on love. We have passion, we have friendship."

Tears pricked her eyes. "You don't love me," she whispered brokenly, pulling the sheet up to partially cover her face.

He cursed again. "I didn't say that. I don't know what I—"

"Yes, you do. Be honest. You owe me that much. You owe yourself that much." With the back of her hand, she swiped at the tears threatening to spill down her cheeks. "All this time, all this time I've wondered why you've remained a bachelor. Why you couldn't find a wife. Why you became friends with all of the ladies you should be courting. I couldn't understand it. It seemed like a mystery. But I finally understand. You *want* to remain unmarried. You *want* to remain aloof, friendly. You don't let anyone in . . . on purpose. And then you act as if you're surprised that you haven't found a wife. It's never been about your clothes or your boots or even your reputation. Do you want to know the real reason you aren't married yet, Christian? Look in the mirror."

She leaped from the bed and grabbed her night rail. She hastily pulled it over her head. The dressing gown soon followed. She pulled it over her shoulders and tied it around her waist. Then she rushed toward the door. Her eyes were blurry with her tears. She placed her fingers on the handle, then turned back to look at Christian one last time.

His hands were on his hips. He was staring at the floor. A muscle ticked in his jaw. "Sarah, don't—"

But she didn't listen. All she knew was that she had to get back to her room. Hopefully without being seen. She took a deep breath and tried to calm herself. Tried to banish her foolish tears. She pulled opened the door and glanced out. The corridor was empty and cool. It smelled like lemons and wood polish.

"Sarah—" Christian's voice followed her into the corridor, but she didn't stop. She ran as fast as she could down the hallway, past a blurry set of bedchamber doors. Just as she was about to turn the first corner, a man came around it. She collided with his chest, and he grappled to save her from toppling over.

"My dear Miss . . ." The man righted her, then stepped back.

She looked up, terrified, her heart pounding so hard in her chest that it hurt. It was Rafe Cavendish. Wait. No. It wasn't Rafe. This man's hair was too long to be Rafe. It was . . . Cade, Rafe's twin. Cade glanced at her, her flimsy attire, her bare feet, her disheveled hair, then he looked down the corridor. Sarah looked, too, to see Christian half-dressed standing at the door, staring out with an equally horrified look on his face.

"Well, well, well," Mr. Cavendish said, a positively roguish grin on his face.

Terror kept words from forming in Sarah's dry throat. She simply stared at him, aghast. This was it. The moment her entire life could be ruined . . . or saved. "Mr. Cavendish, I . . . We . . ."

"I beg your pardon, Lady Sarah," Mr. Cavendish said, crossing his arms over his chest. "Seems I've stumbled upon a most inopportune moment."

"Cavendish," Christian called from the doorway, his voice a harsh, pleading whisper.

"No need to explain," Mr. Cavendish replied. "You may depend upon my discretion. For I myself have done far worse. And *I* have the kinds of secrets that, were I to share, might well get me hanged."

"What are you saying?" Sarah breathed.

"I'm saying you could not have a more ready ally," Mr. Cavendish replied.

Sarah and Christian both stared at the man in disbelief.

"Besides," Mr. Cavendish continued, "what do you think *I'm* up to, roaming the halls at this time of night? No good, I assure you." He winked at them and, whistling, continued down the corridor to his bedchamber.

CHAPTER FORTY

The next morning, Lucy Hunt came to collect Sarah from her room an hour before the wedding was to begin. With the help of her maid, Sarah had washed and dressed and was outfitted in a pretty morning dress of bright yellow, with her hair twisted high atop her head and a bonnet tied securely with a golden ribbon on the side. The only evidence of her hideous night was the slight puffiness to her eyes and the dark circles underneath them. Bother.

"I was hoping you'd accompany me," Lucy explained after Sarah had ushered her into the room. "I cannot wait to attend this wedding. It's been a long time coming."

"I'm certain it shall be quite beautiful." Sarah sighed, trying not to think of her own looming wedding.

"Yes." Lucy nodded. "Beautiful and a bit unusual considering they're already married."

Sarah's mouth fell open. She turned to Lucy with wide eyes. "Pardon?"

Lucy flourished a hand in the air. "Oh, a story for another time, dear. Now, will you come with me? I saw your parents downstairs earlier with Lord Branford."

Sarah decided to hold her tongue regarding the questions she had about Daphne and Rafe already being married. She'd learned that Lucy's set of friends made up an odd bunch. "Lord Branford is here?" she asked instead. "I had hoped he'd cancel."

The side of Lucy's mouth quirked up in a smile. "You wouldn't be so lucky."

"Of course Mother and Father are already dancing attendance upon him." Sarah sighed.

"Of course," Lucy replied. "They look quite enamored of him. Especially your father. I think *he* should marry the man."

Sarah groaned and pressed a finger to her pounding temple. "Don't make me laugh. My head hurts ever so much this morning."

Lucy smoothed one elegant eyebrow. "I wasn't going to mention it, dear, but you do look a little pale, and have you been crying?"

Sarah dropped to the cushioned seat in front of the dressing table. She stared back at her own hollow reflection. "Oh, Lucy. If I told you what happened yesterday . . . and last night, you'd never speak to me again."

In a rustle of skirts, Lucy moved over to her and placed her hand on Sarah's shoulder. "Dear, you know that's not true. And now you must tell me, because you have sorely piqued my curiosity."

Sarah drew a deep, shaky breath. She glanced up at Lucy and saw only sympathy and understanding in the duchess's unusually colored eyes. She opened her mouth to say only one thing, but ten minutes later, she had poured out the entire sordid story, leaving out none of the details, including the fact that Cade Cavendish had witnessed her ignominious exit from Christian's room last night.

"Ooh, what do you suppose Cade's done?" Lucy asked, her eyes wide and interested.

Sarah furrowed her brow. "You do realize that's not the point of the story, don't you?"

"Oh, yes, of course, dear. This is about you now." Lucy tossed her head, her black curls bouncing. "Very well, nothing you've told me sounds bad at all. In fact, I'd say it's all quite good."

Sarah's mouth fell open. The furrow in her brow deepened. "What in heaven's name are you talking about? Didn't you hear what I said? I cannot believe I did that. Any of that. I'm a harlot. A shameless wanton. Lord Branford must never find out."

"You're hardly a shameless wanton, dear. Why, Cass, Jane, and I did much worse than that before we married our respective husbands."

"What!"

"It's true. Don't look so shocked."

Sarah snapped her mouth shut and contemplated that surprising news for a moment.

"It's not unusual at all, and you should in no way feel guilty for it," Lucy continued.

"But I *feel* guilty. Extremely guilty. Surely lightning will strike me when I stand before God in the church this morning." Sarah buried her face in her hands.

"Ridiculous," Lucy replied. Sarah looked up to find the duchess tugging on the end of her glove. "I find it hard to believe that God would have made us all such passionate creatures if he didn't want us to be passionate from time to time," Lucy said.

Sarah blinked at her. "Do you truly think that?"

"Of course." Lucy flourished her hand in the air again. "And you can hardly be blamed for a bit of passion with the man with whom you're clearly falling in love."

Sarah groaned miserably. "But didn't you hear me tell you that Christian doesn't love me?"

This time, Lucy's brow furrowed. "No. I heard no such

thing. I heard the part where Christian didn't *say* that he loves you, which is quite different and of course quite stupid of him, but he's never experienced anything like this before. Besides, we've all had to overcome a bit of stupidity when falling in love. I'm afraid it comes with the territory." Lucy sighed.

"But I asked him outright. And he couldn't say it," Sarah argued.

"Did you tell him you love him?"

Sarah blinked. "No."

"Then why in the world would you expect him to come out with it? I admit one of you needs to be less stubborn and say it first, but these things are complicated, dear, and there are other factors to be considered in this particular situation."

Sarah's hand fell to her side. "Such as . . . ?"

"Such as your engagement to the Marquess of Branford."

Sarah's head dropped into her hands again, hat and all. "What am I to do, Lucy?"

Lucy leaned down and tugged her up to stand next to her. Then she hugged her against her side. "First, you're to attend Daphne and Rafe's wedding. We must set out immediately or we shall be late." She pulled Sarah by the hand toward the door.

"And then?" Sarah asked in a melancholy voice, dragging her feet along the floor in Lucy's wake.

"Then you must decide whether you are going to marry for love or for duty, because the only one who can decide that is you. You must not allow life to happen to you."

"But I can't—"

Lucy turned and shook her finger at Sarah. "See here. When I first saw you in Northumbria, I immediately liked you. I told Cass that any young woman who was willing to take off to Scotland in the winter with nothing more than some borrowed maid's clothing and a stash of pin money was the type of interesting young lady with whom we should very much strive to be friends. Don't forget that you are that selfsame young woman. She may be confused at the moment, but she's still there. I have full confidence. And she's not about to make the wrong decision. I'm certain of it." The duchess finished her speech with a resolute nod.

"I'm not at all as confident of it as you are," Sarah said as Lucy opened the door and pulled Sarah into the corridor.

"You will be, dear. You will be."

CHAPTER FORTY-ONE

Three weeks went by, three torturous weeks in which Christian returned to London and did everything in his power to stay away from Lady Sarah Highgate. The still-very-much-engaged-to-Lord-Branford Lady Sarah Highgate. Christian did whatever he could to keep her from his thoughts. He went riding in the park. He went to the fencing club with Upton. He even went shopping, of all bloody ridiculous things, with Monroe. According to Monroe, a well-dressed gentleman could never have too many fine shirts.

But Christian soon learned, to his chagrin, that while staying away from Sarah was easy enough, keeping her from his thoughts was much more difficult. For his thoughts were haunted by the memory of her in his bed in Surrey, her gorgeous naked body splayed in front of him. Her lips around him, driving him wild. Then, inevitably, his thoughts would turn to the talk they'd had after it was over. *Do you love me, Christian?* she'd asked in the most heartbreakingly vulnerable voice he'd ever heard.

Can you say you love me? Those were the words that kept him awake at night. Made him toss and turn in bed. Those were the words that tortured him. And every time he thought of them, he cursed himself for not having answered them in the way she'd obviously wanted. Every time, he hated himself more for not being the man she clearly needed him to be.

While Christian's thoughts were plagued with her, he spent his days studiously avoiding her, which proved to be somewhat simple. For Sarah was rarely in public. According to Lucy, she was busily preparing her trousseau while her mother saw to the wedding details. When he did attend *ton* parties, he rarely saw her. When she was there, he ensured that he spent his evening dancing with a never-ending slew of young, marriageable ladies. And he refused to look at her.

"I cannot imagine what she's thinking," Lucy declared one afternoon when she and Christian had gone for a walk in the park.

"I can. She's thinking she's about to marry Lord Branford," Christian retorted, nudging up his hat with the tip of his finger.

"But we spoke in Surrey. I was certain she'd—"

He glanced at Lucy, who'd snapped her mouth shut. "She'd what?"

"We talked before the wedding. I was certain she'd leave him. What did you do to your hand, by the by?" She gestured to Christian's right fist, which was wrapped firmly with a clean white rag.

"It's nothing," he murmured. He kept his mouth shut on the other score, too. He made a show of flexing his hand, in an attempt to prove it didn't pain him.

He wasn't about to tell Lucy what had transpired between him and Sarah in Surrey. Besides, if Sarah had ever had a moment of wanting to leave Branford and marry Christian, he'd bloody well put an end to it when he'd refused to tell her he loved her that night.

Damn it. *Did* he love her? Did he even know what love was? He couldn't bring himself to say those words without being absolutely certain. It wouldn't be fair to her. He couldn't ask her to cause a scandal that might estrange her from her parents for the rest of her life without being entirely certain. She'd asked him. She'd put him on the spot. And he'd failed. He'd been unable to say it. He didn't blame her for putting him on the spot. How could he? He was asking a lot of her, to toss over Lord Branford, anger her parents, and cast shame upon her family. Only he'd been convinced he was rescuing her . . . actually, stupidly *believed* she'd be grateful to him for offering for her. He'd been a bloody fool. And an utter arse.

To make matters worse, he'd nearly wished that Cade Cavendish had gone and told the household full of people what he'd seen. That, at least, would have forced the issue. Yes, there'd be an undeniable scandal, but in the end, no doubt, Christian would be with Sarah. The fact that he'd even thought about it, let alone wished it, made him an undeniable cad. The truth was, he wasn't good enough for Sarah. He didn't deserve her.

She'd told him to be honest. Told him he owed her that much. And it was true. Her tears had ripped him to pieces inside, but he did owe her his honesty. *All this time,* she'd said, *I've wondered why you've remained a bachelor. Why you couldn't find a wife. But I finally understand. You want to remain unmarried. You want to remain aloof, friendly. . . . And then you act as if you're surprised that you haven't found a wife.*

Those words clawed at his mind each and every day. He couldn't forget them, couldn't banish them, couldn't keep busy enough to drive them from his thoughts. *It's never been about your clothes or your boots or even your reputation,* Sarah had said.

Was Sarah right? Had he wasted her time in Scotland, asking her to help him become a legend? He'd had the pick of the lot after him, Lady Sarah herself. But when it came to telling her the one thing she needed to hear, he'd bloody well ruined everything. He had no one to blame but himself. Perhaps despite all his protestations to the contrary, he didn't want a wife and family after all. Perhaps he was incapable of love.

Do you want to know the real reason you aren't married yet, Christian? Look in the mirror, Sarah had said.

And he had. He'd taken a good, long, hard look in the mirror. Stared at himself. Couldn't look away. What he saw was a lonely bachelor staring back at him. One whose mother had left him when he was a child. She got sick one day and he never saw her again. It was a memory he rarely allowed himself to dwell upon, but he'd stared it down and let it torture him again for seconds, minutes, an hour. He'd taken that good, hard look in the mirror, and then he'd punched the bloody thing, shattering it into a hundred tiny pieces.

In the end, he'd realized why he wanted to be every lady's friend. Friendships were easy. Love. Love was difficult. Love caused pain.

The three weeks before her wedding passed with both an alarming alacrity and an excruciating slowness that Sarah thought would drive her mad in turns. Lucy Hunt's words echoed through her mind. *You must not allow life to happen to you.* Blast Lucy for putting a bunch of rebellious notions in her head. The duchess knew full well how the lives of ladies in their positions went. She knew full well what was expected of them. Sarah wanted to do what Lucy thought she should. She wanted to call off the wedding and choose Christian. If only Christian had given her a reason, a *real* reason . . . love. But Christian couldn't have been more clear. She'd asked him if he loved her and he'd said . . . nothing. He couldn't bring himself to say the words. Obviously, he didn't feel them. He'd mentioned passion and friendship, but nothing about love. She couldn't defy her parents and damage her reputation for anything less than love. It just wasn't good enough.

It didn't help matters that Meg was firmly on Lucy's side. "The duchess is right," she'd said on more than one occasion.

"About which part?"

"You must decide whether you will marry for love or for duty."

"I've decided," Sarah had insisted. "I'm marrying for duty. I have a responsibility to."

Meg had given her a sad look that reminded Sarah a bit too much of Fergus II when he was denied a treat, but in the end her friend had respected her decision and told her she would be there to support her on her wedding day, regardless of the groom's identity.

But in her more quiet moments, when she wasn't shopping for the final bits of her trousseau or being wished well by scores of callers and friends, Lucy's other words haunted Sarah. *Christian didn't say that he loves you, which is quite different . . . he's never experienced anything like this before. We've all had to overcome a bit of stupidity when falling in love.*

Was Lucy right? Could she be? Did Christian truly love her but was incapable of telling her because he'd never been in love before? Didn't recognize the feeling? Or was all of it just wishful thinking on her part? Idiotic, useless wishful thinking?

When she wasn't plagued by such thoughts, Sarah's

days were spent with her mother making repeated visits to the dressmaker's for the fittings for the wedding gown. Sarah couldn't even look at herself in the thing. It was a gorgeous gown, everything she'd ever wanted, with a fitted silver bodice and a long trailing white satin skirt. It had tiny blue and silver beads threaded in swirling patterns along the hem and across the skirt, and she looked absolutely breathtaking in it (or so both the dressmaker and her mother assured her). But every time Sarah tried to look at herself in the mirror, guilt made her look away. She was a fraud.

Her nights were a different matter altogether. They were spent awake in bed, unable to forget about the night in Christian's bedchamber when he'd made her feel things she couldn't have imagined.

When she wasn't thinking about Christian, she was fighting the fear that rose in her chest, the panic that threatened to bring the walls of her room crashing in on her, when she thought about spending the rest of her life with Lord Branford.

Sarah avoided Lucy and Meg the same way she avoided looking at herself in the wedding dress. And then one day she woke up, and it was the day before her wedding.

CHAPTER FORTY-TWO

Brooks's was the club of choice for Christian's set. On any given day there, he might encounter Claringdon or Swifdon, Upton or Monroe. Perhaps all four of them. Even Rafe Cavendish and his twin were known to make an appearance once in a while, ever since Rafe had been made a viscount by the prince for his work bringing the former Earl of Swifdon's murderers to justice.

Christian himself was a member of Brooks's, but he rarely went to the club. Drinking wasn't his pastime the way it was for, say, Monroe. He usually preferred the quiet solitude of his study or library to the busyness of the club. But today Upton had talked him into it, and today Christian had reason for going. Sarah was getting married tomorrow. Tomorrow. *Tomorrow.* From the moment he'd got out of bed today, the word had played like a death knell in his brain over and over again. He'd spent the better part of the morning in his study going over the same row of figures in his ledger. It had been maddening, but his attention wandered again and again with one word in mind. Tomorrow. Tomorrow. Tomorrow.

By the time Upton had stopped by and asked him to accompany him to the club, Christian was more than ready to throw down his quill and leave with his friend. Perhaps a drink was in order today.

The two men had been ensconced in leather chairs in one of Brooks's salons drinking brandy and talking about politics for no longer than half an hour when Owen Monroe came sauntering up. He was accompanied by Sarah's brother, Hart.

"Monroe, what are you doing here? Your wedding is in days. Shouldn't you be preparing or something?" Upton said, offering him a seat.

"I'm as prepared as I expect to be," Monroe replied, taking a seat and ordering his own brandy from a passing footman.

The word *wedding* stabbed at Christian. He curled his lip and took another long draught of his brandy.

"Do you two chaps know Highgate here?" Owen gestured toward Hart.

"Of course, good to see you, Highgate," Upton replied.

"Highgate," Christian intoned, acknowledging the man. He could barely look at him, though. With his black hair and green eyes, Hart reminded Christian too much of Sarah.

Upton invited the two men to join them, and they accepted.

"What's the matter with you today, Berkeley?" Monroe asked as soon as his drink arrived. "You look as if you could kill a man with your bare hands."

"Eh, don't let it be you, Monroe," Upton replied. "The lad's in a state today. Been downright surly since I first laid eyes on him."

Christian merely grunted.

"I don't suppose it has anything to do with Lady Sarah's wedding tomorrow morning," Monroe said, straightening his already perfectly straight cravat.

Highgate's brows rose.

Christian narrowed his eyes on Monroe. Why did he have to bring it up in front of Sarah's *brother*? "I'd keep such comments to yourself, Monroe, unless you want me to take your fancy cravat and shove it down your—"

"Whoa!" Monroe said, putting up a hand as if fending Christian off. "I didn't mean to offend."

"Are you going to the wedding?" Upton asked, obviously trying to create a more jovial atmosphere.

"No," Christian shot back. Perfect. Even Upton seemed intent upon talking about Sarah.

"But you were invited, weren't you?" Upton prodded.

Christian glowered at his friend in reply.

"Let's ask Highgate here," Owen continued. "I'm curious. What do you think of your future brother-in-law, the marquess?"

Highgate shrugged. "Can't say I think much of him, but my parents seem delighted with the match."

"And your sister?" Monroe prodded.

Christian wanted to murder Monroe with his bare hands.

"She doesn't seem to be as delighted," Highgate replied. "I never thought the wedding would happen, to be honest."

"See there," Monroe said to Christian. "Yet another person who doesn't think it's the best match."

"But what do I know about matches?" Hart continued. "I've been studiously avoiding my own for years." He chuckled.

Monroe's eyes never left Christian. "Do you love her, Berkeley?" he asked simply, settling back in his chair and taking a sip of brandy.

That was it. Christian *would* murder Monroe with his bare hands. He began a reply, a scathing one. He'd even opened his mouth, ready to deliver it posthaste. But in that moment, the anger completely drained from him. He took a long, deep breath and answered the only way he could. Honestly. "I have no bloody idea."

"That's a start," Upton said, a grin on his face, raising his glass in a salute.

Highgate took a sip of his own brandy.

"How am I supposed to know?" Christian groaned, rubbing his knuckles against his forehead. "Lord knows I tried to court other women over the years. I liked them. I might have married them if they would have had me. How am I supposed to know if it's different with Sarah?"

Monroe spent a silent minute lighting a cheroot and proceeded to blow his famous smoke rings into the air. "If you promise not to take a swing at me, I'll tell you something I think you may desperately need to hear today, Berkeley."

Christian snorted. "I promise no such thing." He waved down a footman to refill his glass.

"What if *I* promise I'll hold him back if he tries?" Upton asked with a devilish grin on his face. "Because I for one want to hear what you have to say."

"I do, too," Highgate added. "I'm bloody well fascinated by you men who fancy yourselves in love. It's completely baffling to me. Especially you, Monroe."

"Just wait, Highgate. When that emotion comes looking for you, you'll find there's very little you can do to escape it. God knows I tried," Monroe said with a devilish wink.

Christian sighed. "Go ahead, Monroe. Something tells me you're going to say whatever it is you want to say whether I agree to act reasonably afterward or not."

"It wouldn't be the first time we've come to blows," Monroe said to Highgate. Monroe settled farther back into his chair. "Consider this, Berkeley. If you had truly loved one of the other ladies you say you've courted, neither hell nor high water would have kept you from her. That's how I feel about Alexandra, and I presume to say that's how Upton here feels about Jane."

"It's true." Upton nodded. "If you're truly in love, you'll do crazy things. Things you'd never normally do. That's one way to tell."

Highgate merely rolled his eyes and took another sip of brandy.

Monroe inclined his head toward Upton. "Listen to him. He knows whereof he speaks."

"Now that I think on it," Highgate interjected, "my sister did ask me about you."

Christian's head snapped up to face him. "She did?"

Upton laughed. "I believe that answers it, chaps. Methinks our lad here was a bit too happy to hear that news."

"She asked me what I thought of you," Highgate continued. "I told her you were a good man."

Christian took the brandy the footman had just presented him and tossed it back in one gulp. There was no use denying any of it any longer.

"By the by, Berkeley," Monroe said, "what did you do to your hand?"

"This?" Christian asked, raising the bandaged hand in question. "It's just something crazy I did for love."

CHAPTER FORTY-THREE

Christian went to the wedding. Of course he went to the wedding. He might have been racked with guilt and tortured by memories for the last three weeks, but he couldn't stay away. And it was even harder today. Today he had to mentally fight against his friends' words. Upton and Monroe had been right yesterday. Sarah was different to him. She'd always been different to him. But his own fear had kept him from admitting it to himself . . . and to her. Now it was too late. He was sitting in the audience at St. George's Church to attend her wedding. It was far too late. He reminded himself repeatedly that it would be a selfish act to tell Sarah that he loved her. It would be greedy to declare himself and tell her he wanted to spend the rest of his life with her. She had clearly made up her mind. Lucy had even spoken to her about it, and she'd made her decision. Calling off the wedding would be a scandal for any reason, even if Christian declared himself and she accepted him. Not to mention he couldn't imagine her father agreeing to any of it. No. Christian would not, could not, ruin her life, but by God, he also hadn't been able to keep himself from the church today.

She'd invited him. Why, he didn't know. Perhaps because, as she had said so many times, he was such a good *friend*. He'd said it that night, too: *We have passion, we have* friend*ship.* She'd asked him if he loved her, and he'd bloody well replied with, *We have friendship.* Idiot. He deserved to spend the rest of his life alone. *Friendship.* God, the word made bile rise in his throat. But like a dutiful *friend,* he was here and he would smile and wish her well and clap her new husband on the back. And he would pretend the entire time that he wasn't being ripped to shreds inside.

A flurry of emerald-green skirts caught his eye as Lucy slid into the pew next to him, followed closely by her tall, broad duke of a husband. The two men greeted each other.

"How are you holding up?" Lucy asked, pity in both her eyes and her voice.

"Don't you dare," he whispered to her out of the corner of his mouth without looking at her. Instead his eyes were trained on the altar, where the bishop stood, waiting.

"Don't I dare what?" Lucy asked, her voice all innocence this time.

"Don't you dare pity me," Christian ground out.

"I can't help it if I think this wedding is wrong and you need to stop it," was Lucy's reply.

Christian glanced around to make certain her outlandish words hadn't been heard by any of the nearby guests. A few older people gave them condemning glares for their whispering.

"Lower your voice," he exhorted her.

"You are making the biggest mistake of your life," Lucy hissed under her breath.

Christian opened his mouth to reply, but the music began to play from the organ in the balcony in the back of the church and the entire congregation stood. First, the Marquess of Branford and the Prince Regent himself came out to stand at the altar. Then Sarah's mother and Hart and an elderly lady whom Christian presumed to be Branford's mother, the soon-to-be dowager marchioness, came down the aisle and were seated. He noted Meg Timmons seated near the front of the church, her blond curls laced with daisies and a resigned look on her face. Then the music rose to a crescendo, and moments later, Sarah herself came walking slowly down the aisle on her father's arm.

Christian swallowed. She looked so beautiful. Beautiful and perfect. Her hair was gleaming, her gown breathtaking. She was lovelier than he'd ever seen her. But her face was pale and drawn, her cheeks without a hint of pink. Her father, however, had a huge smile on his face. They proceeded down the aisle together for what felt like an eternity to Christian. Sarah kept her eyes trained straight ahead. If she saw him, she did not indicate it in any way. When she passed their pew, Lucy elbowed Christian in the side and he elbowed her back. The duchess uttered an "Oomph" and fell lightly against her husband, who righted her and gave her a warning glance.

Sarah's father escorted her up to the altar, where she took her place next to Branford. The marquess also looked quite pleased with himself. A smug smile hovered over his face. Christian squeezed his fists against the back of the pew in front of him. His grip was so hard, the knuckles on his uninjured hand turned white while a spot of blood bloomed across the bandage wrapped around the other hand.

The bishop began the ceremony, and Christian watched Sarah's ramrod-straight back as the words rang throughout the church. The memory of how she'd attempted to brandish the broadsword at him in Scotland flashed through his mind.

"Dearly beloved, we are gathered together here in the sight of God, and in the face of this congregation, to join together this man and this woman in holy matrimony."

How she'd deftly made biscuits and played with a servant's dog.

"Which is an honorable estate, instituted of God in the tome of man's innocency, signifying unto us the mystical union that is betwixt Christ and his church."

How she'd soundly beaten him at chess and helpfully carved out a spot in the snow for Fergus II to go outside.

"And therefore is not by any to be enterprised, nor taken in hand, unadvisedly, lightly, or wantonly, but reverently, discreetly, soberly, and in the fear of God; duly considering the causes for which matrimony was ordained."

How she'd been so worried for poor Mrs. Goatsocks despite her own troubles, and how she'd thoroughly charmed Mrs. Hamilton.

"First, it was ordained for the procreation of children."

The rest of the bishop's words blurred for Christian. They were just a mass of nonsensical sounds that blended together in his mind. Children. *Children.* Sarah would be having children. Branford's children.

The words that Monroe had said to Christian yesterday slashed through his mind. And he realized, he finally realized. Monroe had been right. If Christian had ever *really* loved one of the other women, he would have fought for her. He would have imagined one of them being the mother of his future children, as he was imagining Sarah right now. He would have fought for true love.

Because, by God, true love was worth fighting for.

The bishop turned toward the congregation. "If any man can show any just cause why these two may not lawfully be joined together, let him now speak or else here-after forever hold his peace."

Out of the corner of his eye, he could see Lucy's elbow headed toward him. "No need," he whispered, leaning down to her ear.

Then he stood up and in a voice that was full of confidence and loud enough for the entire congregation to hear, he declared, "I can!"

CHAPTER FORTY-FOUR

A collective gasp sounded through the church. The bishop's mouth fell open. Lord Branford's face was quickly turning purple. Hart seemed to be trying to squelch a smile. Meg didn't even attempt to squelch hers. Sarah's father swung around, looking as if he wanted to punch first and ask questions later.

But Christian was looking only at Sarah. She turned slowly, no doubt recognizing his voice, and when she saw him standing there, she closed her eyes. But not before he saw pain in them. Pain and . . . regret?

"What is your reason, sir?" the bishop asked, clearing his throat.

Christian stepped out of the pew into the aisle. "I have something to say that may greatly affect the continuation of this wedding."

Sarah opened her eyes again. Yes. There they were. Pain and regret. Her eyes pleaded with him to stop.

But he couldn't stop. Even though he knew in that moment that she might never forgive him, he couldn't stop.

"Out with it, then," the bishop said.

Sarah's father stepped out of the first pew, where he'd been sitting. He turned to the side so that he was halfway facing the bishop and halfway facing Christian. "This is preposterous," the earl said in a booming, angry voice. "This man must leave the church immediately. I don't think—"

"I want to hear what he has to say." Branford stepped forward, his face turning more purple by the moment.

"As do I," the Prince Regent agreed, pulling his embroidered morning coat over his wide belly.

Sarah's father clearly couldn't argue with the two most esteemed gentlemen in the church. The earl stepped back, but his eyes burned like hot coals into Christian's shirt-front.

"The truth is," Christian intoned, "you all may have heard some rumors several months ago. Rumors about Lady Sarah running away."

Sarah mouthed the word *No*.

His gaze fell from hers. Instead, he turned his attention to Lord Branford. For Branford was the one who would have every right to call him out after he finished listening to what Christian was about to say.

"The rumors are true," Christian continued in a voice loud enough for those in the farthest pew to hear. "Lady Sarah did, in fact, run away. She came to Scotland, where I live part of the winter, and she and I were alone together for several days in my hunting lodge there."

An even louder collective gasp reverberated throughout the church. Before Christian had a chance to take a breath and say another word, Sarah ran. She raised her delicate white skirts and flew down the steps from the altar, past her father, past Christian, down the aisle, and out the back doors of the church. Meg Timmons and Hart quickly ran after her. Sarah's mother, pressing a handkerchief to her mouth, promptly fainted.

A few of the women sitting near the front eased the countess off the floor and helped her into the first pew, fanning her repeatedly.

"This is indecent! Stop this immediately!" Sarah's father thundered.

Christian glanced over to Lucy, who gave him an encouraging nod as if to say, *Go on. Finish what you started.*

Christian grasped the lapels of his coat and straightened his shoulders. He met the bishop's gaze. "It's true. All of it."

Branford spoke in a strangled, incensed, voice. "May I have a word with you, *Berkeley*?"

Lucy nodded to Christian. Christian leaned over to Claringdon. "If I don't return in ten minutes, please come retrieve my dead body," he whispered.

"I surely will," Claringdon whispered back, still facing forward.

Christian proceeded to walk down the aisle and up to the altar, where he followed the bishop, Sarah's father, Branford, and the Prince into the room off the back of the altar.

As soon as the door closed behind the men, Sarah's furious father turned to Christian with a savage look in his eye. "What in the devil's name is the meaning of this, Berkeley?"

The bishop held up his hands in a calming manner. "Kindly allow the man to speak, Lord Highfield."

Branford stepped forward, a sneer on his face. He stood toe-to-toe with Christian. It was the first time Christian truly respected the marquess. "I have only one question for you, Berkeley."

Christian nodded. "Yes?"

"Is it true?" Branford spit the words between clenched teeth.

Christian nodded again. "Yes. It's true. She ran away.

She ran away because she didn't want this marriage. She became lost in Scotland and came upon my hunting lodge." He turned to stare at her father. "Absolutely *nothing* untoward happened, but it's true that she was with me, alone, for several days."

Branford's entire face was a mottled shade of purple now. "Didn't want the marriage?"

"Egad," the Prince Regent said, pulling a bit of snuff from his lacy cuff and snorting it with great fervor.

"That's preposterous," Sarah's father said. "Sarah wants the marriage. He's obviously lying. He—"

"What reason would I have to lie?" Christian said calmly. "I wish only happiness for Lady Sarah."

"Didn't want the marriage?" Branford echoed, his voice a positive gurgle in this throat. "Didn't want the marriage to *me*? Are you serious?"

"I am. You can ask Lady Sarah herself if you like," Christian said.

"That will not be necessary," Branford intoned. His nostrils flared with indignation. "Why, if that silly chit doesn't want to be married to *me,* I certainly can find someone who does." He turned away in a huff. "I'm leaving, Highfield. My solicitor will contact you immediately to have the marriage contracts destroyed. I rescind my offer. I'm not about to marry your ungrateful little daughter now."

Christian watched the marquess leave, trying to squelch the smile that desperately wanted to pop to his lips.

As soon as the marquess was gone, Sarah's father turned on Christian, pointing a finger in his face, spittle flying from his lips when he spoke. "I have two choices at the moment, Berkeley. I can either call you out, thereby exposing my family to even more shame and scandal, or I can demand that you marry Sarah immediately, thereby mitigating as much of this debacle as possible. That option will not erase the damage done, but it seems to me at the moment that it is the best of two impossible choices."

"I firmly agree," the bishop said, nodding his regal headdress.

"By all means," Christian replied. This time he did allow the smile to appear.

CHAPTER FORTY-FIVE

Sarah was sitting in her father's coach when Hart and Meg found her. The two had apparently run after her. With the help of the footman who'd remained with the conveyance, she'd managed to climb into the luxurious sapphire velvet squabbed seats and pull her long train in behind her.

Hart helped Meg up first and then climbed up to sit next to Sarah's friend in the seat opposite his sister.

Sarah had both hands braced against the seat next to her and was gasping. She couldn't catch her breath.

Meg was the first to speak. "Are you all right, Sarah?"

"No. I can't breathe." She tried to do as Christian had taught her and lean over, but her stays wouldn't allow it. "I can't believe he did that," she gasped. "I'm ruined."

"It's not so bad as all that," Meg said loyally, leaning forward to pat her knee.

Sarah gave her friend a look that clearly indicated she believed she'd lost her mind. "Are you mad? Mother and Father will never forgive me."

"Who cares if they forgive you?" Hart asked.

Sarah blinked at him, surprised at her brother's words. "What happened after I left?" she asked.

"I didn't see much, but I believe Mother fainted," Hart said.

"And you didn't stay with her?" Sarah asked, aghast.

"Mother has made her own bed and must lie in it. I was more concerned for you."

"That's sweet of you, Hart. You may want to give me one last hug. After this scandal, I'm sure I won't be allowed out in polite Society ever again."

"I'm glad he did it," Meg announced.

Sarah's mouth fell open. "What are you saying?"

"I'm glad Lord Berkeley stopped the wedding. I'm only being honest. I saw the look on your face. You looked as if you'd been sent to the guillotine. I was about to say something myself, only I couldn't think of anything properly scandalous to say."

"I have to agree," Hart chimed in.

Even in her state of abject misery, Sarah noticed that Hart and Meg were studiously avoiding looking at each other. Normally, they ignored each other—well, at least Hart seemed to barely notice Meg—but today he was actively *not* looking at her. Curious.

"You agree," Sarah said. "Have you no loyalty?"

"I have nothing but loyalty," Hart retorted. "And yes, I agree. It's no secret that you've been avoiding Branford for months. I happen to have it on good authority that you have feelings for Berkeley. Furthermore, I have it on even better authority that he has feelings for you."

"What?" Sarah felt dizzy, as if the world were tilting on its axis. She braced her hand against the side of the coach to steady herself.

"I saw him at the club yesterday, and let's just say he wasn't happy about this wedding."

"What does that have to do with anything?" Sarah cried.

"He stopped it, didn't he?" Meg pointed out. "That must mean he has feelings for you."

"It means he's lost his mind," Sarah replied. "And ruined my life."

"I think he saved your life," Meg replied.

"I agree," Hart said.

Meg blushed, but they still didn't look at each other. Sarah narrowed her eyes on the two of them. "What's going on with you two?"

"Absolutely nothing!" they burst out in unison.

CHAPTER FORTY-SIX

True to his word, before ten minutes had passed, Claringdon came looking for Christian's dead body. When the duke was told what had transpired, he immediately offered to procure a special license from the archbishop of Canterbury.

"It won't be the first one I've got and I doubt it will be the last," Claringdon said with a wry smile.

He left immediately to arrange the matter while Christian and Sarah's father left for Highfield's town house to see to the new marriage contract.

"May I come in?" Lucy Hunt's voice filtered through Sarah's bedchamber door. The words had been preceded by a soft knock.

"Come in," Sarah called blankly. She'd been doing nothing more than staring unseeing out the window.

The door creaked open slowly and Lucy walked in. She was dressed in the formal clothing she'd worn to the wedding earlier.

"Are you all right?" Lucy asked, coming to stand

behind Sarah at the dressing table, a sympathetic look on her face.

Sarah patted her coiffure. She'd long ago removed her veil, but she remained dressed in her exquisite gown. "Expected me to be crying, didn't you?"

"I didn't know what to expect, to be honest," Lucy replied with a sigh.

"Well, I'm not crying. I refuse to cry. I'm not sad, I'm . . . angry." She lifted her chin and faced Lucy.

Lucy nodded slowly. "Angry at Christian?"

Sarah raised her gaze to the ceiling briefly. "Yes, and at myself. . . . This whole thing . . . it's turned into a complete mess." She flicked a hairpin across the top of the dressing table.

Lucy stopped it with the palm of her hand before it flew off the end of the table. "If it helps at all, I do think Christian loves you madly."

"That's what Hart and Meg tried to tell me, but I still have my doubts."

"I don't. Not one."

Sarah braced her elbow on the table and let her forehead fall onto her palm. "Why in God's name did that man wait till the very last minute?"

Lucy squeezed Sarah's shoulder. "I agree. He hasn't handled it well, any of it."

Sarah groaned. "And *why* did he do it in such an ignominious fashion? My parents will never live down the shame. Father will never speak to me again."

"Your father just needs time."

"You don't know my father."

The anger that had been bubbling in her since she'd run out of the church finally spilled over. Sarah slapped a palm against the top of the table. "Christian had no right to do what he did. Absolutely no right."

Her mother had come to visit her when they'd first

returned home. Sarah had tried to calm her down at first, but her mother had continued to hurl accusations at her and even accused her of planning Christian's announcement with him. In the end, Sarah had asked her to leave her room. She didn't know where her father was or Christian, either, for that matter. She'd asked Hart and Meg to give her time alone to think. Apparently Mother wasn't about to keep a duchess from calling. And at the moment, Sarah was thankful to have Lucy to talk to. Sweet, kind, unconventional Lucy.

Lucy squeezed her shoulder again. "I agree that his timing was hideous, but aren't you the least bit glad not to be married to Lord Branford?"

Sarah groaned and rubbed her hand across her forehead. "Ah, yes, a reprieve from one man's whimsy only to end up at the mercy of another's. I'm sick of being treated like a valuable doll."

"Good," Lucy replied. "You should be. It's high time."

Sarah's head snapped to the side to face the duchess. "You agree with me?"

Lucy pushed a curl aside. "Of course I do. I'm a lady, too, aren't I? We should be treated with nothing but decency and respect and allowed to make all our own choices as far as I'm concerned. I'm only sorry that you didn't see fit to tell your father to go to hell before the wedding."

Sarah couldn't help the smile that popped to her lips. "I would have liked to see the look on his face if I had."

"As would I," Lucy replied with a conspiratorial grin.

Sarah stood, turned around, and smoothed her skirts. There was no use wishing things had gone differently. All she could do now was face the future with courage. "What's going to happen now, Lucy?"

Lucy tapped a finger against her cheek. "If I don't mistake my guess, Berkeley is downstairs in the study with your father, writing your marriage contract." She smiled. "All things considered, I would not make his wedding night easy for him."

CHAPTER FORTY-SEVEN

The archbishop was a tall man with white hair, grand white robes lined with sable, and a permanently unsmiling face. Sarah had watched out the window from her bedchamber as the prelate arrived at her father's town house at approximately eight o'clock that evening. Apparently, when a duke, an earl, and a viscount required his presence, the archbishop complied. The Duke and Duchess of Claringdon were there, as were the Earl and Countess of Swifdon. Along with Sarah's parents, Hart, and Meg, they were the only witnesses. Lucy Hunt was smiling from ear to ear.

Sarah's bridegroom, while devastatingly handsome—which was annoying given the circumstances—looked somber. A bit as though he might vomit, actually. Which was exactly the way Sarah felt. How in heaven's name had she gone from complying with her parents' wishes and trying to do the right thing to becoming the biggest scandal in London—all in the space of a few hours? Her mother could only sob quietly, and her father looked right through her as if she didn't exist. But Sarah knew he'd ap-

proved the wedding—demanded it, according to Lucy—
or it wouldn't be taking place.

The archbishop read the same words that the bishop
had read earlier, and Sarah's head hurt remembering that
she'd attempted this same sacrament just hours earlier
with an entirely different man. The world had obviously
gone mad. What sort of a fickle changeling was she that
she was agreeing to this? She was a coward. She let her
parents tell her what to do and when to do it. But hadn't
that always been the way? *Do what you're told, Sarah.*

She might have to marry Lord Berkeley because of
the damage that had already been done to her reputation,
but she didn't have to like it. Of course, she'd been informed that Lord Branford had promptly cried off, dis-
gusted and disgraced by the hoyden he'd nearly married.
Father hadn't put up a fight at all. Apparently, he'd readily agreed to end the contract and let Lord Branford go in
order to more quickly move on with the contract with
Lord Berkeley.

They'd spent the afternoon going over it, Lucy had informed her. And now, what? Sarah was supposed to be
pleased? Thankful that she'd been saved from her own
reputation? A small part of her realized that she'd brought
all this on herself. If she hadn't run off to Scotland to begin with, she wouldn't be in the situation she was in now.
But she'd nearly got away with it. She had been moments
from putting the past behind her, and then Christian had
gone and done the most incomprehensible thing in the
world.

She'd sat in her room alone, quietly, after Lucy left.
Sarah had had hours to think this afternoon. And that's just
what she'd done. She thought about her mad trip to Scotland, her return to England, Christian's transformation into
a legend among the *ton,* and their time together in Surrey.
Finally, she'd determined she *would* marry Lord Christian

Berkeley. It seemed she had no other choice, but she knew she did. She could run away again, from all of them. Leave and never come back. But the truth was that after all that had happened and even after what he'd done today, she loved him. She loved Christian. Whether he ever was able to say it back, she knew she loved him with her whole heart. But that didn't mean she wasn't incensed with him.

"Wilt thou have this woman to thy wedded wife?" the archbishop intoned.

Christian's face was a mask of stone. He looked as though he already sorely regretted his decision.

"I will," he replied solemnly.

"Wilt thou take this man to thy lawful wedded husband?"

The words stuck in her throat. Christian tensed beside her, obviously worried that she would say no. Or flee. Even after all that had happened, she couldn't do that to him.

"I will," she replied just as solemnly.

There were more words, more vows, but Sarah didn't hear them. All she could hear was the pounding of her own heart as her life was linked inextricably to the man standing at her side. A completely different man from the one she'd expected when she'd climbed out of bed this morning.

"I pronounce that you are man and wife," the archbishop declared.

There was a bit of clapping, some hugs, and some congratulations and best wishes. But Sarah didn't remember any of that, either. There was a wedding dinner, quite out of the ordinary, given that weddings were usually held in the morning. But the group ate, toasted, and drank wine. By far the most joyous people in the room were the duchess and her set, while Sarah's parents glowered at everyone else. All the while, Sarah couldn't even look at her new husband seated next to her.

An hour later, she woodenly got into a coach that was set to take her to Viscount Berkeley's London town house. *Her* new town house. She was a viscountess now. Her trousseau, the one she'd picked out for a life with Lord Branford, was loaded onto the coach and the conveyance rolled off.

When they arrived at Christian's town house, he waited for the footmen to pull down the steps, then he got out and helped her down. He tucked her arm over his and escorted her up the stairs into the foyer.

The butler was pleasant. The housemaids smiling. The house was finely decorated and smelled clean and fresh. And slightly . . . masculine, a little like her new husband. All of the servants bowed and welcomed her. But Sarah was still in a daze. The footmen rushed about to carry her trunk to her room. Her new husband showed her to her bedchamber on the second floor.

"I'm directly next door . . . if you need anything," Christian said.

"I never want to see you again." Sarah promptly walked into the room, shut the door, and locked it.

CHAPTER FORTY-EIGHT

Christian was out of the house the next morning long before his bride was awake. He proceeded to complete every errand that needed attention, including several matters that would normally be seen to by the servants. Then he spent a sweaty midmorning fencing at the club. Finally, he ended up at Brooks's, where he stared sullenly into a glass of brandy that he barely drank. Some of the other patrons gave him odd looks. Apparently, the story had traveled fast. He'd known it would. But no one approached him or said anything. Good. The way he was feeling today, he might bloody well punch one of them in the face if they so much as coughed in his direction.

He didn't blame Sarah for being angry with him. He wasn't certain why he'd done what he'd done. He only knew that he'd had to stop the ceremony. Knew it wasn't right. Knew he couldn't sit there in an uncomfortable church pew and watch the woman he loved—and he was quite clear on that score now—marry another man. He'd thought she loved him, too. But she certainly was angry.

Upton slid into the seat next to him. Christian hadn't even heard the man approach.

"I hear congratulations are in order," Upton said.

"Yes," Christian replied woodenly, pushing his glass back and forth on the tabletop between his palms.

"You've got to be the most unhappy bridegroom I've ever laid eyes upon. And what in God's name are you doing *here* of all places? Shouldn't you be, say, in bed with your new wife?"

"My new wife doesn't want me in her bed," Christian ground out.

"That bad, eh?" Upton replied.

"I merely interrupted her wedding, ruined her reputation, and brought the censure of her parents and friends down on her head. Not much."

"Yes, it does sound a bit dramatic. Seems you might have picked a better time and place, but the point is that you love her, don't you?"

"Madly."

"Have you told her?"

"No."

Upton slapped his palm against his forehead. "Why not?"

"Again, the ruination of her life. Even when followed by the words *I love you*. It makes them sound a tad insincere. Oh, and there's also the bit where she told me she never wanted to see me again."

Upton winced. "Sometimes ladies need time. Whenever Jane's angry with me, I give her time and plenty of space."

Christian slid his glass over to Upton. "That's exactly what I intend to do."

CHAPTER FORTY-NINE

On the second day after her wedding, Sarah awoke, rubbed the sleep from her eyes, and sat up. The events of the last few days came rushing back to haunt her. She groaned. She hadn't seen Christian yesterday. He'd left early and been gone till long after she'd retired. She'd spent the day alternately worrying and exploring her new home. She'd met all the servants and spoken at length to the housekeeper. Being the lady of a great home was a role she'd been born to. It seemed only natural that she begin immediately. Everyone had been perfectly lovely and welcoming. She was already feeling at home.

When Christian hadn't returned by dinnertime, she began to regret her last words to him. *I never want to see you again.* They were harsh and said in anger and untrue. Of course she wanted to see him again. They were married, for heaven's sake. They needed to speak. They needed to decide their future. The night of their wedding, Lucy's words had hammered in Sarah's skull. *You must not allow life to happen to you.* She'd decided that day that she *wasn't* going to allow life to happen to her. Not anymore. Never again. *Do as you're told, Sarah.* Those words held no power over her any longer. She'd been angry. She'd been sad. She'd been a hundred other things. But she wasn't about to marry someone she didn't want to marry. She'd sooner flee to Scotland again and never return. And so it was with a fully determined—if still outraged—mind that she'd stood in front of the archbishop that night and allowed the wedding to proceed. But when they'd arrived at his town house and Christian had shown her to her room, the anger she'd felt earlier had flared and she'd lashed out at him. She hadn't expected him to take her words so literally.

Her gaze fell on a note sitting on her bedside table. It was folded and sealed with Christian's stamp. Dread clutched her heart. She slowly pulled it off the table and unfolded it, breaking the seal with her finger. Christian's handwriting filled the page.

Dearest Sarah,
I know you have no wish to see or hear from me. I intend to honor your request. I'm going to Northumbria for a few days and then on to Scotland. It's inadequate, I know, but my deepest apologies for everything I've done. I hope someday you can find it in your heart to forgive me. For what it's worth, I do love you, hopelessly.

Christian

Tears spilled down Sarah's cheeks, and she read the letter over and over. He loved her? He loved her, the lout? He'd handled everything awfully and been a complete idiot, but none of that mattered anymore. He *loved* her.

But he was gone. She'd driven him away with her disapproval. What did she expect him to do when she'd told him she never wanted to see him again? He thought he was giving her what she wanted, what she'd requested. Oh, she'd made a complete mess of things, too. They were quite a pair, the two of them.

She rang for her maid and promptly dressed. Then she set about writing a letter of her own.

At precisely four o'clock that afternoon, the traveling chaise of the Duchess of Claringdon pulled to a stop in front of Christian's town house. Lucy, Cass, Jane, and Meg alighted.

As soon as the ladies were ensconced in the silver salon, Lucy wasted no time in announcing why they'd come.

"I received your letter, dear, asking for our help. Of course you may have it. We realize what Berkeley did was a bit of a problem for your reputation, but nothing a duchess, a countess, and a future countess can't overcome. We know everyone who's anyone in the *ton,* and we've begun courting favor with our friends. We've already told half the town how your poor thwarted love story has ended happily after all and you're properly married now, so who really cares? All's well that ends well."

Sarah blinked at them. "You're here to . . . stop the scandal?"

"Of course, why else did you think we'd come?" Lucy asked.

"We want to help you, Sarah," Cass said softly.

Meanwhile, Jane was helping herself to tea cake.

"We'd like to help Meg here, too, if only she would stop being so stubborn and allow us to purchase a few new gowns for her," Lucy added.

"I appreciate the thought, Your Grace," Meg replied with a wide smile, "but we're here for Sarah at the moment."

Sarah bit her lip. "I wanted to . . . I mean, I . . . The *ton* will truly accept that story?" She felt silly and didn't want to admit why she'd asked them to come.

Lucy flourished a hand in the air. "The secret is, darling, that most of the most respectable people in the *ton*, including Cass and Jane and myself, have extremely scandalous stories of how we met our husbands. Everyone's a bit willing to be forgiven when they've needed it themselves a time or two."

Sarah shook her head. "I never knew."

Cass blushed a little. Jane merely shrugged.

"Of course you didn't, dear," Lucy continued. "That's what's so lovely about it. It's all easily forgotten and swept under the rug once a nice tidy wedding takes place, and you've already done that."

"Ooh, what did you do, Lucy?" Meg asked, helping herself to a tea cake, too.

"Stories for another time, dear," Lucy said to Meg with a wink.

Sarah smoothed her skirts. "That certainly makes me less worried. But I'm still afraid Father will never forgive me."

"Oh, pishposh. Your father will forgive you once he's bouncing his first grandbaby on his knee. I'm certain of it," Lucy said.

"It's true," Cass added.

"Babies do tend to be peacemakers," Jane said. "Or so I'm told."

"Forgive us for not coming sooner and putting your mind to rest, but we thought we'd give the two of you a bit of privacy on your first day or two as a married couple." Lucy waggled her eyebrows. "Then I received your letter and, well, here we are. Now where is the happy newly wedded bridegroom?" She glanced about for Christian.

Shame flooded through Sarah. She was certain she was bright red. There was no way around it, she'd have to admit the truth to her friends. "He's . . . not here."

Lucy blinked. "Not here? Whatever can you mean? He

can't have already left for an outing. Why, the two of you should still be indecently in bed all day."

More red heat. Sarah pressed her hands to her cheeks. Meg blushed, too.

"Lucy!" Cass scolded.

Jane Upton merely rolled her eyes and helped herself to more tea cake.

"Not only is he not here," Sarah admitted miserably, tugging at the collar of her gown, "but we . . ." She gulped and looked away. "We . . ."

"Go on, out with it, dear. It can't be that bad," Lucy prompted.

"It's worse than bad," Sarah said, meeting each lady's gaze in turn.

"Oh, dear." Cass came over and patted her hand. "It's all right. You can tell us."

"You are under absolutely no obligation to tell us anything," Jane offered.

"No, no. I want to. I need to. I need your advice," Sarah said.

"Of course you do," Lucy replied, giving Jane a dirty look. "Go on, dear," she prompted Sarah.

"Cover your ears, Meg."

Meg did as she was told. Sarah took a deep breath and closed her eyes. She needed to tell them, but she didn't have to *see* them while she told them. "We haven't con-consummated our marriage," she blurted out, then bent over and hid her face in her hands.

There was a slight gasp—she wasn't certain from which lady—but soon she felt Cass's comforting pat again. "There, there. It's not so bad as that."

Sarah sat up again and opened her eyes. Lucy motioned to Meg to uncover her ears.

"I'm so ashamed," Sarah whimpered. "I've been such an awful wife to him and he . . . he . . ."

"He what?" Lucy asked, sympathy in her voice.

"He left for Northumbria," Sarah managed through a dry throat.

"What!" Lucy plunked her hands on her hips, looking positively outraged.

"He left for Northumbria. This morning." Sarah slowly dragged the note from her pocket and handed it to Lucy. "Here. This explains it all."

Lucy read the note aloud so the others could hear, and when she finished she shook her head and clucked her tongue. "That coward. How could he run from you?"

"I've run from him often enough. Besides, he's not a coward," Sarah admitted miserably. "He was just doing as I asked."

Cass's head snapped up. "You asked him to leave?"

"I didn't know he'd go to *Scotland,* but I told him on our wedding night that I . . ." Sarah made a small moaning noise in the back of her throat. "I told him I never wanted to see him again. Oh, I've ruined everything."

"There, there," Cass repeated. "You haven't ruined everything."

"Not at all," Meg stated loyally.

"Yes, I have. He's left me and he loves the north. He may never return," Sarah said.

Lucy, who had been busily tapping a finger against her cheek, obviously plotting, pointed a finger in the air. "It's true, he may never come back, *unless* he has a reason."

"What reason?" Sarah asked, brightening a bit.

"I can't think of a good reason," Lucy replied.

Sarah's shoulders slumped again.

"But I can think of an alternate plan," Lucy said, a smile slowly spreading across her face.

CHAPTER FIFTY
Scotland, June 1817

After Christian finished rubbing down Oberon in the barn, he hiked up to the front door of the lodge. Scotland was lovely and green this time of year. It was so different from the last time he'd been here. Snow knee-deep and . . . Sarah.

Damn it. He'd promised himself he'd stop thinking of her. A promise he was slowly coming to realize was going to be impossible to keep. The entire journey to Northumbria had been torturous. The four days he'd spent at the estate seeing to his business affairs had also been unpleasant. The servants, including Mrs. Hamilton, had obviously heard the news about his abrupt wedding, and they were baffled by the fact that he'd come home without his new wife. Mrs. Hamilton alone had peppered him with so many questions he didn't want to answer that he found himself hiding from the woman in his own damn home. It was ridiculous. He'd planned to stay at Berkeley Hall for a sennight. He'd left after only four days. And ridden hell for leather to Scotland. The place where he always felt safe, at home, happy. But looking at the front door of the lodge now and remembering the last time he'd been here was making him feel anything but happy. Memories of Sarah flooded his mind. Surrounded him. Haunted him.

He'd spent the entire journey here trying to think of some way he could make it right for her. The obvious answer was a quiet annulment. He'd be willing to give it to her, but he suspected she'd refuse it. An annulment would drag her family into even greater scandal, which was exactly what she'd been trying to avoid. Not to mention her father would no doubt call him out immediately if an annulment was offered, let alone took place. No. The only thing to do was write Sarah and ask her what she wanted of him. If she wanted him to stay in Scotland and Northumbria, he would. He would not make her life more difficult. If she needed him back in London to mitigate the scandal or face it with her, he'd return. He'd left merely to give her time and space. He'd do whatever it took to make it right. But his greatest fear was that she'd write back and tell him to stay here indefinitely. Funny. Something he'd always wished for was no longer what he wanted. He wanted Sarah. Wherever she was.

When he opened the front door, he didn't hear the familiar bark of Fergus II. Instead, the scent of stew cooking reached his nostrils. He glanced around. The rug was near the hearth where Sarah had left it. And sure enough, a pot of stew was bubbling on the stove top. The chessboard was sitting on the table. Biscuit dough sat rising on the countertop.

And then he heard . . . singing. Coming from one of the bedchambers. A woman, singing. He immediately headed toward the sound of it.

He pushed open the bedroom door and blinked. Was he seeing an illusion conjured by his imagination? Sarah was there, sitting in a chair next to the bed, knitting.

Fergus II, wearing a new blue sweater, was sound asleep on the rug next to her feet.

The knitting needles dropped to her lap and Sarah looked up into Christian's eyes. It wasn't a figment of his imagination. She was here. She'd come to him.

"You're early." Her voice was a hoarse whisper.

"You're here." So was his.

She stood up, set her knitting in the chair, and smoothed her skirts.

"You're here, aren't you? This isn't my imagination?" he asked.

"No, it's not your imagination. Of course I'm here. It's my duty as a wife."

"Your duty as a—"

She stood and turned down the bed. Then she motioned for him to sit on it. He did so, still watching her carefully.

She knelt and motioned for him to pick up his foot so she could assist him in removing his boot. He complied. She pulled off first one, then the other.

Christian watched her with wide eyes. He had absolutely no idea what she was about. Was she still angry with him, or did she want to make love to him? He couldn't tell. He braced his hands behind him on the bed and leaned back, his eyes never leaving her.

Sarah stood, walked over to the wall, and hefted the sword that still rested there. She came back to the bed and, after lifting the weapon with both hands, held the tip of the blade to Christian's throat.

"Sarah, I—"

"I'm the one with the sword. That means I get to speak first."

He swallowed against the blade. "By all means."

She straightened her shoulders and tossed back her hair. Her arms strained under the weight of the sword. Her eyes flashed like green ice. She looked magnificent.

"If you ever take me for granted . . . if you ever treat me with disrespect . . . if you ever again make a life-changing choice without consulting me first . . ."

"You'll slice me in half?" He didn't smile. Didn't dare smile.

"I'll make you regret the day you were born."

"Understood."

She lowered the sword away from his neck and propped it against the nearest wall. "Now, I'd like you to tell me what I've been waiting to hear for days but you only saw fit to write in a letter you left on my bedside table before you fled from me."

Christian jumped to his feet and pulled her into his arms. "I love you, Sarah."

"You do, Christian? You truly do?"

"Yes. I think I've loved you since the *first* time you threatened me with a sword."

She smiled at that and he hugged her tightly.

"I love you, too, Christian."

"Helplessly?"

"Yes."

"Hopelessly?"

"Yes, and not only that, I missed you, my darling," she said.

Christian picked her up and swung her around. "Good, because if this is a dream, I don't want to wake up." He kissed her long and soundly.

"Neither do I," she breathed.

He set her back on her feet and held her hand. She lowered herself to the bed, sat on the edge, and patted the space next to her. He sat beside her.

"Christian, I'm sorry. I let my stubborn pride and my idiotic need to please my parents get in the way of our happiness."

"No, I'm sorry, Sarah. I'm sorry that I didn't tell you I

love you weeks ago. I let my fear keep me from finding the happiness I've always wanted. But I know now I cannot be happy without you. And I hope you feel the same way."

She cupped his cheeks. "I do, my darling. I do."

Christian reached out and touched her face gently. He ran his fingers along her cheek, along her jawline, along her smooth neck. She arched her chin so he could touch her more.

"I want to make love to you," he whispered.

"Yes," was her only reply.

With a slightly shaking hand, he reached out and began to unbutton her gown. He pushed it off her shoulders. She turned for him and plucked the pins out of her hair while he set about the painstaking task of unlacing the back of her gown. He had to pull each lace through the series of brackets, and he stopped every few moments to kiss the back of her neck, sending shudders throughout her body.

When he was finally done, she was able to lower the gown over her hips and she stood there in only her shift, her stays, and her stockings. He pulled her close and kissed her deeply while his strong fingers worked on the laces to her stays. Finally, that garment, too, gave way and she tossed it aside.

"Now you." She nodded to him.

Christian had forgotten that he was still fully dressed. His boots were already gone, so he had only to remove his stockings, his breeches, and his shirt. He nearly ripped his cravat from around his throat and tossed it aside.

"Careful. That looked expensive." She smiled.

"I don't care. I'll buy ten new ones if I must." He pulled his shirt over his head with both hands.

When his chest was bare, Sarah sucked in her breath. "Oh, Christian, you're so, so . . ."

"I spend a lot of time fencing," he said with a wicked grin as she traced her hands down his flat abdomen to the muscles that stood out in stark relief along his middle. "Your hand on me is like torture," he whispered.

"Now your breeches," she whispered back, excitement filling her.

His hands were at the buttons of his breeches, and he watched her while he undid each button of the placket. Sarah held her breath.

He shucked his breeches and stockings in one quick move and stood naked before her, tall, lean, muscled. His manhood jutted out toward her, hardened by his desire.

She had the sudden urge to touch it but was immediately reminded of the fact that he was naked and now she should be, too.

She turned toward the bed and crawled onto it. Without saying a word, she pulled off her shift and tossed it on the floor. She had only her stockings left. She reached down to push them off, but Christian's hand stopped her. "No. Leave them on. I find them completely alluring."

She nodded and reclined against the pillows. Christian watched her, her long hair spread out black against the stark whiteness of the sheets. Her full, perfect breasts, her tiny waist, her long, sleek legs. She was breathtaking.

She was watching him, too. Her eyes devoured his frame from the top of his head to the bottoms of his feet. He lay down on the bed next to her and she flinched.

"I won't hurt you, darling. Trust me," he said.

She bit her lip. "Mother told me it will hurt terribly, but—"

"Your mother doesn't know everything," he said.

"Kiss me," she breathed, and he complied. He took her face between his fingers and moved his mouth over hers.

"Sarah, I'm going to do something. Something that

won't hurt you at all. Something I hope you'll like. Something that should make you wet, ready for me."

She felt herself blush. "Is it . . . what you did in Surrey?"

He grinned wickedly again. "Yes."

"Then by all means, I trust you," she murmured.

He kissed his way down her torso, stopping to ravish each breast with his mouth and hands. By the time his head descended toward the apex of her thighs, she was panting and mindlessly wanting him. "Christian, please," she breathed.

"Patience, my love," he replied.

Her hands dug into the bedsheets as his mouth covered her most intimate spot and his tongue licked deep between her cleft, finding that perfect point and torturing it with the tip of his tongue. Sarah's eyes rolled back in her head. "Oh, God. Christian!" she called, wanting it never to end.

The feeling that surged through her began between her legs and pulsed throughout her body, spreading like fire to every nerve ending in her body. She cried out and splintered apart, cradling his head between her legs.

He lifted up on one elbow and grinned at her. "Did you like that?"

She couldn't answer. Panting and a nod were all she could manage.

"Good." His hand slipped between her legs and he slowly pushed one finger inside of her. She groaned. "You're so wet. So wet for me, my love."

"Yes," she murmured.

He took her hand and moved it down between his legs. "Don't be afraid. That's how much I want you. It won't hurt you."

She nodded.

He lifted himself above her and braced both hands on

either side of her head. Then he dipped his head and kissed her long and lovingly. "I love you, Sarah."

"I love you, too, Christian." She traced her fingertips along his cheek.

His manhood prodded at the opening of her body, but when he slid in, there was only the gentle glide of him and a soft pressure. No pain.

"Is that it?" she asked, biting her lip.

He barked a laugh. "Not exactly what one hopes to hear the first time one takes his wife to bed."

"No, I only mean . . . It doesn't hurt, Christian. It's rather—"

He moved his hips then and she moaned. "Nice," she finished, already panting.

" 'Nice' is one word for it," he said, already pulling out and levering his hips again. "But I can do better than 'nice.' " He pulled out and pushed in again and again, closing his eyes and kissing her as though his life depended on it.

The pressure built within her again, and the intense pleasure rolled through her one more time. She cried out against his rough cheek.

"Oh, God, Sarah," he cried when at last he pumped into her for the final time and spilled himself inside her.

Moments later, he rolled over and pulled her atop him, cradling her against his chest.

"What do you think?"

"You're right. It was better than nice," she said, tucking her head under his chin and kissing his chest.

"I'm infinitely glad to hear it."

She slapped at his shoulder and laughed. "You didn't have to make all this so very complicated, you know."

"You didn't have to almost give me a heart attack by nearly marrying another man, you know."

Sarah laid her head back against Christian's chest. "I'm

only glad it worked out the way it has. It frightens me to think how close we came to ruining our happiness."

He wrapped his arms around her and squeezed. "I'll never take you for granted, Sarah."

She returned his embrace.

"What were you knitting, by the by?" he asked her.

"A new sweater for Fergus."

"The man or the dog?"

"The dog, though I wouldn't mind making one for the man, too. I believe I shall begin after Fergus Two's new summer coat is finished. Though Mrs. Goatsocks may well take exception to my making a sweater for *Mr.* Fergus."

"Mrs. Goatsocks? Is she still here?"

"Yes. She's found work in town as a lady's maid. Mr. Fergus visits her each Sunday, or so he told me. That's where he is right now, in fact."

"Is that so? I wondered where he'd got to."

"I expect we'll hear an announcement between them, shortly. He was infinitely pleased to hear that *we* had married, incidentally."

"Just think, you created two couples when you ran away to Scotland."

"Do you know Mrs. Goatsocks had the nerve to tell me that she decided to give you her blessing to take me to Northumbria the moment she discovered you were the viscount?"

"What?"

"That's right. Apparently, she already had in mind that we'd make an excellent match for each other. 'No better way to form a match than to let down one's strictures for a bit.' She said it with a wink. Can you imagine?"

Christian nearly fell off the bed laughing. "No, actually. No, I cannot imagine."

Then he kissed Sarah again, long and deeply, and when he raised his head, she had a contented smile on her face.

"You know, I think I shall quite like living in the north most of the time."

"You won't miss—what did Branford call them?—the *amusements* of London?"

"I only want to be where you are." She rested her chin against his shoulder.

"I think I can manage to bring my wife to town from time to time. Whatever you like. My home is wherever you want to be." He hugged her close.

"We may want to stay up here for a while. At least until Mother and Father come to terms with our marriage and Lucy works her magic."

"Lucy?" Christian asked. "What magic is she working now?"

"Oh, she fully intends to scrub my reputation clean. She's already begun."

Christian's crack of laughter bounced against the walls. "All of my money is on her. Make no mistake."

"I agree. I fully expect us to be back in the *ton*'s good graces again in a matter of days."

"But in the meantime?"

"In the meantime, I think we should remain here and do wicked things. I might as well earn the reputation I've got."

Another crack of laughter. "You mean like how I found you quietly knitting a sweater?"

"I think we can think of things much more wicked than that."

"Like chess?"

Her fingers traveled slowly down to where the quilt covered him below the waist. "Is that what we're calling it?"

An hour later, after he'd thoroughly made love to his wife again, Christian met her in the kitchen to partake of the stew she'd made. "I'm famished," he said as she set about preparing the biscuits, just as she'd done all those months ago.

"I am, too." She blushed at his leering look.

She set out the wine and served the stew.

Just before Christian took his first bite, Sarah said, "What do you think poor Branford will do?"

"Find someone as interested in himself as he is, no doubt. The *ton* is full of ladies who will put up with a great deal to become a marchioness."

"It's sad but true." Sarah sighed. "Perhaps Lady Claire would be a good candidate. Branford does have a penchant for the belles of the Season."

"I think they might make *quite* a fine couple, actually."

Sarah laughed. "Yes, well, they're welcome to each other. I must turn my attention to helping Meg find a proper husband. Lucy and Cass have agreed to help."

"What about the man Meg is helplessly in love with?"

"Unfortunately, *he* is not an option." Sarah sighed again.

"Never think it. True love and all that."

"Well, there was something quite odd about the way . . ."

"About the way what?"

"Never mind. I'll have to dig to the bottom of it when we return to London. I may have to enlist Lucy to help me with that, too, though she's already set her sights on someone else to be her next project."

"Already? Who is the poor girl?"

"It's not a girl. It's Cade Cavendish. I told Lucy what he'd said about having done things that might get him hanged. She's intrigued."

Christian shook his head. "Lucy's always wanted to be a spy."

"What do *you* think Cade Cavendish has done?"

"I can't even begin to guess," Christian replied.

"Lucy says she intends to find out."

"*That* cannot possibly end well," Christian said.

"Why not? All her other schemes have ended well, haven't they? Her last one got us together."

"You may have a point, but *you* were also instrumental in getting us together. You ran away from London and broke into my house."

"Yes, well, it wasn't entirely easy. You asked for my help finding *other* ladies."

Christian picked up her hand and kissed Sarah's knuckles. "You made me into a legend."

She squeezed his fingers and stared at him with love in her eyes. "Yes, and now you're mine. My legendary lord."

Thank you for reading *The Legendary Lord*.
I can't tell you how much I enjoyed writing Lord Berkeley's
love story. I think he finally met his perfect match in Sarah.

I'd love to keep in touch.

- Visit my website for information about upcoming books,
  excerpts, and to sign up for my email newsletter: www
  .ValerieBowmanBooks.com.
- Join me on Facebook: http://Facebook.com
  /ValerieBowmanAuthor.
- Follow me on Twitter at @ValerieGBowman, https://
  twitter.com/ValerieGBowman.
- Reviews help other readers find books. I appreciate
  all reviews whether positive or negative. Thank you
  so much for considering it!